GIRELF STOOD, AMAZED.
"IS IT REALLY A CRYSTAL,

or some wondrous made thing, something even from Earth itself?"

"It's a crystal," Barc said. "Anyone can see it's a crystal."

The mantee glanced about, and her eyes fell on the bronze panels. "Can you read that stuff?" she asked, indicating the patterns.

Barc almost said *Read what?* Thinking quickly— for a bors—he stopped himself. As she believed the geometrics to be writing, his question would have sounded ignorant. If it were indeed writing, and she understood it . . . "Not well," he said. "How much of it can you understand?"

She eyed him suspiciously. "Me? Not a word. Where would I learn ancient Universal?"

STEPWATER

An Arbiter Tale

L. WARREN DOUGLAS

A ROC BOOK

ROC
Published by the Penguin Group
Penguin Books USA Inc., 375 Hudson Street,
New York, New York 10014, U.S.A.
Penguin Books Ltd, 27 Wrights Lane,
London W8 5TZ, England
Penguin Books Australia Ltd, Ringwood,
Victoria, Australia
Penguin Books Canada Ltd, 10 Alcorn Avenue,
Toronto, Ontario, Canada M4V 3B2
Penguin Books (N.Z.) Ltd, 182-190 Wairau Road,
Auckland 10, New Zealand

Penguin Books Ltd, Registered Offices:
Harmondsworth, Middlesex, England

First published by Roc,
an imprint of Dutton Signet,
a division of Penguin Books USA Inc.

First Printing, October, 1995
10 9 8 7 6 5 4 3 2 1

Cover Art by Mark Gerber

REGISTERED TRADEMARK—MARCA REGISTRADA

Printed in the United States of America

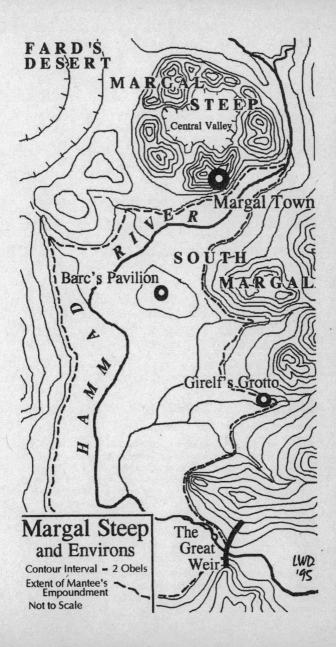

FARD'S
DESERT

MARCAL
STEEP

Central Valley

Margal Town

R I V E R

SOUTH

Barc's Pavilion

H A M M A D

MARGAL

Girelf's Grotto

Margal Steep
and Environs

Contour Interval = 2 Obels
Extent of Mantee's
Empoundment
Not to Scale

The
Great
Weir

LWD
'95

Acknowledgments

Jack Vance, for setting the standard I aim for. Jack, when I finish writing a novel, the first thing I do is reread one of yours, and ask myself if I'm getting any closer.

Sue, for putting up with the clutter, the chores left undone, the long evenings of being a "computer widow," with no more reward than an occasional WorldCon. Thanks, my love.

William Foster "Bud" Potts, for a million zany ideas and suggestions, at least ten thousand good ones too, and for being a friend. Leo Frankowski, for conversations, adventures, stories, and beer. John Pigott, for high school, college, and all the witty repartee.

Shawna McCarthy, agent extraordinaire, for everything, and Allan Cole, for getting us together.

STEPWATER

An Arbiter Tale

PROLOGUE

The Duchy of Erne, on Newhome, is the seat of
the Arbiter, who oversees a thousand inhabited worlds
orbiting as many stars. On Newhome dwell
members of all seven races of Man. It is said that
the Arbiter observes the interactions among the human
types on Newhome, and from his observations draws
the requisite conclusions for the making of general
rules and laws for the Stream. Thus it is claimed
that Newhome mirrors, in microcosm, the fate of all
the worlds of the Xarafeille Stream.

Kelosodill's Cosmographics,
Newhome, Year 12098 of the Rule of Law

John Minder, Arbiter, hammered his fist on the dark wood
of his father's coffin. Then he rested his head on folded
arms, and he wept. There he remained until the honor
guard and the pallbearers arrived. Rober Minder, the Arbiter Rober VIII, was dead. Johnny Minder, his eyes brimming with tears that he only later, retrospectively, decided
were insincere, followed the procession on foot all the
way from the Carnelian Hall to the family plot on the
high end of the Fields of Man. Onlookers remarked what
a dutiful and loyal son he was. A pity, they said, that he
was not firstborn, and thus Rober's heir, instead of that
wandering rascal Shems.

The insincerity of Johnny's tears resulted from something he knew that those onlookers did not know—that
Shems was not coming home, and that he, Johnny, en-

tirely unprepared for the burden, was indeed the Arbiter's heir, and that he did not want to be.

Before the rich soil of Newhome had settled over the grave, young Minder made himself a promise: never would his own children be left so unprepared. He would teach them everything an Arbiter had to know, so that whichever of them took up the burden would be ready for it. But his first years in his office were hellishly difficult ones, and though he somehow found time to marry and to sire the three who now sat with him, he had hardly thought of that vow he had made, until now.

"Tell us, Daddy! Tell us what Uncle Shems did!" Parissa blurted.

Young Rober frowned at his littlest sister, a sharp rebuke for her impetuosity forming on his lips—but he did not voice it, which demonstrated to his father that the Minder genes still bred true; the Minder genes, cultivated, culled, and manipulated, encouraged their bearers to be easy and accommodating—however unnatural that was for a child, any child. The Minders were not power-hungry, testosterone-ruled, or inclined to dominate those about them. Given a choice, any one of them, male or female, would prefer a life spent in quiet academic pursuit to the hustle and confrontation that was an Arbiter's lot— though having a little sister was a burden that would try a saint's patience, the elder Minder suspected. "Parissa," John Minder asked, "do you remember the Vault of Worlds?"

The very day Rober Minder VIII had died, Johnny sent word to his brother Shems, who was an archaeologist working a dig on Fyobar, Xarafeille 903. He got no reply. Postponing the funeral, Johnny left his father's body in stasis in the Carnelian Hall; until Shems returned to take up his post, there would be no Arbiter at all. Johnny sent a courier by fast ship to Fyobar, which was a week's travel away.

"I'm sorry," the courier said when he returned alone. "There was no one there. The dig was closed down and backfilled, and no one knew where Shems has gone."

Johnny sent more messages and more couriers. Because he was not himself Arbiter, he did not have the authority or the proper codes to use his father's starfleet or his *poletzai,* his enforcers, though he sent many messages via the vast network of agents and consuls on the worlds of the Xarafeille Stream. None reported word or trace of his brother Shems.

Finally, two months after his father's death, Johnny Minder accepted the inevitable: Shems was not coming home. He himself was going to be the next Arbiter, John Minder XXIII. There was no avoiding it. He scheduled the funeral and his own installment ceremony—it was not a "coronation," because there was no crown, and he would be both less and more than any king. The day after his father was interred, Johnny entered the Vault of Worlds. If any human not of the Minder line had placed palm to door seal, the Vault would have remained locked, and alarms would have shaken the palace from the Vantation Turret to the deepest footing bonded to Newhome's most stable, ancient bedrock, but the iridescent alloy door swung open, then sighed shut again on Johnny's heels. The lights within remained low, and a laser holoimage formed in the dimness ahead of him: Rober Minder VIII, Johnny's father.

"I'm sorry, Johnny," the image said, shaking its head. "Since you're viewing this, it means Shems has not come home. I didn't really think he would; we Minders walk a delicate line between our ingrained distaste for responsibility and our acquiescence to it. That you are here, and Shems isn't, is an example of one of the selective processes that make us what we are meant to be—Arbiters."

The holoimage informed Johnny of seven datablocks, sealed and ratified by the high councils of the seven human races, each one containing some—but not all—of the codes that would open the archives. There the deci-

sions of Arbiters past were recorded—the solutions to
problems Johnny could expect to confront, as Arbiter
himself. Within the databases were the secret location of
the Arbiter's mothballed fleet of starships and the navigational instructions to certain worlds far off the starlanes;
those worlds, without ships or the knowledge of making
them, were home to a militaristic warlike race of old humans, poletzai, who would man his warships.

Fleet and poletzai, Rober Minder's image remarked,
had not attacked a world of the Stream in seven generations. Most often, their threat and their legend were
enough. If not, the appearance of a thousand ships in orbit around an offending world sufficed. Rober's holoimage
stated that it hoped Johnny would find no need of them
during his own career, but they were there, and the
knowledge would bolster his confidence that his own
edicts would be obeyed.

When the image faded and the light level rose, Johnny,
following instructions, went to the case where the seven
datacubes were kept. Seven, one for each of the races of
man, no one sufficient to release all of the information he
would need to perform his unwelcome duties.

The case was empty, except for a single sheet of slightly
rumpled paper. "Johnny," he read. "If you're reading this,
I can assume you're already the new Arbiter, John Minder XXIII. Congratulations, I suppose. I wondered what
was on these cubes, but they're so old no terminal in the
house can read them. They're dated thirteen centuries
ago, and since anything that old is practically archaeology,
and since there's a cybernetics museum on Fyobar that
has a dozen old terminals, I'm taking them along with me.
I'll send them back when I'm done. They're probably
nothing but old arbitration records anyway.

"By the way, in case you haven't guessed yet, I'm not
coming back. Don't even try to find me. I don't intend to
spend my best years cooped up in that palace. Good luck
with your new job. Shems."

* * *

"They weren't just old arbitashins, were they, Daddy?"

"We all know that, Priss," Rober grumbled.

"Parissa, dear," their sister Sarabet murmured, "Robby let you have your way, but now it's his turn. Let Daddy tell us about Stepwater now, and how he got the backup datablock."

Parissa's mouth opened as she prepared to protest. She wanted to hear—again—how Daddy found out about the backup cube, and where they were hidden. But genes will tell. Instead of demanding what she wanted, Parissa clamped her lips shut, and with meaningful silence, composed herself on Sarabet's lap to listen to the tale Rober wanted to hear. . . .

PART ONE

INCEPTIONS

Margal Steep and Karbol City,
on Stepwater, Mirrim IV,
Xarafeille 578

CHAPTER 1

The star Mirrim, Xarafeille 578, has one inhabited
planet, Stepwater, home to the city of Garloom, the
interworld capitol of the wendish race. The wendish
homeworld, Forest, lies outside the Xarafeille
Stream, and the elfin wends have forgotten its location.

Wends inhabit Stepwater's subtemperate woodlands
and cool coastal rain forests, sharing their world
with several other human variants. Trogloditic bors
occupy highlands except in the continental deserts,
which are home to scattered tribal groups of nomadic
fards. Reclusive aquatic mantees claim rivers and
floodplains to a distance of fifty obels* from water's
edge. Only on Newhome itself are more human types
found living shoulder to shoulder. Racial conflicts are
common, but are usually nonviolent, involving
conflicting land claims, and the tourist who does
not stray from cities and main roads need not be
overly concerned about becoming involved in
them.

Parkoon's Guide to the Worlds of the Xarafeille Stream,
Parkoon and Parkoon, Newhome, 12125 R.L.

Barc Doresh did not like mantees, though not because of
anything the slippery water-men had done to him. He had

---

*An obel is the height of the monument in the courtyard of the wendish
archive, and is the official standard of measurement on Stepwater, as
wends hold the original grant to the world and are keepers of all records
and standards. The obelisk, or obel, is approximately 100 borrish feet, or
one-fiftieth of a fardic mile.

simply acquired an attitude about them from listening to his uncle Grast.

"Damned gypsy thieves, that's what they are," the elder Doresh had been heard to exclaim. "Make them pay in advance, you hear? In advance, or those circuit boards we sold them will corrode to uselessness before we see our shipment of scentweed. In advance, hear?"

Today, though, Grast Doresh expressed no such sentiments. The mantees were not here to trade, though their visit would theoretically facilitate trade in future. Traditionally, several times during the adolescence of a Doresh heir to the tiny principality of Margal Steep, such visits were arranged. When Barc, Grast's sister's son, ascended to the malachite dais beside his sister Blet, he would already know the names and faces of his mantee trading partners. Now the whole family cavern was suffused with the noises a large party makes, and the central hall's glow lights were turned to full brightness. Their gleam reflected from polished native rock walls, floor, and ceiling inlaid with slabs of select beauty—lapis lazuli, jasper, pink quartzite, and white quartz shot with veins of soft gold. A basalt table ran the length of the irregular chamber, draped with fine cloth from wendish looms, bright with polished metal tableware made by the best craftsmen on Stepwater: the bors of Margal Steep.

Barc knew his place at the feast table would be right beside Girelf, the mantee heir. This was not the first time he had met Girelf, heir to the Hammad River Valley, but at least this time she would have clothes on, as befitted the formal occasion.

It had been quite hard for Barc to maintain his inculcated dislike of mantees all along. The year before last, Girelf had taught him to swim—underwater, like a mantee, something few bors ever master. Then last year . . . It was impossible for him to forget what had occurred the last time he had met her.

Grast Doresh did not have any idea what had transpired

between Barc and Girelf last year—and thus he did not have an inkling of what could happen this year. If he had, being Barc's mother's brother and thus responsible for the boy's education, he might have taught him more about mantees than their thieving, hard-bargaining ways.

He might also have taught Barc more about the "facts of life," as tender-minded folk called them. If he had done so, perhaps the subsequent history of Margal Steep might have taken a different turn. Surely, the personal history of Barc Doresh would have, if he had known what he was getting into . . .

Margal Steep is a range of mountains surrounding an uninhabitable desert valley. North and west of the Steep are desert playas, slightly less bleak, where the fardic tribe of Musal Bhjak roams, wresting meager sustenance from sand, rock, and occasional patches of thin, brown vegetation, and from the sale of crystals precipitated from the foul waters of their wells, whose varying flavors they cherish and give a thousand distinct names, and of muslins tinted a rare, bright crimson with a secret, unfading dye. West and south lie forests inhabited by the most primitive tribes of Stepwater's dominant wendish subspecies, who weave tree fibers and carve wood into unique multi-harmonic flutes, and into Ouije figurines to sell in the tourest bazaars. Southeast and east of the Steep's bare, rocky massif runs the Hammad River, dividing Margal in two parts. South Margal is smaller and lower, its peaks covered with fine, tall trees to their summits. Though both are one principality, the single road between them, and the single bridge, cross the mantees' land and water, and the river-dwellers exact a toll on all traffic.

Equatorial Stepwater is a land of extremes. Desert pans abut forested, glacier-sculpted valleys in turn enclosed by bare granite, sandstone, limestone, and metamorphic ridges and peaks; the moist river valley exudes itself through Hammad Water Gap and wanders south through thick wendish forest and vast, grassy steppes to the garish, dashing, busy city of Karbol; snow and heat, moist and dry, lush and barren, all lie cheek to cheek, nowhere a week's walk apart.

Last year Barc and the bors entourage had visited Girelf's folk during the mantee summerthrong, when they all gathered ashore to enjoy the thick humid air of the season, to bask on sunlit rocks, and to chatter about the long, lonely winter past. He had thought Girelf quite pretty, for a mantee. Of course, her brown fur was short and slick, not black and fluffy like his own, and her short, pointed muzzle and large, childlike green eyes were unlike his broad, blockish face and his ice-blue irises, but Barc had been quite attracted to her. Of course all mantees seemed feminine to a burly bors, even the males.

Still considered children by mantees and bors alike, Barc and Girelf had been exempted from the most tedious ceremonials. It was more important to their elders that the young ones come to know each other. If they liked each other as well, that would be good. It might make the difference between successful trading and unprofitable misunderstanding in years to come.

"Can you swim?" Girelf asked him, sprawling gracefully on sun-warmed streamside gravels. "You didn't forget how, did you? Are you bors that dumb?"

"I didn't forget," Barc snapped. "I never forget. But swim? What for? Why would I want to do that? The spalk aren't running yet, and I'd get wet for nothing. I'd have to go to dinner all wet."

"There are no spalk here anyway. They're cold-water fish. And who cares if you're wet? We're eating at the outdoor pavilion anyway, and it will be quite warm all night. You can't swim, can you?"

"I can! But not in this muddy trickle. There's no room."

"It's quite deep. And there's a cave, a secret cave, under that bellfruit tree over there. I keep all my treasures there."

"A cave?" Bors, troglodytic by nature, miners by tradition, were of course intrigued with new, unexplored caves. That a mantee should claim one only sharpened his interest. It was not natural or proper for a mantee to claim proprietary interest in a cave, Barc thought.

"Right over there. You'd have to swim, to get to it."

Two aspects of bors nature warred in him—curiosity, and dislike of being wet. His fur did not shed water like hers did, any more than hers would protect against abrasive rocks and icy mountainside blasts. But it was summer, and the worst he would suffer would be to take all night to dry out. Like all bors, he could slow his metabolism at will; he would not run out of breath for several minutes underwater. Curiosity won. Besides, there was another force driving Barc—one he had not quite identified yet.

The cave was a disappointment, little more than a rootbound burrow beneath the ancient tree. Barc rested just inside, catching his breath. Girelf, wondering if he was all right, knelt beside him and put a hand on his cheek; Barc, responding to that yet-unidentified motivation of his, put a hand around her slender, smooth-furred waist and curiously, uncomprehendingly, drew her close to him. Her breath caught in her throat, and she wiggled to get away—but not nearly vigorously enough. Then, just as Barc felt a strange, hot sensation in his middle, as he tensed to pull the soft, wiggly mantee closer still, she jerked convulsively, and pulled away from him entirely. "No!" she said, firmly but not angrily. "No. Not yet."

Barc did not understand her or himself. What had happened between them? Needless to say, after that intense moment, Girelf's treasures failed to impress him—a waterworn rock crystal, some azure mahkrat eggs, their shells blown dry, and an old wendish doll whose ceramic eyes opened and closed.

Barc's disappointment must have shown. After all, rock crystal was common in the honeycombed mountain that was Margal Town. There were blue ones, yellow-gold, smoky, even lavender amethyst crystals. And someone, Barc remarked, had already sucked the mahkrat eggs. Dolls, even clever wendish ones with carved heads and eyes that responded to a counterweight, held no interest for him. "Maybe I can find an amethyst crystal for you," he offered, trying to undo his silent offense. "Maybe I can find a whole cluster of them."

"I don't want your stupid crystals," Girelf snapped, and plunged down through the dark water, and out of the cave.

"I'm sorry," Barc said later, after the visiting party had feasted on fresh curdles, rocksnapper, and steamed mussels. "The mahkrat shells were pretty. It's just that I was hungry then, and . . ."

"You bors! You can't think when your stomachs are empty, and you don't want to when they're full." It was an old joke among mantees. Girelf's smile robbed it of offense.

"I'm thinking now," Barc said, eyeing her slyly, sideways. For a mantee, she was very pretty. He had, he thought, missed a bet when they had been alone in the cave. He should have tickled her, or something. He had finally realized just what the intense feelings had been. He did not understand them well, because no one told young bors about such things, not until it was absolutely necessary that they know. Still, he felt himself a very dumb bors. Then, when he had seen the blue eggs, and was disappointed when he found they were empty . . . But he did not want to think about any of that, right then. It was true, what she said, he thought. Now that I'm full, I really don't want to think. But then, Barc was young, barely adolescent by bors standards.

They had no time to pursue what Girelf too might have considered an interesting line of thought, for Barc's uncle Grast approached, accompanied by the mantee throngmother.

That sight alone was enough to dissipate Barc's last libidinous thoughts. The throngmother, Shillemeh, was larger even than Uncle Grast, and so fat she must have preferred to slide though the lush riverine grass on all fours instead of walking properly upright. Like mother, like daughter. Was she really Girelf's mother? Mantee kinship seemed an impenetrable maze. Would Girelf look like that, someday?

The throngmother wisely chose not to accompany the mantee delegation to Margal Town. How would she have sat at the table to eat? Was there a chair wide enough for her? Girelf, however, had no difficulty mastering table and chair, or holding her meat knife properly. Barc wondered if the mantees had tutored her, as he had been tutored in the etiquette of mussel-cracking.

"I've changed my mind," Girelf said, eyeing him coyly across the glitter of soapstone platters, silver tureens, and candlesticks fabricated of gold beads and garnets.

"Huh?" Barc replied.

"An amethyst rock crystal! You said I could have one."

"Oh. I did. Now?" Barc's mouth was full.

"Why not now? You can show me where they come from." She sighed. "Barc, I was wrong to be offended, last year. My little 'cave' is nothing compared to this. Does Margal Town take up the whole mountain?"

"Aw, your cave was nice," Barc said. "I was just . . ."

"Hungry! And you bors . . ."

"I know, I know. Can't think, don't want to . . . It's true, I suppose."

"What about it?"

"What? I'm not hungry, now."

"Not that. The rock crystal."

"Oh. Of course. I know where there should be some good ones. Come on."

Margal Town did extend almost halfway to the top of Mendeb Peak, the southernmost mountain on this side of the river, and its deepest, oldest caves plunged well below mean sea level, too. Northward, an arm of the tunnels reached almost to the edge of the waterless central valley,

Margal Steep's useless hub, a wasteland of sinkholes and
dry, crumbling caverns created by meltwaters during the
long-departed last glacial age. Girelf seemed properly impressed with "real" caves. Barc led her through Ambo
Deep, where glow lights on a ceiling a hundred meters
high flooded roofless shops, squares, streets, and a half-
dozen busy marketplaces with bright, eerie light. He led
her down narrowing passages lined with doors—working-
class residences—ever deeper into the mountain.

At some point, when the doors they passed were no
longer painted, where they hung loose on rusty hinges and
opened on dark emptiness, she became uneasy. "Where
are you taking me? There are hardly any lights, and no
people, and my feet are getting wet."

"You're a mantee. You should like wet feet," he said un-
sympathetically, remembering his own wet fur the last
time he had been with Girelf, and a gray, furry fungus he
had acquired in the water or her cave that had taken
weeks of stinky medication to eradicate.

"I'm scared, Barc."

He relented, and explained. "We're in the oldest caverns now," he said. "These were the first ones bors settled
in when we came to Stepwater and bought Margal from
the wends. We're below the level of the river, now, and
water seeps in. Don't worry, we're almost there. Look!
There's a bunch of crystals now." Indeed, a cluster of hex-
agonal quartz filled a niche near the ground. They were
not violet, only dark, like dirty glass. Girelf sniffed, unim-
pressed, though they were larger and shinier than her own
treasure was. "Well, there are better ones," Barc said.
"Come on."

Barc, caught up in his own enthusiasm, lulled by his
own familiarity with the dark, damp caves, hardly noticed
her hesitancy. He did, at their next stop, notice her diffi-
dence. He thought the cluster of finger-thick smoke crystals was beautiful, even in the dim illumination of a single
glow light a hundred yards away. Individual crystals
seemed to trap the green-white light and convert it to a

red, emberous glow deep within. "Where are the amethysts?" Girelf asked him.

"There were some, the last time I was here," he mused. "Someone's been harvesting. We'll have to go deeper."

"Oh, no. I won't. I have decided that I'm really not interested in crystals after all. You can come back later, and find some. If you find amethysts, you can show them to me. But now, I want to go back."

"Aww . . . Honest, we're almost there. You'll see."

"Hah! I don't think there are any amethysts. You just wanted to tease me. All Margal's crystals are dirty and dull and brown, aren't they?"

"No! Why, there's one that's . . ." Barc hesitated. He had never told anyone about *that* crystal.

As a cub, Barc had explored the oldest caves by himself. Even though he was heir to Margal Steep—or perhaps because of that—he was not a popular youngster, and early on he developed the internal resources of the estranged. Exploring was his fancy, his escape from surly cousins, Uncle Grast, and his mother, Sheb, who was always too busy for him. His father? A merchant in Karbol, he was told. Fathers were mere conveniences to the bors of Stepwater. Descent and inheritance were reckoned in the female line. Grast ruled the Steep, but at his sister's sufferance, and his sister's son—Barc—would inherit it. Barc's sister Blet—and female bors always gave birth to twins, one of each sex—would in turn rule him, and Blet's children would succeed her and Barc. His own offspring, inheriting from their own mother, whoever she might someday be, would not be in the line of succession.

In those lower caves, in an unlit corridor not far from where Barc and Girelf would later wander, a very young Barc had discovered an old door almost concealed behind thick, dark fungus. It was an iron door, not wood or bronze, a rarity indeed. Rarer still, it had been left to rust, but he was able to pull it outward until it crashed to the cavern floor with a painfully loud thud. Immediately, a trickle of water pooled behind it. There was always water in the deep caves. Barc was cautious, because he had encountered several participants in the deep caves' unique ecology before: there were several species of slithers, which were innocuous, and fed on mold; there was a single type of mahkrat with tiny pink eyes and large, poisonous claws, that was not. It fed on slithers, other mahkrats, and anything else foolish enough to be caught unawares. He waved his small light globe, sheltering his eyes from its direct glow, and surveyed the chamber within. Blue-white light flashed back at him, and he froze in place.

A crystal. A blue crystal as big as his fist, wrist, and half his forearm. Its rectangular body facets returned much of the light from his globe, and he immediately noticed several unusual things about it. First, it had been cut or ground flat on both ends, against the ordinary cleavage planes. If that had not been enough to convince him that he was not the first to discover it, the glass case it resided within would have. The glass was hardly dirty; this far down in the caves, there was little air movement, and even the mahkrats moved slowly, most of the time. The case was a domed top, with six rectangular panels forming the sides. The muntins that held all seven pieces of glass together were some dark metal, probably bronze.

The assembly rested on a polished stone plinth, almost like an altar—though bors were not religious by nature, and the nebulous god they acknowledged demanded no artifactual manifestations of their faith. What was it? Or rather, as it was a crystal in a case, on a plinth, in an abandoned room that had obviously not been visited in generations, what was it for? And who had placed it here?

Barc explored. The room had once been finely decorated in an austere style, its buff limestone walls carved geometrically, its ceiling a tessellated negative bulge shaped like the domed top on the crystal's case. The walls, all six, each had a bronze inset that looked like a door with no fittings or latch. There was writing on them, or so Barc thought, geometric characters like nothing in

the oldest books. Bors, unlike wends, had no innate interest in old things, and considered the past dead and irrel-
evant.

Finding nothing else of note, he returned to the glass
case, and lifted it aside. The blue crystal gleamed brighter
still. It was cool to the touch, no heavier than a crystal of
that amazing size should be, and when his ring clacked
against it it made a sound much like any crystal might
make, but still, Barc felt uneasy handling it. Perhaps it
was the setting he had found it in—obviously, someone
had once thought it important, and worthy of great respect. Though Barc could not explain his own feelings, he
set the blue gem down gently, and replaced its cover. He
was hungry and thirsty. The sodden feel of the surface underfoot reminded him that water ran from the room. Did
it come from somewhere high enough to be clean, free of
mahkrat feces and slither slime? He searched, holding his
globe high and slightly behind. There! It was coming from
behind one of the wall medallions, the "doors." Poking
and prying, he pulled an edge of the heavy metal rectan-
gle free. It *was* a door. It swung open without much
effort, on a narrow passage.

The water on the floor was still suspicious, but the passage seemed to lead upward. Barc followed it. He followed it and continued to follow it, ever slightly upward.
The trickle was undiminished. By now, he had forgotten
his thirst, and was consumed with interest in the passageway. It seemed an entirely natural passageway, and it was
unlike the wide, branching ways he was familiar with.
Where did it lead?

A scent tickled his nostrils. It was nothing strange, but
for a moment it surprised him. It smelled like rain, like
the ground outside smelled after a shower, when soil bacteria freshened and bloomed. Barc pushed on. It *was* rain.
When he muffled his globe in his shirt, he saw a glow not
from his own lamp or another glow light, but from outside.

Barc's thoughts raced. Outside? Had he found a secret

exit from Margal Town? One without gate guards to stop
him and humiliate him by calling his mother for permission to let him out? One unknown to his nosy cousin,
Dird, and even to Uncle Grast? The possibilities the discovery promised were limitless. "Barc, where are you?" he
imagined his mother asking. "Just exploring the old caves,"
he imagined his reply. "Ah well," he imagined her say,
sighing, "at least it's safe." Safe. Even the oldest caverns
were stable. There had not been a cave-in in a century.
They were safe, stable, and to Barc's dismay, they had begun to become . . . boring. Today was different, of course,
but in how many old rooms could he expect to find things
like the blue crystal? The most exciting thing he had
found before this was old bones, perhaps of an explorer
less skilled or lucky than himself. The thought of death in
the lower caves had spiced his wanderings for a while, but
the more he looked at the bones, the more they resembled leftovers from some old-time barbecue.

The enticing, fresh glow inspired him to great effort. It
was a very small glow, from a minute hole—the source of
the water. He had to dig his way out. He had to claw past
cobbles, push past roots, then scrabble over rubble and
through dense brush but, finally, he got out.

He stood in cloudy daylight within a few paces of the
river, just a few obels downstream of the South Margal
bridge. He was outside. He was . . . free. Glancing behind
him, he could see no trace of his exit. Next time, he
would have to bring something down from the upper
caves with him, something unsuspicious to mark the spot.

Becoming aware of the time, of the low sun-glow behind the clouds, he realized it was already late. Barc
pushed back through the brush, then scrambled over the
rubble, and ran most of the way down the long, narrow
passage. It was clean and clear; he had encountered nothing on the way up it that might have caused him to stumble, and he was comfortable in the dark, even more than
most of his kind.

Exiting the crystal's shrine, he could not replace the

fallen door—but then, no one but he had discovered the
place in ages, anyway. It did not matter. Barc hurried back
through familiar caverns and passageways. About halfway
home he realized that, with the river so near, he had forgotten to assuage his thirst as had been his initial intent.

Girelf stood amazed. "Is it really a crystal, or some wondrous made thing, something ancient, even from Earth
itself?"

"It's a crystal," Barc said. "Anyone can see, it's a crystal." He had intended to show her a crystal, and he had
done so. No one, he was sure, would ever be able to show
her a bigger, clearer, or prettier one. He was not pleased
with her talk of "made things," as if his treasure were an
artifact, thus duplicable. Had he been more introspective,
more perceptive, Barc might have wondered if Girelf was
merely revenging herself for his negative reception of her
own treasures. She reached out to remove the cover.

"No!" Barc's own vehemence surprised him. "Don't
touch it."

"Why not?" she asked, arching her brow. "It's only
a . . ."

"Only a crystal? It's in a case for a reason, you know. It's
not just a crystal." *It's my crystal,* he almost said, *my discovery.*

She hesitated. Of course it was not just a crystal. It was
a . . . But she did not voice her thought. "Of course not,"
she replied. "It's very special." She glanced about her, and
her eyes fell on the bronze panels. "Can you read that
stuff?" she asked, indicating the patterns cast or carved in
them.

Barc almost said *Read what?* Thinking quickly—for
him—he stopped himself. As she believed the geometrics
to be writing, his question would have sounded ignorant.
If it was indeed writing, and she understood it . . . "Not
well," he said. "How much of it can you understand?"

She eyed him queerly—suspiciously, almost. "Me? Not
a word. Where would I learn ancient *Universal?*"

A name. She did know something of it. It was a language, then. He resolved to find out more about it. The only problem was that he would have to show it to someone else, wouldn't he? And he did not want to do that. "At least you know what it is," he said. "Most people don't." She smiled, seeming flattered.

"We have to get back soon," she said. "They'll be worrying, and I'm all dirty." It was true, he saw. Her fur's oils, which made it waterproof, also collected every bit of loose dust and cobweb she had brushed. Barc thought long and hard. "There is another way back," he said. "Today, if the city portal guards see us approach, they will say nothing. They'll wonder how we got out of Margal Town, but they won't dare say anything. They'll fear a reprimand, thinking they let us slip by, earlier. I've done that before."

"Whatever do you mean?" Girelf asked, not understanding. Barc showed her the panel that moved, and the passage beyond. "Then are these others doors also?" she asked. Barc, for all his explorations, had not given that much thought. Girelf examined the edge of the open panel. "See? That nubbin of rust used to be a latch, of a kind. As there are no handles, I think it opened with a push, in the right spot." Since the door swung outward, how could an inward push open it? Barc wisely kept that thought to himself. Girelf pushed on each door in turn, with no result, until the last one, which emitted a distinctive click, and then popped open enough for eager fingers to wiggle behind its edge. "See?" Girelf said. "What's in there?"

Barc lifted his glow light. He checked for mahkrat sign, then slipped inside. "Come in and see," he said, his emotions mixed; this whole place was his discovery, and he did not want to share it—except, as with the crystal itself, as a grandiose gesture, to impress her. He would rather have had time to explore this new room himself, before showing her.

"Someone lived here!" she exclaimed. Together, they peered at perfectly ordinary furnishings. Only the style was a bit odd. A sofa, and chairs. Small tables with long-dead reading lamps. And another door. Girelf darted toward it, and Barc, holding the glow light, followed. "See? A bed." She glided over a floor laid with thick carpet. Barc had at first glance thought it was merely darkmoss, but it was, he realized, quite dry. He followed. She patted the dark coverlet, which gave off only the slightest musty smell. Obviously, this room had remained dry.

He brushed past her to examine the fabric, and static from their shuffling over the carpet caused her fur and his to raise up where they brushed. "Ooo!" she exclaimed as they exchanged tiny crackling blue sparks, and she turned suddenly. Barc found himself holding her. He had only once held a female before—Girelf herself, the year before—but the immediate sensation was enticingly familiar. She was so small and delicate. She was warm. She wiggled, as if to escape his sudden, clutching grasp. Sudden, urgent, and ill-understood sensations flooded Barc's body. He felt hot, then cold. His hands moved of their own accord, big bors hands that covered Girelf's back and waist. The twin pressures of small, firm nipples fell just halfway between his belt and his shoulders. She made a small, strange sound deep in her throat.

Girelf's hands were busy too—and she was not trying to push him away. He felt the pressure of each of her slim fingers individually, five in the small of his back, and five more burrowing into the fur of his left buttock, beneath the loose trousers he wore for cave explorations.

Neither mantees nor bors are ordinarily clothing-conscious. Bors wear garments on formal occasions, denoting status, position, or wealth. They wear, as Barc did, loose utilitarian smocks and trousers to perform possibly dirty tasks, to protect their lush, soft fur. Mantees wear clothing even less often, perhaps only as a relic of ancient human tradition. Nonetheless, as Girelf pulled loose the drawstring that held Barc's trousers, and as he slid her silky smock up over her head, the motions were sensual, the acts suggestive and arousing—if further arousal was possible for either of them. The mustiness of the bed did not bother them at all, when they tumbled together upon it. That the coverlet, dry with age, tore under their combined weight and their intense activity went without notice.

"Now we really have to go," Girelf murmured, her face buried in the soft darkness of Barc's chest. Barc's big hands pulled her tightly against him. "No, I mean it," she said. The metenkheh will be furious with me." *Metenkheh,* Barc knew, meant something like "assistant throngmother," the mantee in charge of the delegation. Girelf wriggled away from him. Through his fur, he felt the damp cold that had entered the room through the newly opened door.

His hands reached for her. "Again?" he almost whined.

"The third time would get me pregnant!" she replied, sounding shocked. Barc knew little of mantee reproduction, but the thought of pregnancy frightened him. Was it so? He was not really all that sure of what it took to get a female bors pregnant, let alone a mantee. But he did know that if Girelf got pregnant, it would be a total disaster for both of them.

Such a child would be horrible. He shuddered to contemplate it, and his ardor dampened immediately. He pulled away as if she exuded slime like a slither. "I'm *not* pregnant," she said, indignant now. "I would not let that happen. Everyone knows what happens to crossbreed babies." Everyone knew, indeed, and it was not a subject either wished to dwell on.

"I need a swim," she said. "I'm all dusty."

"There's a bathtub in there, I think," Barc responded, gesturing. "I saw a toilet, anyway."

"None of the plumbing works," she said, shaking her head. "I tried to get a drink while you were sleeping. Besides, that's *stagnant* water. I need to swim to get clean." Barc remembered then: mantees considered water that was not running to be dirty, even if it was not. He explained that the passage out led right to the riverbank. Girelf immediately brightened at the prospect of a quick plunge in the river. He had noticed the year before that her fur, unlike his own, did not stay wet and soggy after immersion, just as his did not collect sticky cobwebs or the dust of crumbling bedclothes.

"Come on," he said.

His earlier work clearing the adit—which he had used many times in the years since its discovery, on secretive expeditions outside the underground town—allowed them to slip out without getting his own fur muddy. A good shake and a quick combing with his fingernails sufficed for him, while Girelf swam. Shortly later, they mingled with residents and visiting mantees, and passed back into the town unnoticed by the guards.

"How come, Daddy?" Parissa queried insistently. "How come they don't want to make a baby?"

"Because babies are ugly, and they grow into noisy little beasts like you," Rober muttered, too low for Parissa to hear—but not too softly for Sarabet, who jabbed him in the ribs with her elbow. "I'm going outside," he said, rising. "You can tell Pariss about that. I already know."

"Daddy?" Parissa said again.

"I have work to do, dear," he said apologetically. "I think Sarabet can explain it to you." He always had work—fleet or no fleet, with or without deadly poletzai, that never changed—but this time, he really just had to get away, to think. . . .

There were always plans to be made, ends to be furthered. Just as Barc and Girelf seemed unlikely individuals to merit the attention of an Arbiter, there were others, too: small, insignificant folk in far and seemingly unimportant places upon whose petty and self-centered actions the fates of planets, stars, and the Xarafeille Stream sometimes hinged. It was an Arbiter's job to find them, to seek out just those little folk who were in the right place at the right time, people whose personal flaws and selfish

desires—if not their loyalties, politics, or ideals—
coincided with an Arbiter's needs, or could be turned to
his advantage . . . and mankind's.

Sarabet could explain, and did. "There are several kinds
of humans." she said to Parissa. "Old humans like us
Minders and then all the rest. Once there were only old
humans, but when they went out to many different
worlds, they could not live on all of them. Some were too
cold, or too dry, or too wet . . ."

"Babies!" Parissa demanded. "Why didn't G'relf want a
baby?"

"Because it would have been an old human like us,"
Sarabet answered her patiently. "It would not have been
able to live in the water, like a mantee. Girelf would have
been very sad, to give up her baby to some old human
tribe."

Parissa was not ready for a history lesson, but Sarabet
knew the story well. The first old-human colonies had
been seeded from Earth by slow-time ramscoop spaceships. Many stellar systems had been visited and explored,
but only six were found with planets even remotely habitable by humans. Even those were inhospitable, barely
suitable for exploitation. They had important resources,
though, resources Earth needed. And the vast corporations that had financed the explorations needed profits
from them.

Earth, back then, had not been a wonderful place to
live. It was crowded, dirty, noisy, and impoverished. It was
not hard for the corporations to find volunteers willing to
indenture themselves for years, even a lifetime, to escape
it. The mines and plantations on all six colony worlds
grew, and the ships sent back refined metals and stasis-
preserved produce to the starving Earth. The profits were
great—but what, to an interstellar corporation, was
enough profit? Indentured workers sickened and died
breathing alien atmospheres, or they thrived in protective
domes, vehicles, and suits, but at great expense. They

produced babies who did not pay for their nourishment, training, and upkeep for twelve, fourteen, even twenty years, but who had to be supported. There had to be a better way.

A "better" way was found. Indentured workers light-years from civil-rights laws, courts, and even the worst democratic governments had little control over their lives, their futures, or their children's. They had little to say about the fate of their genes, any more than did black bears, dugongs, kangaroo rats, seals, otters . . . and all those genes were used to design the new generations of corporate slaves. The new children were adapted to their worlds as no old human could be, and they were cheap to support. Corporate profits soared.

Bors shared certain genetic traits with black bears— their rich, dark fur and their ability to hibernate when cold became extreme and food scarce. The mining companies did not have to feed or shelter them in the off-seasons, when access to the mines was impossible. They did not even have to transport them from northern to southern hemisphere when the seasons changed; they just allowed bors to breed freely, and selected their workers from northern or southern populations as needed. During the off-seasons, the bors could fend for themselves.

Mantees were adapted for a different world, a wet place for the most part, and their genes owed much to dugongs, seals, and otters. They were versatile, able to cope with differing watery environments and climates, adapting as need be. The mantees of the Hammad River would have seemed otterlike to Earth humans who had seen the originals.

Fards had kangaroo rat and jackal affinities, and ikuts surely owed as much to polar bears as did bors to the woodland and mountain varieties. Wends' borrowings were unknown. Weasels, perhaps? Squirrels, mongooses, or ferrets? Tarbeks' sulfurous metabolisms seemed unearthly, but who knew what genes they owed to bacteria that lived in undersea volcanic vents?

The original John Minder, the first Arbiter was a physicist and the discoverer of a faster-than-light spaceship drive. Of course it did not really allow ships to exceed the velocity called "C," it merely found a loophole in the universe and pulled itself—and anything firmly enclosed or attached—through it. Minder, testing his first small craft, discovered the fates of the slave races, and was appalled. He decided to do something about it. But that was another story, and Parissa had fallen asleep long before Sarabet got to the part about babies. . . .

John Minder XXIII pulled a stubby wood-staved barrel from its niche on his small private balcony that overlooked the Rhend marshes to his left, the Sofal Hills directly ahead, and the Meridite Aridity far away on the right, beyond a grassy savanna that almost touched the horizon. There were few clouds, and visibility from his high place was unlimited. On the far side of the forested Sofal Hills, threads and trickles of smoke rose. There lay a city, Nort, occupied by wends, mantees, fards, and the occasional tarbek. It was very much like Karbol, on Stepwater, he knew, and there had been riots there only a week before. They had started over some sexual impropriety, but he had not been able to track down the actual triggering event. Nort was quiet, now, but for how long? And how many other cities were there, on how many worlds?

The barrel John Minder sat on was the right height for a stool, and that was what he used it for, as had his father and forefathers. It had been an antique when the first John Minder had bought it many centuries before. Like the famous battle-ax of the legendary hero Washington, that had been given a dozen new handles and several new heads throughout the years, the stout container had been "restored" and "repaired" so many times that Minder doubted that a single original stave or wrought-iron hoop remained.

He gazed toward the smoke from Nord's chimneys. Humans were indeed a diverse lot, he reflected, and diversity made for friction. Friction created heat, and sometimes fire. Even when there had been only old humans, there had been genocidal wars. Minder dredged the names of peoples and policies from ancient histories: Jews, and the "Final Solution," "ethnic cleansing," "manifest destiny." . . .

The lesson of history was clear: whenever geographic borders and cultural ones coincided, as long as the technology of warfare and the economy to support it had remained weak, most clashes were peripheral and fleeting; when empires arose and when early versions of the Rule of Law were superimposed on diverse peoples, they mixed and mingled, and for the most part their ancient enmities were suppressed—for a time.

For a time, under one ancient Rule of Law, Serbs, Croats, Slovenes, and others ignored ancient borders and worked side by side. In another place, ex-slave and former master, immigrant and indigene, plowman and herdsman, had created a nation—for a while. But ancient differences faded only slowly, if at all, and whenever the Rule was lifted for a decade, a year, even a moment, those small "differences" loomed large—and then men died, and kept on dying. Then they fought house to house, neighborhood to neighborhood, because there were no longer borders, logistic limitations, or separate economics to divide them.

Without the Rule of Law—and without an impartial, unambitious, and empathetic Arbiter with the power to enforce it—the worlds of the Xarafeille Stream would ignite in a conflagration the scope of which history had never seen, because never before had there been so many humans so well distributed on so many worlds, and never had there been so many differences between them. Bors would turn against mantees against wends, ikuts, tarbeks, and fards, and separately or together, all would turn against the despised old humans.

The current John Minder sat on his many-times-restored barrel, and the hard, raised ends of its staves cut uncomfortably into his buttocks. It was a hard seat, but more than that, it was a symbol: perhaps the last putatively genuine powder keg in all the worlds of the Xarafeille Stream.

CHAPTER 2

A cautionary note: if old humans are among your
traveling party, it might be wise to conceal their nature
while touring rural Stepwater. Though urban folk
are tolerant to a fault, old humans are a distrusted
minority, and though dozens of origin myths have
obscured the nasty details of their exploitation of the
other six variants, old humans are unpopular among
rural habitants. On Stepwater in particular, only the
Arbiter's protection has kept them from being
exterminated. That and, of course, that the product
of breeding between separate human subspecies
invariably resembles neither parent, and is virtually
indistinguishable from an unmodified old human. Such
crossbreeding is less uncommon than admitted, and
may account for much of the disgust old humans
evince. Whatever the causes, caution is advised;
several visitors have reported disguising themselves as
fards and tarbeks, with varying degrees of success.

Parkoon's Guide to the Worlds of the Xarafeille Stream,
Parkoon and Parkoon, Newhome, 12125 R.L.

Girelf and Barc arrived in the palace hall only minutes before anxiety and annoyance ballooned into panic. "Where
were you?" Barc's mother snarled, her voice too low for
the mantee delegates to hear. From Girelf's stiff posture,
Barc suspected the metenkheh was asking much the same
of her. Barc told the agreed-upon tale that they had been
exploring, and had merely forgotten the passage of time.
His mother seemed mollified. Barc was unharmed, and

the mantee heir seemed less distraught than her guardian, surely. Sheb was relieved that Barc was so young for his age, though. Heaven help them all if he had been sexually mature. Young bors too often imprint on their first sexual partner and never find complete satisfaction with any other—and she had already selected a mate for him, the daughter of a mining magnate from South Margal.

Though Barc's mother noticed nothing amiss, younger, keener noses sniffed and snuffled, and young minds, cynical for all their youth, drew uncomfortable conclusions. Though Girelf had gone swimming, Barc had not. When Barc drew Girelf aside just before she departed with the other mantees, an older cousin, Dird, caught them with their hands entwined. "Ah, the new queen of Margal Steep, one presumes?" she said in falsely courtly speech. "And will you bring a furless mahkrat-child here to live?"

"Get out of here, Dird-bird. Your fur needs licking." Barc turned away. His was a mild slur—only infants and besotted males forgot essential hygiene. Dird's accusation that Barc and Girelf had engendered an old-human infant could have been a mortal insult. Had Barc not been on his best behavior with Girelf, it would have resulted, at the least, in the two bors rolling about, all teeth and clawed fingernails, growling and bloody. That Dird was female would not have mattered at all.

As it was, Girelf looked first at Barc, whose anger was confined to his eyes, then at Dird. "I thought Barc said your mother was a fard," she said conversationally. "But you smell like a tarbek. What did your father Grast see in her? Did he think to breed little sulfur matches to light this cave cheaply? Or is it you who carries a sulfur pot under that smock?"

Dird howled, and sprang at Girelf, her fingers cupped as if they were really claws. Girelf darted away. Mantees were more agile than bors, even on land. "Muckwhore! Vile swamp tart! Child-fucker! I'll pull out your eyes."

Barc grabbed her as she dashed past him to get at

Girelf, who was now behind him. He caught Dird's nostrils with two fingers, and yanked her back from Girelf. "You'd better go," he said to the mantee. "I'll calm her down."

"You'd better cage that misbegotten, diseased creature and sell it to the hairless gypsies or to a zoo," Girelf said. "I am insulted." She drew herself up stiffly, and departed.

Barc, staring at her, almost forgot about Dird, who tried to break free from the painful hold.

"Now see what you did?" he snarled. "You made her angry."

"Her? I made her angry? The muckwhore! You fucked her, didn't you? You fucked a mantee! Dirty little beast-fuckers, both of you. I won't be ruled by a pervert. I'll . . . yowp!"

Barc's fingers came away bloody as he yanked Dird's head back. He kicked his cousin and then growled, "You'll keep your nasty mouth shut, is what, or I'll decorate the rest of your ugly snout!"

Barc's threat was meaningless. Girelf was gone, whisked away by the offended mantees who had seen, if not heard, the exchange. If Dird kept silent, others with sensitive noses and suspicious minds did not. Barc was thenceforth confined to the town. The gateway guards were given strict instructions not to pass him out under any circumstances. His mother refused to see him at all. Uncle Grast, much the worse, spent all too much time with him.

Perhaps Grast Doresh was too harsh with his nephew. If so, it was only because he was angry with himself; it had been his responsibility to teach the youngster about sexuality—about certain odd quirks of bors sexuality in particular. *What you don't know,* he thought too late, *can indeed hurt you.*

"Did you?" he demanded. "Did you do it with her?"

"Do what, Uncle Grast?" Barc asked, all innocently. "I showed her some crystals. I didn't let her take any. Honest."

"Crystals! Phah! Did you . . . did you . . . do it with her?"

Barc maintained both his innocence and his ignorance. The nature of bors sexuality was in his favor. Most bors males were incurious about sex until they came fully of age. Then, usually confined within the premises of town, farmstead, or mountain fastness, their first sniffling interest in sisters, female cousins, even domestic animals of the other sex were laughably obvious. And Barc had exhibited no such behaviors.

Barc, Grast realized all too late, had spent far too much time alone, away from other bors. The older bors realized his own error: he had been happy to have the young heir away, wandering empty caves, while his own offspring learned the ins and outs of adult life in the town. Though they could not inherit his own status, they would have strong and influential positions as civil servants and merchants—the stronger for the frequent absence of the future heir, and for his ignorance.

Perhaps his sister's idea for Barc was better than Grast's for his own offspring. She sought a mate with a wealthy mother for Barc, from whom his children would inherit something worthwhile. Grast had unfortunately mated with a Karbol merchant's daughter, who had owned nothing of her own, and who had inherited only a miserable plot of waterlogged farmland now entirely flooded by the Hammad River's slow rise. Grast had been young enough, and stupid enough, to be impressed by the father's show of wealth, fine clothing, and a vast, well-lit cavern near the top of Mount Bez. He had not examined his mate's mother's assets, until it was too late.

Shillemeh, the throngmother, eyed Girelf speculatively. What had transpired between her and the bors whelp? And why did her daughter, her chosen heir, look so very smug?

Girelf rolled over on the flat rock where she basked, aware of Shillemeh's gaze, aware also that her mother had no idea what momentous events she, Girelf, had set in motion. Yet the young mantee was not really smug at all. How could such a little thing, such a brief, sweet dalliance, have such effects as she envisioned? Could the tiny ripples of water droplets falling from her wet fur nudge a wave out on the open water into a different course, and could that wave perhaps cause a tree to fall on the far shore?

Girelf pondered such small beginnings and what might result from them if only the right water droplet had been let fall at just the right time. She imagined the fallen tree drifting into the sluiceway of the Great Weir, blocking it. She pictured the immense dam cracking with the weight of water behind it and the roar when the dam collapsed, the wall of water rushing all the way to Karbol, carrying even that great city before it, scattering the rubble of men, buildings, and artifacts far out across the bottom of the sea.

She shuddered. Such a small beginning, but once begun, no one could control the events set in motion. Girelf was not smug at all; she was terrified.

Barc's explorations stopped after that, though no one in Margal Town would have known it. He still disappeared for long periods. Now, though, he invariably headed straight for the crystal room and the passage out—and down the narrow waterside path that led to the mantee's basking shores. The crystal remained in its case, undisturbed by more than Barc's glances as he passed by.

He saw Girelf from time to time, but he was not able to get near her. Always, she kept a barrier of water and other mantees between herself and Barc. Once, he tried to swim out to her, but his reward was only wet fur, because she, seeing his approach, slipped into the river herself and disappeared underwater. She might have swum right under him, for all he knew. On another occasion, when he was nearer the water than she was, he approached her, but the throngmother herself thrashed and waddled toward him, hooting in the incomprehensible mantee dialect, and the entire throng followed her. Barc retreated the way he had come.

"She has gone to Garloom on business of a private nature," a young mantee called Simolf told him one time. Garloom was the capital city of Stepwater, an exotic place where the Arbiter's consul held court, and the home of the vast wendish archives, the records of all their race, everywhere across the Xarafeille Stream, and repository of all Stepwater's deeds, contracts, and treaties as well. What possible "business" did a young mantee have in Garloom?

Barc decided that Simolf was lying to him, and that Girelf was purposefully avoiding him. That much was obvious, even to a lovesick bors. He accepted it, but not entirely. Was that what *she* wanted, or had the old fatbag, the throngmother, restricted her much as Uncle Grast had tried to restrict him? Still, he lurked on the edges of mantee gatherings, seeking a glimpse of her. When he was successful, he became morose and melancholy for the rest of the day, and ignored his studies in the evenings. When he was not, he merely daydreamed of her.

Dird and her gaggle of friends tormented him unmercifully, but always from beyond the reach of his strong arms and too-often-bunched fists. Bors males and females were of a size, and ordinarily so evenly matched that no custom of protecting females from male aggression existed. Barc would have attacked any number of the cousins—with no real hope of being the winner—but for the females' avoidance of close contact with him.

"He did it," Barc's mother snarled between clenched teeth. "He imprinted on the mantee slut."

"We don't know that for sure," Grast murmured, eyes averted. His sister's wrath was to be feared, and Barc's ignorance—which resulted from Grast's own neglected responsibility—put him straight in the way of her ire.

"Oh, I didn't think so, at first," she said. "He was quite

convincing, and besides, he never left by the gates, did he?"

"He hasn't gone outside once since the mantees were here," Grast said, now sure of his ground.

"Then why," his sister spat, "has the throngmother sent this?" She presented a course sheet of reed paper at the end of a stiff, trembling arm. Grast took it from her, and scanned the stiffly written characters on it. It was a letter from the mantee ruler requesting that the bors queen restrain her male child, and curtail his lurking, his trespassing, and his continual harassment of her folk. It described Barc's visits in detail, with times and dates.

"But he was not outside then," Grast protested. "He has not left Margal Town at all."

"Not by the gates," she snapped. "But he's been out. He's found another way—down in those old abandoned caverns. You don't think the first settlers had no gates of their own, do you? Our present gates, the passages leading to them, weren't even dug, back then."

"I'll have him followed. I'll have his exit walled off."

"He'll find another. I know him. If he's imprinted on her—and he has, believe me—then nothing will stop him. Nothing but a hundred thousand creds, at any rate." Grast raised an eyebrow. How did she plan to accomplish that? A mindskinner?

"No!" Grast protested, picturing the drugs, the restraining devices like instruments of torture, the electrodes. . . . "It is too cruel. Even if the imprinting is successfully broken, he will be a wreck of a man, and his future mate will hate us for it." His sister Sheb's willingness to contemplate such a course of action—and for her own son— horrified him.

"Then I will apprentice him to Nidleg Marboon," she said.

"Oh, no! That rakehell? He'd ruin the boy."

"Niddy's returning to Karbol town next week. He can put Barc to work for him. It's our only hope."

"Marboon will corrupt him. Karbol town will. The boy

will never have a normal sex life after that. He'll be ruined."

"And he won't be, if he's 'in love' with the future mantee throngmother? How could you do your job, your trading with the mantees, if you were imprinted on Shillemeh?"

Grast shuddered at the mental picture of himself creeping and mooning after the great, fat hulk of the throngmother. He could not even imagine such a thing. He had imprinted on his mate, a lovely thing in her youth, and since she had run off (since he had run her off, to be honest about it) he had been entirely disinterested in fleshly things. He was one of the lucky ones who did not have to chase females or employ chemical stimulation to stave off the madness that resulted when a male bors' monstrous libido remained unsatisfied. Still, he knew that if she returned, he would again be as much the slave of his imprinting as after their first time, even if Mellif was as old, paunchy, and scarred as he himself. Had he imprinted on old, fat Shillemeh in her lovely youth, he had to admit, he would be no less vulnerable to her now, and Margal Steep would be the poorer for the terrible bargains in trade that he would have made with his ugly lover.

Among ordinary folk such misogamy might seem trivial or merely ridiculous, but when the stakes were wealth or rulership, they took on grave importance—and of course the rulers set the cultural ideals, and the taboos. Ordinary folk, with less to lose, might have dared experiment with compassion, but Grast was neither imaginative nor especially compassionate. He prided himself on being pragmatic and practical. And Barc's alliance with a mantee was neither one.

Mantees, to the best of his knowledge, did not imprint on their mates in the same way. A mantee ruler imprinted by a bors would not be under any of the disadvantages of a male bors. If Barc had truly imprinted on Girelf, then the imprinting had to be broken, or Barc could never be allowed to rule in Grast's stead. And, as he well knew, there was no legal way to disinherit him. If Barc's urges could not be redirected to a less dangerous mate, he would have to be killed. There was no alternative. But Nidleg Marboon? The man was an astute trader, or he would not be Margal Steep's factor in Karbol, the area's central trade nexus. But Marboon was a pervert. He mated with anything—fards, old humans, even tarbeks, Grast supposed. He said as much to his sister.

"And he's a better trader for it," she said. "He understands all their languages and customs, because he learned them in their beds. We use the tools at hand. In Karbol, if necessary, Niddy can send Barc to the best mindskinners on Stepwater. If his imprinting can be broken, they'll do it. Then when he gets back, we'll mate him with the Mitbrok heir right away. We won't let him even see the Girelf slut until she's been impregnated and had popped a few dozen mantee sprouts herself. He won't even recognize her, by then."

Mantee reproduction was not well understood by outsiders, but what was known indicated that the throngmother was, literally, the mother of all her throng. Fatherhood was not reckoned at all. Only the heir received, from the present throngmother, the essences that made her fertile. Then, for a period of several years, she mated promiscuously. Her eggs were fertilized during each mating, but they remained inert in her womb until, at the retirement of the throngmother, when her final fertile egg had flourished and her final offspring was born, another essence was transferred—a secreted drug? A pheromone? No outsiders knew. Then Girelf's eggs would develop and, until the last of them was gone, she would be the throngmother. She would grow immense, and would experience only maternal desires. The entire next generation of mantees would be her children, and from them, she would select one, the healthiest and smartest, as her heir. Would she select a "backup" heir? No one not a mantee know.

* * *

It was decided. "But I don't want to go to Karbol," Barc complained bitterly. "Karbol is a spaceport, a big, noisy place with no caves. I'll have to live in a house!" I'll have to live with . . . Niddy Marboon. He shuddered. His cousins told tales of Marboon. He was abnormally tall and skinny, and though he was old, the fur on his back was still jet black, not silvery white. He did not age, but remained a perpetual adolescent. He had, the tales claimed, been born when Margal Town was a single natural cave, uncounted thousands of years before.

None of the tales were true, of course, except that Marboon was tall and skinny. Barc knew that the young Nidleg Marboon had been apprenticed to his own paternal grandfather, which was how his mother had come to mate with Barc's father. Though Barc did not know his father at all, his mother had kept a holo of him, taken in Karbol, standing next to a very young, but recognizable, Niddy Marboon. That knowledge did not make an apprenticeship to the trader less unappealing, though. Marboon was indeed an unmated pervert—Barc's dark nose warmed at the memory of his own . . . perversion. Suddenly, the trader did not seem quite so despicable. Still, he was far too talkative, far too open in his speech and his manner, he had no status whatsoever in Margal Steep, and he lived in Karbol, where Barc did not want to go.

The journey to Karbol was not unpleasant. River travel was a mantee monopoly, and though they furnished a pilot and groups of laborers to pull the barge around obstacles and through certain broad, slow stretches of water, like the headwaters of the mantees' Great Weir at Kapstabble, the barge itself was a bors product, and was comfortably appointed for them.

The central portion of the two-obel craft was piled high with crates of Margal Steep's products for sale in Karbol. Stacked low were wrapped ingots of zinc, lead, platinum, and silver dug from the ever-growing caverns of Margal Town, of Endash under South Margal, and of a host of smaller towns under the mountains that ringed the dead central valley.

Stacked above were finished goods—integrated circuits and special-purpose boards laced with the rarer elements mined under Margal Steep: germanium, indium, the lanthanide series of elements. Circuitry—actually, all manner of delicate instrumentation—was a bors specialty, as was mining. Some bors produced fine mechanical devices like the clockwork gadgetry that adorned wealthy mantels and hallways, and others made heavier machinery for roadbuilding or construction. Margal's specialty was electronics, and it was no accident that they shipped many tons to Karbol, a spaceport. Most Margal product ended up offworld, often installed in the very ships that carried it.

In the barge's passenger cabin was a great iron trunk, locked and solidly bolted to the boat's broad, flat keelson, where were stored the most precious articles of trade—sometimes ingots, sometimes rare natural crystals destined for industry or fashion. In that cabin also dwelt Barc Doresh and his new, unwelcome mentor, Niddy Marboon. Obviously, either Grast or Barc's mother had told him of Barc's "problem."

Barc's initiation to Marboon was immediate and shocking. The older bors grinned knowingly, and as soon as he was alone with Barc, began asking him about . . . Girelf. "Did you happen to notice if she had a bifurcate clitoris?" Marboon's questions were, invariably, coarse, rude, even humiliating. Worse, Grast had obviously told him his suspicions. Worse still, no subject was sacred to Niddy Marboon, not even Girelf. "The northern ones that look like seals have them, but I've never had my nose up an otter-phase mantee, so . . ." Barc's eyes narrowed and his ears flattened against his head. Angry, embarrassed, and offended, he maintained a stolid silence. Marboon had no shame. He talked constantly, and every phrase seemed a question, an importunity, an obscenity, and an offense. Barc did not think he could take six months of Niddy

Marboon. He would kill him, if he did not leap from the barge, screaming imprecations, before they even arrived at Karbol.

As the barge neared Corabund, upstream of the Great Weir across the Hammad River near Kapstabble, it was steered aside into a man-made canal and lowered through several locks. Barc was disappointed. He had heard that there was no sight as impressive, no sound so mind-shaking, as the plunging, roaring Hammad as it slid down the spillways and roiled below the great obstruction, lay-ing dewlike mist on leaves and stones a mile from the river, but it was evident that he was not going to get any-where near the dam itself.

"You can catch a far glimpse of the mantees' pride from the heights on the land road," Marboon said, "but no one not a mantee gets within ten obels of the weir itself."

Downstream, the river was first narrow for a day's travel, then gradually widening as it approached the con-fluence with the Kulee, where Karbol Spaceport had spawned the town itself.

Karbol. It was everything Barc suspected—an offense to the eye, nose, and sensibilities. It was that, and more. Even a day's float upstream, the immense silvery shapes of spaceships could be seen ascending or descending twice a day, or more often still, like silent soap bubbles in the clear, dry air. From a half day out, towering structures—buildings—rose like glass and metal needles above the rolling yellow grasslands that the river cut through.

An hour from the outskirts Barc, sitting atop the cargo, where the disgusting Niddy Marboon could not easily speak with him, could hear the dull roar of ten thousand vehicles, of machinery, perhaps even, he imagined, of great crowds of shouting, babbling folk of all seven races, shoulder to shoulder in the streets and warrens of the town.

There was no time to sightsee when the barge docked at an ordinary wooden wharf deep among the towers of

Karbol, where no direct sunlight impinged. The cargo had to be off-loaded and either secured in the warehouse there or loaded into yawning cargo carriers that awaited it. Barc and Niddy himself were not exempt from stevedores' tasks; when all was done, long after dark, Barc was so exhausted he hardly remembered the smooth, silent ride to Marboon's quarters, the flash and glare of lights through the windows, the two-minute ascensor trip up through one of the towers, or even the rooms themselves. He hardly saw the bed, except to fall upon it without opening it. Even the constant all-night roar of traffic on the thoroughfares below was, as he slept, like a comforting murmur of voices, a susurrus of ventilation fans in the caves at home.

(HAPTER 3

Interbreeding among human types is less uncommon
than admitted, though it is most often considered
perversion, and among the decadent gains the luster
of dissolute sophistication. Interracial prostitution
is rife in large cities on Stepwater, as on most worlds
of the Stream.

    Parkoon's Guide to the Worlds of the Xarafeille Stream,
    Parkoon and Parkoon, Newhome, 12125 R.L.

When he woke up, sunlight was shining on him. Barc
went to the window, and immediately backed away, struck
with vertigo—or as close to it as one born and bred in the
mountains could be. He was sure, from his brief glimpse,
that he was higher than the Steep's highest peak. A short,
cautious step forward again, and could see the upper stories of surrounding buildings, and reestimated that he was
no more than a thousand feet above the ground. His surroundings were far finer than his room in the palace
caves, he discovered. There was a shower, should he need
it, and better, a dusting-powder bath and vacuum hose.
The bathroom was tiled in maroon and gold, and the bedroom paneled in some silky wood of no common species.
There was another room, a study, he thought, or an office.

The desk reminded him that he was here to work. But
what use would Marboon have for him? Clerking? Lug-
ging crates and boxes, like last night? Brief glimpses seen
from the vehicle—the limousine—the night before
flashed through his head. He did not want to work, not

yet. There was a whole huge city out there, a universe, practically, that he had not yet seen. He remembered bright, colored lights that spelled out words. BAR. He had heard of bars, but had never seen one. Margal Steep was a quiet, rural place, for all its sophisticated products. There were no bars, no colored lights. He was not sure what HOTNSWEET was—cocoa, perhaps?—or FUR YER PLEA-SURE.

Since he did not know what Marboon had in mind for him right away, he did not dress. If manual labor were to be required, he could get his smock and pants. He took a quick dust bath and vacuumed his fur, and set out to find breakfast.

Marboon at work was not the same man as Marboon at loose ends. Breakfast was hard rolls and dried meat eaten at his desk, washed down with coffee, a bitter offworld brew. "Do you know ledgers, cub?" Marboon said, motioning Barc to a desk with a terminal. "How about inventories?" Barc, schooled as heir to a principality, was insulted. He proceeded to demonstrate his knowledge not only of ordinary accounting software, but of underlying principles as well. Marboon confined himself to specific questions as he tested his new apprentice.

By lunchtime—again ordered in, again austere, and eaten while working—Marboon was beaming at him. "Tonight, I have a mind to celebrate the fine days ahead, with a smart apprentice like you to make my headaches disappear."

By suppertime Barc had a fair knowledge not only of Marboon's trading, but of its importance to the economy of Margal Steep as a whole; everything went through the Karbol warehouses, it seemed. Every payment, deposit, and outside investment went through Marboon's hands. Barc suddenly realized that Uncle Grast had not simply fobbed him off on an obnoxious merchant as punishment or to get rid of him, but had put him in the hands of someone astute, someone Grast surely trusted implicitly. After that, Barc's burning resentment cooled considerably—and that, before he had yet ended his first full day in Karbol.

"Done! Enough!" Marboon said abruptly, slapping his littered desk. He was delighted with his new aide, who was as smart as if he were Marboon's own son, and he felt expansive, generous, and . . . paternal. "Let's eat, and then . . . I'll begin to acquaint you with the delights of city life."

"Bars?" Barc asked hopefully, envisioning the brightly colored signs.

Marboon laughed indulgently. "Bars it will be, for a start, at least," he said. "And after that? I imagine your education back on the mountain has been . . . limited, at best."

Barc did not know just what the merchant alluded to, so he supposed he was probably right.

At first glimpse, Barc thought that Girelf had followed him to Karbol, because the mantee woman looked so much like her. Marboon did not miss the way his eyes lit up when she approached their private booth, a U-shaped seat with a table in the middle, open to the main room. A succession of females had stopped by to greet Marboon as the two men sat nursing their beers, letting the remains of a rich meal settle within them. At first Barc was shocked by their easy familiarity—one, a jittery, abrupt fardish woman, had tweaked the merchant's ears, and another, a bors, had reached intimately under the table as she snuggled against him. She exuded woman-scent, not perfume. Barc became slightly aroused, smelling it, and remembering. . . . Woman-scent did not seem to differ much from one kind of female to the next. Even a tarbek dropped by, wearing a veil that was really a filter, catching her noxious hydrogen sulfide breath, like rotted whertle eggs, before it could escape and offend.

The mantee slid gracefully into the booth. As was Girelf, she was slight—small enough to slip onto Marboon's lap, over him, and onto the seat between the men. "And who are you?" she cooed, smiling and wriggling in the way only a mantee could. "Are you Niddy's new toy? Has he forgotten how much fun *we* used to have?"

"My apprentice, Barc," Marboon said quickly, before Barc had time to digest the comment. Later, much later, he found out what she had implied, but it was far too late to be embarrassed or offended by it. "He'll be my boss someday, Shilleth, so be nice to him."

"Mmmm . . . How nice? This nice?" Her slim hand slithered down Barc's chest, his belly, and found something of interest beneath the table. "You're nicer than some bors I know," she murmured, wiggling even closer to him. "You aren't hiding from me."

Marboon rose. "I see a friend at the bar," he said. "When he gets talking, he's hard to stop so don't expect me back for a while." As he turned away, he whisked a curtain across the front of the booth. Barc had not known it was not purely a decorative drape. The booth, now lit solely by a single flickering electric candle, seemed to warm several degrees.

Shilleth was warm already. Warm and busy. Her hands darted over him here, then there. . . . Her breath was sweet, woman-scented, and even her fur seemed to waft musky odors his way. Barc groped clumsily for her. With a casual motion, she flicked the table aside. It hummed softly, folded in on itself, and retracted under the benchlike seat. Barc had not known it could do that, either, but he did not give it the attention such thoughtful design deserved. He did not even wonder what had happened to the glasses that had rested on it. He was much too busy.

When Marboon returned, he flicked the curtain aside without an apparent thought, and found Barc sitting alone, with a full glass of beer in front of him. Barc's fur was rumpled, damp in places, and he wore a vaguely sheepish expression. "Ah, Shilleth is gone? Did you find

something to talk about while old Kambrath occupied
me? I hope you weren't bored."

Barc had not been bored. Neither did he wish to discuss what had occurred. Marboon did not seem to suspect. How could he help it? The girl had been so . . .
Even as he thought it, he knew that "girl" was a misnomer. He had been around mantees enough to know that
breasts as full as hers, much softer than Girelf's hard little
teats, meant that she had birthed infants. He was puzzled
that it could be so, and that she was not enormous and fat
like Shillemeh the throngmother. He suspected that the
ease with which he had penetrated her had significance
as well, and her easy skill, her knowledge of the minor
differences between bors and mantee anatomy. "You
weren't gone too long" was all he said.

"There's a drama I want to see at the Encomium," his
companion remarked. "Would you be up to it?" Barc
pleaded that he was tired, that he had not yet become accustomed to late city hours. Marboon did not insist. "Tomorrow," he said, "there's a shipment to be loaded, textiles
mostly, going to Margal. You won't have to lift bales, but
I want you to be familiar with the process, and to meet
the regular warehouse crew. Drink your beer, and we'll be
off to bed, then." Barc drowned it in two gulps. Perhaps
it would help him sleep. In spite of his words to Marboon,
he was not tired, and he was not at all comfortable with
what had happened. He did not feel warm and elated as
he had with Girelf, eager for more even when they had to
force themselves to leave the crystal chamber. He felt, instead, soiled and stinking, and more than a little ashamed.
After his initial spasm, he had withdrawn not only physically, but emotionally, and when Shilleth could not rouse
him from his sudden, cold passivity, she had left him,
with a promise of a "next time" that he knew would never
come.

Barc applied himself to his work. Marboon became
even more pleased with him. "Look at this," Barc said af-

ter a morning spent reading through a stack of contracts.
"Did you realize that Pedimet Enterprises agreed to reim-
burse Margal for all shipping costs?" Marboon had not.
Ordinary customers orders were shipped Freight on
Board, Margal. A few large-lot buyers' shipments went
FOB Destination, and the rest paid either COD or entirely in advance. The reimbursement clause was unusual
enough, and came up rarely enough, that some past aide,
perhaps training his own successor and eager to get on
himself to a new posting, had forgotten to pass that special knowledge along. Barc had only discovered it because
he was more responsible, and more interested in Margal's
business, than any other aide before him.

"Imagine how happy they must have been when Margal
stopped billing them for that," Niddy remarked. "I wonder
how much they owe us—not that we'll ever be able to collect it all."

"A hundred forty-two thousand five hundred and forty-
seven creds," said Barc, grinning.

When Niddy sat down at his console that night to make
his periodic report to Margal, he shook his head. Old
Grast was a fool not to see what a treasure Barc was. The
boy was a natural at whatever he chose to do. Not only
was he good with figures and unafraid of taking on extra
work, like reviewing all those contracts, but people liked
that potty, bumbling manner of his. They always wanted
to help him—and thus, to do things his way.

The next time, it wasn't a mantee. For several nights,
Marboon took him to different places to eat, and to drink
while they waited for one entertainment or another to
open. He was introduced to fardic epic plays—theater-in-
the-round, with occasional unwitting audience participa-
tion when actors, overcome with the import of their roles,
dragged watchers into the circle to dance, or fight, or . . .
He watched and listened to Old Earth operas by Wagner
and Puccini, saw recorded dramas ancient and modern,

and even learned how to square-dance. Few lovelies interrupted him and Nidleg Marboon at their suppers, and Barc did not see Shilleth again.

One night after Barc had been in Karbol more than a week, Marboon pleaded off about dinner. Barc did not mind, especially. He had quickly learned about the local currency and, after the first week, he got a paycheck. With cash in his belt pouch, he set off alone. As he had no real plan and no particular craving, he visited the bar where he had met Shilleth. It was close by, and in one of the booths he could pull the curtain if he did not wish company. Besides, who knew him, there?

The curtain swayed aside, then back. He glanced up, at first thinking someone outside had brushed it. The someone was already inside. She was a fard, a delicate creature with downy white belly fur, her breasts mere pink circlets of exposed flesh, and the rest of her was covered with a short, smooth pelt of an ocher hue. She wore tiny bells in her pierced ears, and a thin gold belt with a flaccid pouch that seemed empty. "Please?" she said. "Hide me? May I stay?"

"What's wrong?" he asked, his curiosity and his desire not to get involved with trouble warring with another motivation he did not wish to examine.

"A man followed me. He is at the bar, now, asking about me. I do not know him, but I am afraid."

"I . . ." Barc began.

"Oh, please! I won't bother you. I will be silent, while you eat and drink, and I will not ask anything for myself. Let me stay?"

Why not? Barc thought. The only fards I've known were the dried-out old men the desert tribes send to trade with Margal Steep, at the north adit, by the central valley. And she speaks Standard, at least. *"Fla teksit, pirgil tilip ska,"* he said. "Sit down then, and tell me your name." She giggled—a high, bell sound—and smiled, flashing her tiny

pink tongue. It matched her nipples, Barc thought.
"What's funny?"

"You asked me to lie down, and then asked my name.
Should not you ask that first, and pretend to know me,
before we make love?"

Barc restrained an astounded snort. "I didn't mean that!
I thought I said '*Sit* down.' "

She smiled, and sat gracefully, on his side of the booth.
"In the desert, '*fla teksit*' is 'sit down,' but it really means
'assume the most comfortable position.' On the hot sand,
that is usually sitting, on the pillow the speaker offers. In
the city, it means . . ."

"I get it. I'm sorry." Barc's nose paled with embarrassment. "I didn't mean to offend . . ."

"Oh, no. I am flattered—or I was, that such a fine, important bors like you would want to . . ."

"I said I was sorry. I didn't mean that."

"It is I who sorrow. I have offended you. I will go."

"No! Stay. I'll order something for you . . ."

"I could not. Just let me wait, and peer through here.
Ah. See? He is gone. I will slip outside, and be away."

"But you didn't answer my question. I still don't know
your name."

"It is of no importance, is it?"

To his surprise, Barc discovered that it was. "Stay. Please?"
He felt as though his fur was standing out from his skin.

Something was indeed standing out from him; his companion had discovered it too. Again, the table slid away,
and again he did not see it collapse, taking his unfinished
meal and drink with it. The seat seemed softer, now. Did
it deflate a bit when the table went away? The smooth,
trembling bundle of femininity on his lap was soft, too.
Some distant part of his mind told him that all fards trem-
bled, that it was natural for them, with their rapid metabolisms, yet he was trembling too in his eagerness. She was
the most desirable creature he had ever known. His fingers brushed her nipples as she lowered herself onto him.

She made a funny buzzing sound deep in her chest, and began to move on him, slowly at first, her small, quick hands on his neck, and then . . .

He had not thought about Girelf at all while he was with the fard girl, who, he belatedly realized, had never told him her name. He thought about the mantee now. Why did he feel dirty again? He had not, with Girelf. What was so different this time, and the last? He did not bother to retract the table when he slipped outside the curtain. A wall clock told him it was late, past the time he normally went to bed, but the bar was still as busy as it had been at dinnertime. No one seemed to notice him as he walked to the door. Of course, not many of the patrons present now were the same ones who had been when he had pulled his curtain closed.

He punched the streetside call button, and a long, silent cab slid up only a moments after. It had felt so good, he thought to himself as the gaudy, tawdry, ugly signs flashed by outside the window. He had wanted it so much. How could anything he wanted like that seem so pallid and sour, now? He could remember the intensity of desire, the glorious moments of penetration and shuddery culmination, but he could no longer imagine why any of it had been so important to him. Instead, it seemed ridiculously compulsive; he remembered being a small cub, and eating until he bloated and was sick. It was like that; even after the stomach pain was gone along with his excessive meal, even after the nausea and the terrible bitterness in his mouth faded, the revulsion had remained.

No more, he told himself. I'll order dinner in, from now on. Even if my body's urges surge, there'll be nothing to trigger them. I'll watch recorded entertainment in my room. The ugly feeling will go away. He did not let his mind dwell on Girelf at all. He could not afford to hang on to that. She was gone. Deep inside, he began to wonder if he would ever feel like he had with her again. Perhaps, he thought, the first time was a onetime thing and it was always like this, from then on. He did not think that could be, but still, he was a young bors, and there was no one he dared ask.

CHAPTER 4

The cautious tourist is aware of subtle differences.
Among mantees, for example, *speleth* is a throngmother's
title, and *metenkheh* signifies a sterile female aide.
The similar *meteket,* though, refers to a fertile
mantee who has birthed hybrid infants. Enzymes
produced by her half-foreign embryos trigger the
production of antibodies that thereafter attack all
but their father's kind of seed.

The difference between a mantee made sterile by
a throngmother's deliberate secretions and one who
cannot conceive among her own kind is subtle to
a bors or an ikut, but, used incorrectly, is a terrible
insult that might have fatal consequences.

The Cautious Tourist,
Parkoon Publications,
Newhome, 12120 R.L.

Barc did not order his meals in, or otherwise isolate himself. His workaday tasks were straightforward enough that
he did not have to question Nidleg Marboon often, so it
did not matter what exact hours he worked. Niddy, who
had come to like his apprentice, felt hurt when Barc more
and more often came to work just when he was ready to
leave; but then, he rationalized, he's an independent type,
and he's been raised to be a ruler. Maybe he just works
better on his own. To be sure, Niddy found no cause for
complaint about Barc's work.

After one night spent supervising the Margal barge's
off-loading, and after spending much of the following day

asleep, Barc found himself walking the streets of Karbol during the bright, sunlit hours instead of going home to bed at dawn.

Karbol by day was not the same city as Karbol by night. The holographic signs were faded images, and the neon tubes were mere black scrawls without import. Doorways enticing at night were barred and locked, and seemed small and insignificant, dark unwelcoming porticoes where no daylight reached.

Little else about the daylit, working city seemed small or unimportant to Barc. He watched from yawning archways as monstrous presses stamped out parts for groundcars, aircraft, and spaceships. He observed wendish weavers at work with toe-looms and tatting-boards. Sometimes the weavers were grannies, their fur brindled with age, who worked seated on bare curbstones in the ethnic quarter, their long-toed feet spread wide into the street; sometimes they were young wendish girls seated in rows upon cushions in production shops that turned out bale after bale of "unique" craft for offworld markets. He visited graving yards, mostly owned by bors, where half-built starships towered above machine-shop sheds, surrounded by skeletal, predatory cranes. He peered through the dust-dulled windows of datashops where people of all varieties entered paper data into terminals, converting the commerce of worlds into crystalline memory.

At one such, spotted just before he was ready to return home for a snack and bed, he watched as technicians lifted a multiterabyte datablock from a processor. It glinted greenly like a pale emerald. He watched, and his own memory leaped backward over months and miles to Margal Steep, and to the crystal cave. A datablock! The mysterious blue crystal was a datablock. It was not pale beryl like the one he saw now, but rich cerulean. Still, it was a datablock nonetheless.

It was not odd that he had never seen one before, to know what they looked like. Such crystals held so much information that they were seldom removed. All the terminals of Margal Steep probably used no more than a fraction of one's capacity in a year, and much old data was periodically purged, freeing memory for current business. The only reason he was able to see the Karbol shop's datacrystal at all was because the business of the place was data itself, not business. Such data, in large volumes, was not purged but packaged in just such crystals for shipment—perhaps to the great wendish government archives in the capitol at Garloom, or offworld. Perhaps that very crystal was destined for the Arbiter himself, on Newhome.

What then did "his" crystal—his datablock—contain? It had to be important. Or rather, it had to have been important, once, or it would never have been treated with such care, such . . . reverence. Barc had long since guessed that the reason a convenient bed and bath was behind the graphic panel was because the crystal had merited a full-time keeper. Once he had thought that meant a priest or a guard. Now he suspected the man's title might have been archivist. Perhaps when he returned to the Steep he would recover the block. Here in Karbol he could have it read out for him.

The thought of returning to Margal Steep generated mixed emotions, now. On the one hand Karbol had become a fascinating place to live. He enjoyed his work and his wanderings. On the other, Girelf was there, not here. He refused to think long on that, but thoughts of his first love led to others—of Shilleth and the fardish girl, and of his own unhappy state. He had been too active and busy for much thought of sex, but now, abruptly, his body was reminding him that its demands were long unmet, and he had recently found it difficult to concentrate on anything at all. The reminder did not have the intensity of his encounters with the mantee Shilleth or the fard, and he did not embarrass himself with a visible physical manifestation of his state; it was, instead, an empty yearning, a sad craving for something that he was not sure existed, and a profound disorientation. Love? Did he want more than just sex?

Love did not lurk about on street corners in Karbol but, in the late afternoon, certain early rising purveyors of bodily lust did. It was fortunate—or unfortunate—for Barc that he happened to pass such a corner that day. If he had not, his relief—and his further disillusionment— would have been postponed at least, though not avoided.

The female was a wend. Barc had decided that he was done experimenting across the subspecies line and that, if ever he pursued a female, she would be a bors. He had come to suspect that his disillusionment with sex resulted from his choice of partners. But the female whom he almost bumped into as he rounded that corner was not a bors. "Oooh!" she crooned. "Aren't you a big fellow?" Barc tried to step past her, but she grasped his arm. "Hey, come on," she said. "Give a lady a chance, won't you? You can't just rub all over me like that, and then just leave me."

"I'm sorry. I didn't mean to bother you. I mean, it was an accident and . . ."

"Then buy me a drink, okay? You're a gentleman, aren't you?"

Her patter made little sense to Barc, who saw no relationship between bumping into someone, being a gentleman, and buying a wendish female a drink, but if that would get rid of her . . . If she had been a bors, he thought, he might have been more interested. He would have been wrong. . . . He shrugged, and let her guide him by the arm, across the street to where a tavern was just opening to serve workers coming off first-shift jobs. As they entered, he glimpsed what appeared to be recordings of couples having sex with each other, shown in dozens of tiny viewscreens mounted on both sides of the door.

He tried to steer her toward the bar, but her insistent grip led them to a booth instead. That brought back certain memories, and Barc found himself becoming slightly aroused. He sat down quickly to conceal that, thinking not for the first time that it would sometimes be convenient to be an old human or a tarbek, and to wear clothing all the time instead of fur. He wished he could wear tight underwear and trousers without looking out of place on the streets, or as if he was on his way to some dusty or dirty job.

The wend slid in beside him, and pulled the curtain shut with a practiced motion. "Ummm, I like you," she murmured, fondling him. Instantly, when the curtain closed, he felt a rush of desire for her. He wanted her touch, and expected it whole seconds before he felt it. He wanted much more than that. He had time for only one odd, rueful thought before there was no room in his mind for thoughts: How do they ever manage to make babies at Margal Steep, where there are no bars, and no booths?

Barc dozed. A soft, sharp hissing sound caused him to open one eye slightly. He was still in the booth, and for a change his partner was still with him. She was spraying herself with something from a tiny bright-pink aerosol container. The first sound had been a puff aimed between her legs—the fur was damp there, and clumped in little spikes. The second time, she raised an arm and sprayed beneath it. The third went beneath her chin. "What's that?" he asked. She jerked, surprised. "Oh, nothing," she said, avoiding his eyes, returning the container to her waist pouch.

Barc intended to insist, but just then, seeing a pinkness almost as bright as the aerosol as she shifted her position—a wet pinkness—he forgot his train of thought. He reached for her with an eagerness that surpassed the first time, though not before she turned around quickly, and offered him a new vision of herself, and a new method of penetration he had not imagined, moments before. Even subjectively, the second time was as quick as it was intense, and moments later Barc shuddered and jerked, his hands on her slim hips, his eyes fixed on the nape of her neck. When she began to pull away, he held her against him.

"You want to do it again? You don't get a discount, you know."

"Huh?"

"I mean, there's no 'third time for half price' rule here. You have to pay for all three."

"Pay for what?" he asked, puzzled, forgetting that he was standing there still half inside her. Instead of answering him, she reached toward the curtain, and behind it. Outside the booth, he heard an unmelodious buzzer ring. Before he could ask her about that, the curtain was flung aside, and an enormous male tarbek loomed over them.

"You gotta deadbeat, Tathabel?" The tarbek's voice was like hard soles grinding over broken glass. He was not, definitely not, wearing a veil or a filter-mask. Barc gagged at the rotten odor that filled the booth, his last vestiges of ardor gone.

"He asks me 'what for' he has to pay, Mfapkot. Like he doesn't know."

"You trina stiff the lady, fat boy? You ower two times. Twenny creds."

Barc began to understand. His partner—Tathabel—was a . . . a whore. But there had been no bargain. He had not known. How could she expect him to pay for what he thought was freely given? The others had not been paid. And how did the tarbek, whom he decided was the bartender, know how many times? Feeling put upon, deceived, and belligerent, he asked him.

The tarbek grabbed him by the nose, painfully, and half-dragged him from the booth. Tathabel slipped quickly aside. "It's getting busy out there," she said. "I have to get back on my corner." She departed.

The tarbek, having led Barc to the bar, still gripping his nose, pointed to a viewscreen. "There," he said. He punched something into a small keyboard set in the counter, and the screen lit with a picture like the ones Barc had glimpsed outside. This time, though, he was not rushed. He recognized his own face, teeth drawn back, eyes glassy and staring as he busily humped someone whose rounded arch of back alone showed in the screen. "That 'us the last time," the tarbek grated. "You want I wind it all the way back? You gotta pay five cred tuh see the whole thing, ten tuh buy it—an' not until after I get my twenny fuh Tathabel's work. Otherwise, it goes on the door screens wit the other deadbeats."

Barc understood, in spite of the tarbek's grammar. If he did not pay, his coupling with Tathabel would be displayed at the door to the place, like merchandise in a shopwindow, advertising what could be purchased within. Starting up at his own stupefied, glassy-eyed visage in the screen, at his hanging jaw and protruding tongue, he realized his momentary ecstasy would indeed make a fine testimonial from a "satisfied customer."

Thirty credits, he thought, was almost all he had, but he paid silently. He did not wish to remain there any longer, even though the bartender had released his nose, and he did not wish his coupling to become part of the bar's public display.

Departing with the tiny metallic recording cube in hand, he saw Tathabel on her corner, and observed as a hurrying man rounded the building there and bumped into her. He could not hear what was said, but he saw her grasp his arm with practiced skill, and look into his eyes. Even that was all staged, he realized, entirely disillusioned now. She could otherwise have stood by the curb instead.

The next day Barc's wanderings deliberately took him in a different direction, into a marginally finer part of Karbol where, even at night, there were few streetside whores. Most of the main floor suites housed retail stores, which he had, for no real reason, not explored in earlier forays.

Everything in the world, he decided with a new cynicism, was for sale somewhere. He supposed that if he looked hard enough, he could find a murderer to kill someone for him, or someone he could pay for the pleasure of murdering someone else. He encountered neither hit man nor snuff parlor that day, though he was correct—both were available in Karbol, to those who knew the right names. What he did find was Scents of Wonder, a perfumery.

Before he looked up to read the sign overhead, he noticed the window display where dozens of bright pink aerosol bottles resided, stacked like a cross section of a pyramid. "Estrokick," he read. Not a very pretty name. He thought of Seduction and Fairy Garden, perfumes on his mother's vanity.

TESTOSLAM, FOR WHEN HE CAN'T, read a sign showing a black bottle and a pink one, AND ESTROKICK, FOR WHEN HE WON'T. A black suspicion darkened his face. Barc pushed through the shop's door. A dark, tiny fard looked up from a counter. "What's in Estrokick?" Barc blurted. "What does it do?"

"What the sign says," the clerk replied, staying cautiously behind her counter. "Makes you want to, if you're a man."

"Want to what?" He did not have to ask. He knew even before the clerk pushed a pink box toward him and said, "Read the label."

"Contains dihydrotestosterogen and an extract of musk pheromone from genuine Earth-origin minks." Dihydro-testostero-gen. Dihydro-testosterone-maker. And Barc knew about minks, or thought he did. Didn't they mate so fiercely they sometimes killed each other? Or was that sphinxes? Or skinks? No, he was sure it was minxes.

"Don't open that!" the clerk said sharply, fearfully.

"I want to smell it," Barc said. "I can smell the *perfumes*, can't I?"

"Estrokick doesn't smell. And if you open that, I'm going to push this button. . . ." Barc set the box down. The dumb fard probably thought he would go crazy and attack her if he sniffed it. On second thought, perhaps that was not so dumb. And he had already had one bad experience with females pushing buttons. But if it did not smell, he could not tell if the other two females had been using it.

He shrugged. "Never mind," he said, brightening. "I've figured out another way to get what I want."

"Good," the clerk snapped as he departed. "You perverts have your own stores in the Kartier Noyre, don't you? They'll probably let you sniff all you want."

"Pervert?" Barc murmured as he walked quickly away. "How did she know that?" He reflected on what he had said. Nothing of consequence. He cautiously rubbed his lower belly fur, then sniffed his hand. Nothing much. Do female wends and fards and mantees smell different from female bors? he wondered. If so, why couldn't he tell? Because he had never poked a female bors?

He wrangled with such thoughts until he was almost in front of the building that housed his home and his office. Then it hit him, and his estimation of human folly rose even higher. Men who want to . . . who want other men to . . . other men who *don't* want to . . . She thought I was one of those! There were perversions, he thought, and then there were perversions. Belatedly, though he was a mile from the shop, his ears paled, though when he thought about it, he considered such other perverts much less disgusting than he himself.

The doorkeeper, seeing his telltale ears, raised an eyebrow and wondered what Barc had been doing, to look so sheepish. Ah, well, he philosophized, they all think their own little foible is the worst kind there is. I wonder what he does? Sniff public cab seats or something?

Barc's ears cooled and darkened while he rode the ascensor. Purposefully, he strode toward his and Marboon's office. Good! It was darkened. Marboon was off to dinner and one of the endless shows he fancied whether alone, with Barc, or with one of his many acquaintances, usually female—and usually not bors, either, Barc reflected.

"Let's see," he murmured as he seated himself at Niddy's terminal. "He forgot to lock it again. Good." He knew right where to look. "Expenses, weeks of 7 Mard and 15

Mard," he muttered. "There. 'Arry's Ore Ouse,' " he read.
" 'Services (nonfood) . . . twenty cred, 8 Mard' and twenty
cred on 17 Mard." Twenty? The others had not been that
much better than the ten-cred wend. Oh, well, maybe
Niddy had one of them later, or while I was . . . occupied.
Let's see, those were charged to account 572—why is that
familiar? Who is 572?

He paled when the in-house service accounts scrolled
up, even before the screen reached 570. Uncle Grast.
Marboon charged my whores to the palace account. Barc
now understood why he was in Karbol: to make him forget
Girelf, no matter how humiliated he was. Never, he told
himself. She was gone from his life, but he would not forget her, no matter how many . . .

The next step in his search was harder. Niddy's corre-
spondence files were encoded. What was his password?
Barc knew he only had three tries. "Short and sweet," he
muttered. "Unrelated to names or significant dates. What
is it? How many clicks do I hear when he logs in?" He
strained to remember. *Click, click, click.* Three. No.
Click-click. Click. Two, and then one. Two easy, one
harder. He unplugged the keyboard, and let his fingers
dance on the dead keys. Sometimes Marboon fumbled
the last one, and had to start over. What keys? Unusual
ones. Z, X, or Q, ones that don't get used much. Zoo? No,
the last letter is the hard one, the one he misses. Subject:
music? Niddy loves music. Jazz? No, that's two z's. Four
clicks. The z's are all double. Something, something X? "It
has to be X. Nothing ends in Q, does it? Sax? That noisy
horn?" He plugged the keyboard back in.

S-A-X, he typed. ENTER CORRECT PASSWORD, the screen
dictated. PASS 1 OF 3. Then Barc smiled, laughed softly.
"What's more fun than music, Niddy?" Again, he typed
three letters. S-E-X. A list of files began to scroll even before he looked up from cautious fingers to the screen.

S-E-X was not Niddy's general password. It only gave
access to limited files. Not coincidentally, they were just
the ones Barc wanted, which simplifed his search. They

were all letters, from two terminals—both at the palace. Uncle Grast's, of course—and who else's? He scanned the files, beginning in the middle of the screen.

". . . Shouldn't have been another *mantee,* you idiot!" he read. "Sorry," Niddy had replied. "I thought it would be easiest, the first time, since he already likes . . ."

Another letter: "A fard? Get him a bors. He's not going to mate with a fard *here,* you fool." The reply said, "There aren't many bors whores. I'm looking, but I may have to call a friend in Garloom and . . ."

Those were from terminal 220. The rest were from Grast on number 222. Who was 220? Whoever it was, he sounded harsh, uncompromising, even cruel. What was done to me was cruel, Barc thought. Could he find out who it was? Again, his fingers danced over the keys, to no avail. He sighed, sat back, and stared at the uncooperative terminal, frowning fiercely. Then, his frown even more severe, he went to his own desk, and activated his terminal. He logged on, entered his password, and pulled up his own letters home. There they were. And there, prominent among the destinations, was terminal 220. Dreading what he already knew to be true, he pulled up the first letter. "Dear Mother," he read, and could read no more.

"Mother? Maaaa?" he wailed. "Muh-therrrrr?"

He did not recover quickly. His hands shook and his eyes blurred. Mother. His own mother did it to him. He did not understand. When the grief and rage abated a little, though, he remembered that he had started in the middle of Niddy's file. There had been earlier letters to and from terminal 220.

"That mantee slut did it on purpose," he read. "I don't know why. The throngmother says she doesn't know either, and I believe her. Mantees nictitating membranes always drop when they lie. I think the bitch has some plot, something to do with her becoming throngmother when the old woman pops her last egg. I know it. Niddy, we have to get Barc weaned of her right away. Can you help?

"Niddy, Brab was your mentor. You owe it to me, and to Brab's family. You must know what to do." As were all the others, the note was unsigned.

"Mother!" Barc whined, sadly now. "Muh-therrrrr . . ."

The "mantee slut" had indeed done it on purpose. Yet had she known, as she even then floated quietly in the small, quiet cove that she thought of as her private place, she would have felt quite remorseful, having so come between Barc and his mother, having caused such suffering. But really, what had she done? She had made love with a sweet, bumbling, sometimes obnoxious bors cub. That was all—or almost all. The rest of it was nature—the natures of bors, mantees, and of the great Hammad River rising ever higher behind the stones of the Great Weir.

CHAPTER 5

The number of missing starships in the Vadissang Sector had doubled in the past six months. It has become obvious that piracy is behind the disappearances—piracy not limited to a single star system. Is this merely a very highly organized group with good communications, *or have they acquired, or built, an illegal interstellar warship?*

The ban on warships is one of the Arbiter's cardinal directives and is the key to our millennia of interstellar peace. Why has the Arbiter not brought down his fleet of great white ships upon the Vadissang worlds? Even repeated requests to the Arbiter's representative here on Thelmin have not resulted in the assignment of even a single patrol ship. According to the consul, the piracy is purely a local matter.

Thelmin Illuminator,
Late Edition

If Barc had owned a portrait of Girelf, he thought, he would have put it away or turned its face, its penetrating, blind gaze, to the wall so it could not witness his shame. If he had owned a portrait of his mother, he told himself, he would have thrown it away, or ceremoniously destroyed it, or sent it to her as a gesture of . . . of what?

For a week, he worked long hours, and his feet never left the short, crooked path from desk to bath to bedroom. Niddy Marboon, for once, said nothing. Barc was sure the trader had both sent and received messages from Margal

Steep, but he no longer cared what Niddy, Grast, even his mother had to say.

It was all downhill from there. The long slide into habitual perversion did not begin fast, but like the wood and metal sled Barc had used as a cub, once it had been given the first few nudges it gained speed rapidly on the long, clear slope before him.

His working binge did not last; there was only so much work for Barc to do. By the end of the week, after seven days without stopping except to sleep and relieve himself, Barc faced Offday, the eighth day, with a clear desk, an empty work queue in his terminal, and a terrible craving for hot food served fresh, for beer in a glass instead of stale coffee, for faces that did not have the too-sharp features of Niddy Marboon.

Barc pushed back his chair and shuffled off to his bed. Tomorrow, he had things to do. Throughout the workweek, his mind had not been running in one single mode, and he had thought much on his situation, and what he intended to do about it. Now, sleep. It would not do to attempt his further self-degradation unrested. Before sleeping, though, he bathed—not just a perfunctory dust-bath and vacuum, but a wet-bath and a half hour under the blower, until his fur was downy-soft and fluffed up like a cub's, black with hardly a tinge of olive.

He did not get up at daybreak. There was no urgency. He was going to take as long as he wanted, do what he wanted, and there would be no complaints from Marboon if he was not back at his desk on Firstday morning. He ate breakfast at Hotnsweet, which was quiet then, halfway through the morning. Instead of the gooey pastries and chocolate drink the place featured during the day (or the different hotness, the less nourishing sweetness offered at night) he ordered a real bors breakfast with red meat, heavy nut-bread, smoked fish, and a brimming cup of buttery ghote-milk imported from a nearby mountain principality—all fuel for what he foresaw as an active day.

He would, he told himself not without quiet bitterness,

show all of them just how well they had succeeded. They would not find out right away, he knew, but Karbol, however large, was not infinitely so. Word would get back to Marboon, first as a raised eyebrow when Barc's name came up, then as hint and workplace gossip among the gate guards, the secretaries, and even the warehouse hefters: "That Barc Doresh is a pervert," they would say. "Every night, he's in one of the bars with someone else—and none of them are even bors." Marboon would not be able to keep his knowledge from Barc's mother, not forever. Not even for long. Contemplating his revenge, Barc set out on the first leg of his long journey into degradation.

Scents of Wonder looked dark from the outside, but the door opened easily and the jittery fard clerk was at her place behind the counter. Barc reached in his waist-pouch and drew out a thick folder of creds. "I want six of those," he said, pointing, "and six of those."

The clerk's bright, dark eyes widened. "Are they gifts?" she asked timorously, perhaps hopefully. "Shall I remove the prices and wrap them individually for you?"

"No need," Barc replied, his mouth curving in what he hoped was a truly decadent, evil grin. "They're for me. They're all for me."

Shrinking back, the clerk's hand hovered near her hidden button beneath the counter. Only the wad of cash creds in Barc's hand reassured her he was not about to do something despicable right there. She took his payment before she opened the glass showcase, though, and only then reached inside for his purchases, which she placed carefully in a glossy black-and-pink shopping bag. She sealed the bag before she pushed it across the counter to him. "Don't open it here," she whispered nervously.

Barc laughed. "Don't worry," he said, leering, hoping he looked rakish and sardonic. "I have a date with this lovely tarbek wench," he explained. "You can imagine how I anticipate it." Then, as if he had forgotten until now, he asked, "You don't have a perfume that's scented with sulfur, do you? Don't you think she'd like that?"

The poor fard had endured all she could. With a pitiable squeak, she spun about and darted behind the storeroom curtain. Barc heard the soft patter of fardish feet and the slam of a heavy door. He laughed again, took up his purchase, and departed. Perhaps he should have charged his purchase to the Margal Steep trade account, he thought, too late. Suspicions of him would have gotten back sooner. Behind him, as he went out the door, he heard the solenoid-operated deadbolt's sharp clack. Scents of Wonder, he suspected, would remain closed for the rest of the day.

"Pervert, eh?" he muttered as he tore open his parcel. "I'll show you a pervert. I'll show you all." He peered into the sack at the mingled boxes, each one with its color-matched aerosol container. Six dark bottles of Testoslam (for when he can't) and six pink ones of Estrokick (for when he won't). "Not yet," he growled softly. "Maybe I'll wait until I really find a tarbek whore." Were there any? He did not think he had ever seen one—just wends and fards and mantees. Are there any ikuts on Stepwater? He pictured a huge, fat female with white fur, a female otherwise much like a bors, but with yellow eyes. Would he have to go offworld to find one, to complete the projected course of the degradation his mother (Mother! Muhtherrrr . . .) had set him upon?

He did not think about bors females, not because, as he had intimated to Marboon, they reminded him of his mother, but because they reminded him of cousin Dird and her friends. Perhaps if Mother had arranged for some sweet, pleasant bors females to visit once in a while he might have imprinted on one of them instead of on . . .

He avoided thinking of Girelf. There were several things he was unsure of, that he did not want to know. Was he truly imprinted on her, or had his subsequent experiences merely made it impossible for him to imprint clearly on anyone? Was he doomed never to know real, genuine love? Or was he, for that brief moment with the mantee heir, merely imprinted on mantees in general? If he could have found out whether the mantee whore had been using Estrokick, he might have known. If she had not, then wouldn't he have known his imprinting was general and incomplete? Contrarily though, if she had used it, he would know nothing more than he did.

He would, he knew, have to try it with a mantee without the hormone jolt. After that, a tarbek (though a willing tarbek was surely a rarity, even in the pits of Karbol) and an ikut (if there were any), and then he would be done with it. Wouldn't he? Obviously he did not even consider an old-human female—they were ugly, furless things, uglier even than tarbeks. Was there such a thing as an old-human prostitute? The only old humans he had ever seen were wraiths draped in long, grimy filter robes with hoods concealing their faces. Did they smell even worse than tarbeks, too? People—real people—avoided them, though as a trader Marboon had probably been forced to deal with them from time to time. No, there was a limit even to revenge—especially since the M-being would never know exactly what he did. Let her imagine that her machinations had led him to bed even an old human. If ever he faced her again, he would not deny that he had.

He frowned briefly. Would even that be the end of it? What had the fardish clerk intimated that other time, that he had not understood until he was almost home? But no, he did not want to think about that, not now. Perhaps if he really had to, but not yet. Not an old human, and not that. Not unless she . . . he found himself avoiding the "M-word" . . . unless she didn't get the message. Then . . .

There were so many bars, whorehouses, and occupied street corners in Karbol; how many could one young bors visit in a single Offday? In a week? A lifetime? Barc did not go to work on Friday, Nextday, or even on Thirdday. Halfway through Midday morning, bedraggled, his fur dirty, stiff, and crusty in places, he shambled to his desk and activated his terminal.

"You must have had a good time," Nidleg Marboon said, looking up from his screen, leering. Beneath drooping, puffy eyelids, Barc observed his boss's expression, and thought that the leer seemed just a trifle forced. He did not reply. "You must have tried . . . everything." Marboon essayed persistently. "I saw you with those two wends, on Nextday afternoon." Barc merely shrugged, and said nothing.

Marboon sighed theatrically. "Ah, there's such a variety of wondrous experiences to be had, isn't there? Such a spectrum of delight, wet places to . . ." His voice trailed off. He rose from his desk and leaned over Barc's, then spoke softly, as if imparting some rare and precious confidence. "I heard there are a couple of *bors* tarts, now, at Fur Yer Pleasure. Have you been there recently? You really should try them—I understand they're fresh in from Garloom."

Barc did not have to feign disinterest. He was tired, in spite of a full night's sleep, and half a morning's. He ached. His member was sore and, even tightly retracted in its fur-covered, fleshy sheath, it felt chafed and raw from overuse. His eyes had sharp, grainy rheum in the corners, and having sex with anyone, anything, was the furthest thing from his mind. He did not think a whole canister of Testoslam would change that. After all, he had not abandoned his debauch until the chemical had already lost its effect upon him, had he?

Niddy Marboon did not give up easily. "There are hardly any bors in the business, you know. It takes years of conditioning and an expensive operation to override their monogamous natures. You really should try one, even just so you can say you did."

"I don't want a bors," Barc finally said. "Fucking a bors . . . I think I'd feel like I was fucking my . . . my mother." There! He had said it. Let Niddy chew on that for a while. Barc wished he could have stepped out of his role long enough to have looked up at Marboon's face right then. In truth, it would have been worth it. The other bor's ears shrank flat against his head, and his lips drew back from his yellow teeth—and not in a smile. Still,

Barc read Marboon's reaction by the way his toes curled, as if trying to get a grip in the thin, hard carpet.

His reading, though, was only partly correct. Niddy was indeed chagrined to know that Barc had discovered his uncle's and his mother's intentions, and Niddy's own part in them, but what Barc missed was Niddy's shame for his involvement, and his sadness that now he had lost the trust of the one apprentice he had ever had whom he would not have hesitated to call "nephew."

Next time, Barc mused with cold, vicious satisfaction, contemplating what his mother would think, if she knew, I really will look for a tarbek whore. Will she have to take off her filter veil? I suppose I should buy some nose filters, just in case, or sniff some teething medicine. Someone, in some bar, had told him that worked on noses, not just babies' gums. I'll get some nose plugs anyway, he decided, thinking how long and sharp that tarbek bartender's claws had been, that time with Stillep, or Spilleth . . . Never mind. Yup. Nose plugs. I wouldn't want to puke, and make a tarbek mad at me.

Realizing that Barc was still off in his private universe, from which he himself was excluded, and that the boy was not responding to his suggestions at all the way Sheb and Grast would have hoped, Marboon desisted, and returned to his own desk. He would have to let the mother know. Marboon knew he had failed with Barc, and that he was going to be in big trouble when the news got back to Margal Steep. Actually, it was not over yet, and he did not know just how much trouble he was going to be in. Barc could have told him.

CHAPTER 6

XPRESS News Service, Newhome—A delegation of
high officials from the three worlds of Sandeb A
converged uninvited upon the Arbiter's summer
palace here this morning to beg him to intervene
in the growing conflict between their homeworlds. "We
need poletzai," they said before entering the palace
grounds. "The rebels aren't going to listen to reason
unless the Arbiter gives them a reason."
When the men departed the summer palace, however,
their spokesman said, "We cannot depend on troops
and warships to settle an internal matter. It is up
to us to bring the rebels to the conference table."

For the second time, Barc missed seeing the mantees'
Great Weir on the Hammad River, this time while going
upstream. Even had the barge floated right under the
dam, it was unlikely Barc would have left the cabin.
He had hardly spoken to Niddy the entire voyage. The
M-creature wanted him home, huh? Home? Home was
Karbol. Home was any convertible booth in any combina-
tion bar, restaurant, and whorehouse, most of the time,
and his room and bed in the high-rise multiplex the rest.
Home was not Margal Steep, not anymore.

The place even looked little, dirty, and insignificant; the
mountains, even Mendeb Peak, looked smaller than ones
the river wound through farther south; the wharf was only
a wooden jetty that had obviously been raised many times
its original height, each time in a flimsier, more haphazard

fashion. It did not compare to the one next to the Margal warehouse in Karbol; Hammad Bridge, between the two Margals, was frail, old, and only two lanes wide, nothing like the great autocar bridges in the city; even the road was poorly paved and dotted with chuckholes the Karbol street maintenance department would never have allowed.

Margal Town itself was a horror. Barc had gotten used to open skies, however narrowly defined by tall buildings, to the airy view from his bedroom windows, to the fumes, stinks, and delicious aromas of the busy city with its all-hours bustle. With his first step inside Margal Town, he felt the weight of warren and mountain press down upon him, making his knees weak, his feet heavy, and his head bang. The closer he got to his mother's chambers, the worse he felt.

When the great door groaned open, pulled by an un-seen servant within, Barc saw that his worse forebodings had been too optimistic. His mother was not alone. He had planned to whine, if need be, and shrink cublike to the floor. He would even have crawled, and nibbled her fingers like a shameless infant, to predispose her to allow him to return to Karbol, to his work and his debaucheries. And after all, it had been her idea in the first place. She could hardly blame him for what he had become. So what if she had to send someone to find his father, and had to breed another heir? Barc was sure he was thoroughly dis-qualified. That should not be too hard, he thought. She still has a few fertile years left. Of course Blet won't like that; my sister, a homeless, husbandless old bag of fur—because if I am not heir, then neither will be her children. Poor Blet. Well, if she had been nicer to me, maybe I would have imprinted on a bors, someone like her, maybe even one of her friends, if she hadn't always goaded them to pick on me. Too damned bad.

His mind, he discovered, was wandering. Blet was there, with the M-thing, and so was Uncle Grast, and even Niddy Marboon. All of them, and only one of him. All thought of ignoble fawning had departed. Barc drew himself to his full height and smoothed his travel-rumpled fur. His brief, stiff bow was the gesture of an outsider to a foreign manarch who held no pledge from him. Sheb did not like that. Her ears flattened.

"Have you no respect?" Grast snarled. "We already know you have no shame."

"I mean no offense, Honorable Grast," Barc said, using a neutral address. "I am nothing, a beast without honor or respect or, as you say, shame." So send me back to Karbol, he silently pleaded. I'm of no use to you here.

"You are heir to Margal, whelp!" his mother spat, ears pale and flat, lips pulled back in a grimace, a snarl, "and you will act accordingly."

Still heir? Impossible. How could that be? He was . . . ruined. He had made sure of that. "Me?" he squeaked, embarrassing himself.

"You, Barc Doresh, my . . . son."

The way she said "son" made Barc cringe.

"Why can't my father . . ."

"Your father? Your worthless, wandering father? Can I chase him offworld, half across the Stream? He won't be back for six more years, I'm told. Oh, yes, cublet, you are the heir."

"But I'm not . . . not worthy," Barc mewed, further embarrassing himself. Old habits, cub habits, popped back at such stressful moments.

"We'll make you . . . worthy—at least, we'll make you functional. Once Blet is empowered, has sired a pair of heirs, then who cares? Go back to Karbol, or go offworld like your miserable sire. To be sure—offworld. I may require it."

Grast's low growl caught her attention, and stopped her ranting. "The boy's tired, sis," he murmured. "Let him go, for now."

His dam nodded. "Tomorrow, then. Tomorrow, we'll begin." She turned to Barc. "Go, shameless cub."

Barc tried to catch Niddy's eye as he backed out of the room, but the skinny fellow would not look at him. His

last impression, before the door groaned shut and he
turned away, was that Marboon looked . . . guilty? But he
must have been mistaken. It had not been the trader's
fault, either. He had only followed the M-beast's orders.
What did he have to feel guilty about?

Barc was almost surprised that no town guard waited to
escort him—where? To his old room? To a cell in the reprobates' prison? Where was he supposed to go, to sleep?
he shrugged. He was not really sleepy. He would wander
around the tiny cramped town a while, savoring its ugli-
ness, for when he returned to airy Karbol.

But . . . His mother intended to keep him here. Abruptly,
her words came back to him: "We'll make you worthy." Just
how, he wondered, becoming anxious, would they do that?

Barc wandered, thinking deeply. First, what did it matter? Let Blet rule. Fine. What did he care? All she has to
do is to pop a pair of heirs, and . . . It was Barc's turn to
flatten his ears. Suddenly, he understood. Oh, yes. He understood, and he shivered. Poor, unimportant females far
removed from the royal line could just pop their twosome
when they wanted. If they sometimes gestated a singleton,
or two of one sex, they might kill them and try again; if
they birthed three, they might slay the weakest or ugliest
or noisiest of the two matched-sex ones—but the ruler
could not do that; the succession was vital to the whole
of Margal Steep. Nothing could be left to chance. There
could be no irregularity.

It was a matter of breeding—and culling. There had
to be two offspring, a male and a female. The trait had to
breed true, and because there was always a chance of an
undiscovered stray gene surfacing, or of a tiny random
mutation, it had to happen not once but twice: the male
heir—the future heirmother's brother—had to breed first,
and had to sire proper twins of mixed sex, before his sister
did, or she could not be empowered. It was a matter of
proof, doubled proof, that the family's genes were un-
changed and uncontaminated.

So they want to breed me to a bors? Barc speculated. But how? They can't. What he knew and they did not— unless Niddy's tattletales and spies had found out—was that he had indeed tried it with one of the bors prostitutes. He had tried and failed, because even with fresh cannisters of Testoslam and Estrokick at hand, he had seen not a lush, wet female, ready for him, but . . . an obscene caricature of his mother. That was when he became sure he was doomed to be a pervert forever.

What Barc also knew now was that he was truly imprinted not just on any mantee, but on Girelf. When he tried it with another mantee, he had indeed needed Testoslam, and a dose of Estrokick, and he had had to pretend she was really Girelf, because every time he remembered she was not, he had . . . lost interest, and required more chemicals. Finally the mantee had become bored, then offended with his experimentation and, demanding her money, had left him.

What would they do when they found that out? What would Blet do when she found out that her cousin Dird was the new heir, founder of the new dynasty of Margal Steep? Barc did not want to know. Blet was bigger than he was, and she had always been mean to him, even to sucking Mother's teats dry while he slept, leaving him hungry. Blet? No, he could not remain in Margal with Blet on his mother's throne or off it. He might not even be able to remain in Karbol. Perhaps Barc's belief in his sister's omnipotence was exaggerated—but not by much. If she had a single flaw (among her manifold flaws) that actually weakened her, Barc had not discovered it.

Looking up, he realized that he was near the Bridge Road Gate. If the guards would let him out, he would willingly walk all the way to Karbol. He turned and, drawing himself to full height, strode purposefully toward the yawing opening lit by the bright, clear light of Mirrim, beyond.

* * *

Not much later, chastised and chagrined, Barc's defeated tread took him deeper and deeper into Margal Town's abandoned caverns and, hardly coincidentally, nearer the shrine of the blue crystal and the passageway out to the riverbank. The guards had been instructed. Barc was thus still in Margal Town.

"You said something a while back about Barc having found an old city gate somewhere deep under the town," Nidleg Marboon reminded Grast diffidently.

Grast chuckled. "I'm sure he's discovering right about now that all those old caves are flooded," he informed the trader. "He'd have to be a mantee and swim out. He'll be back. Everything's all ready for him, and this time it's going to work."

Marboon, having just seen what was in store for poor Barc, repressed a shudder that would have revealed his sudden decision. Barc was a good kid. He didn't deserve what Grast and Sheb planned. He was a fine young bors and . . . and above all, he was Niddy's friend. Niddy Marboon would have had to think long and hard to remember the last time he had said that about anyone. "I should go," he said. "It was a long trip, and . . ."

"Of course," Grast said magnanimously. "You brought him here. Now rest. And tomorrow, you can watch the changes in Barc Doresh as they unroll before your eyes." Marboon did shudder, once he was outside the door, and again as he passed the room where . . . *it* was—where Barc would be, in the morning, unless . . . He shuddered a third time when he passed the room next to his own in the guest quarters, where the mindskinner, Spuk, was staying. There was no light coming under the door, and no sound from within. Spuk spent much of his time in the reprobates' prison . . . experimenting. Niddy shuddered again. Then quietly, without giving himself time to think, he opened the door to the psychiatrist's chamber. There! On the shelf! It was the very book Spuk had proudly showed him and Grast earlier. He removed it, tucked it under his arm, and slipped back into the hall.

"I'm looking for Barc, the heir," he said. "Have you seen him?" Niddy Marboon wondered how many people he had asked, in the hours past. Was he any closer to the boy? He was not sure until the last man to have seen him pointed to a darkened passageway that slanted down. There, in the muck formed of blown-in dust, crumbling ceiling rock, and a trickle of groundwater, he saw a single, new, fresh footprint. Barc had gone that way. Niddy met him on Barc's way back out.

"Following me?" Barc snapped. "Why? Didn't you know I'm trapped here? The water is . . ."

"I know. Grast told me. But you *have* to get out."

"I do? Why? What do you care?"

"Come see," Marboon said, holding up the mind-skinner's book. "There's a globe light back there. You have to see this. You have to escape." Barc, puzzled by Niddy's uncharacteristic intensity, followed him toward the light. He understood all too well, soon after.

"See?" Marboon said, pointing at a holographic picture.

"The bors strapped in the chair? What's he doing there?"

"It's not what he's doing, it's what they're doing to him."

"They? Who? There's no one else in the picture."

"Grast and Blet and your mother, that's who."

"Huh? Where are they?"

"Look at the wires, you fool! See?" Barc looked close, and saw wires that snaked from a black box with dials and switches, across the floor, and up the chair leg, where they seemed to terminate in the neighborhood of the bors's crotch. "And see the holoscreen in front of him? And his eyes, taped open? They're going to put you in the chair, Barc, and show you pictures of females—mantees, wends, bors, even old humans, I suppose—and they're going to jolt your privates every time they show you a picture that's not a bors female." Barc seemed properly horrified,

Niddy saw, watching his ears. "They'll make you hate mantees and ... and everyone but bors. And see that sack? Those tubes? Dihydrotestosterogen, and lots of other stuff. Estro-something."

Barc knew. Concentrated, lab-strength Testoslam and Estrokick, and some other heavy-duty hormones. He had read about them on the little "clinical products" catalogue that came wrapped around every vial of the retail-strength products. They were going to pump his blood full of strong hormones, wire him like an industrial-duty glow light, and skinner his brain. He would be tied up, poking his thing in the air, and getting zapped by every kind of female except the ones that looked like his sister and his ... muh-therrrr. . . .

Marboon saw that his future plight had sunk in. "You have to get away," he repeated, feeling queasy, imagining those wires. . . .

"How?" Barc asked.

"Swim? Didn't you say once that you could swim?"

"But it's too far!" Barc wailed. "I'd drown."

"You're a bors. You can hold your breath for a half hour. You won't drown in a few minutes underwater."

"I can't hold my breath that long, and swim hard too."

"It's only for a few minutes, Barc. And look at this!" Niddy clutched his arm; then, having his attention, he tore a flyleaf out of the mindskinner's book, took a pencil from his pouch, and sketched rapidly. "This is a tunnel, see? And here's a chamber, and another tunnel. . . ." Then he drew a line that snaked and stepped from chamber to chamber, and crosshatched the part below the line. "The water comes up, but it can't fill the high parts, only the lower tunnels, see? You'll have to swim through the tunnels, catch your breath in the chambers, and then . . ."

"It's too far!" Barc wailed again.

Niddy held the book up to his face, still open to the holograph. "It's not too far," he stated, "is it?"

"No," Barc said, subdued, pale-eared, and wide-eyed. "It's not too far." Even if he did not make it all the way, if he died, bloated, and floated there until his flesh rotted and his bones sank to the floor, it was not too far at all.

"I'll wait outside for you, right where you said," Niddy Marboon promised, as Barc waded chest-deep in the black water. He had wrenched one of the working glow lights from a tunnel ceiling. Without power, it would fade and die within an hour, but until then ... if he was not out and free in an hour, he never would be.

How far? He thought he was standing about a half obel, about eight body-lengths, from the crystal chamber, but he could not be sure. The water changed things, and he had not been there in a long time. He shrugged, and lowered the globe into the water. One last look, for his bearings, and he was gone, without a bubble or a trace. He really did swim like a mantee, Niddy thought, tossing the horrid book on the ground and kicking muck over it. Then he turned, and walked away, toward the next, distant light.

Barc heard the plash of his own emergence even before he knew for sure his head was really in air. Then he drew in great, gasping lungsful, and treaded water awkwardly in ordinary bors fashion. When he held the light globe up to look around, the weight of globe and arm almost thrust him under again, but he was rewarded with a brief glimpse of a much-deteriorated ceiling, in considerable disrepair. It was the crystal chamber. Holding the globe low, he dog-paddled about, ducking his head under water and peering through the murk, looking for the passageway, the open bronze door. He looked also for the blue crystal, but though it should have been easy to spot, he saw only the case that had held it, lying on its side on the floor where the encroaching waters had left it. The crystal, smaller, was probably covered with silt.

Was the door to the archivist's or guard's bedroom open or shut? He thought he remembered shutting it, but he could not be sure. He would just have to try the first opening he could find, and hope—there should be air in the bedchamber, too, shouldn't there? If he chose the wrong opening, he might get another chance. Barc took several deep breaths to oxygenate his blood, competing against the toll of his own constant paddling effort to remain afloat. Then, taking a final lung-straining breath, he plunged downward toward a dark, shadowy opening dimly seen.

Niddy Marboon waited in the water, shivering, clinging to a dead branch that threatened to pull loose from the crumbly rock wall. This had to be the right place. The water was higher, so there was no longer a riverside path or a clump of concealing brush—just sheer cliff and fast-moving, silent black water. Where would young Barc emerge? Would he emerge? If the water was so much deeper out here, then what about inside? Had Barc been farther away than he had thought? Niddy clung silently to his flimsy branch, and he waited.

Several times, chunks of weather-fractured rock tumbled from the cliff, pieces of Margal Steep gnawed loose by the water. Each time, he looked up, hoping that the looming cliff was holding firm, that the water's drag on him, and his own pull on the scabby little branch, was not the additional stress that would bring the whole monstrous overhang down on him.

Again, Niddy looked up—but the source of the latest sound came not from near the cliff, but from farther out in the stream. He peered through the darkness, and saw a brief, star-limned, irregular ripple. "Barc!" he hissed. "Over here."

"Whoosh! Whoof!" He heard the younger bors gasping for breath after his long swim.

"This way," he said, louder, but surely not loud enough for the guards on the bridge to hear. "Over here." The ripple-reflections intensified, and came nearer. A hand grasped his. "Barc?" he asked.

"**No.** Whoof!" came the answer. "I'm Uncle Grast.

Weren't you . . . whoosh! whoof! . . . expecting me?" Barc pulled himself up Niddy's arm. The trader cringed, and glanced up at the threatening rock. "Water's really up, isn't it?" Barc said as he recovered his breath. "We'll have to swim to the far side. Can you make it?"

Glancing at the branch, at the ever-more-exposed roots, he replied, "I don't think I have any choice," and he let go.

CHAPTER 7

One cannot assume. Take the "Month Song" sung
to various tunes by children across Stepwater:

> Newarry, Brewarry, Mard, then Quart;
> Persammon, Lectamon, Allomon, Half;
> Selobrate, Ornicate, Vazilate, Twellary;
> Theenary, Tenalong, Lastafol, Leven.

Like many calendars, the months' names may
once have meant something. "Newarry" was perhaps
"New Year," and "Brewarry" when the first new ale was
tapped. "Quart" or "Quarter" is self-evident, as is "Half."
"Twellary" also seems appropriate, but "Tenalong"
is the fourteenth month, "Leven" the sixteenth, and
"Lastafol" is not last of all.

The Curious Tourist,
Parkoon Publications,
Newhome, 12122 R.L.

On the long walk downstream, Barc had time to draw several threads of thought into a single woven strand. He did
not want to think about what he had escaped from, because that gave him visceral twinges, so instead he pondered the ramshackle Margal Jetty. The Hammad River
had risen slowly enough for the Margal wharfmaster to
adjust for it, however sloppily, and thus the water's rise
was a single long-term event. Then, there had been trickles in the lower caves when he had been a child exploring
there—trickles that had surely not been there generations

before, when those caves had been occupied. Now the lower caves were inundated.

So: a single phenomenon, rising water, accounted for several accruing problems for Margal, and though Barc was quite bitter about his recent treatment there, he was not so upset that the damage to Margal did not bother him also: the rising waters had a single cause, and he was sure what it was.

"I have to see it," Barc stated flatly. "You have enough money, don't you? Enough to pay a driver to take us over on the high road? We can catch another boat at Fantol, farther downstream. I have to see the Great Weir."

"But why? We must hurry. If Sheb and Grast send men after us . . ."

"The flooding in the caves, Niddy! Didn't you see how the walls are crumbling? And the cliffs where you waited for me? The mantees are undermining Margal Town."

"The mantees? But how? And why?"

"As for how, that's what I must confirm. And why? That's easy—the fifty-obel rule." Marboon said that he did not recollect the rule. "Everything within fifty obels of a riverbank—that's about five thousand bors feet—belongs to mantees," Barc told him. "It's in the planetary charter, unless it's been specifically revoked by deed. Since the river has risen, they've doubled their territory." He pointed out into the vast empoundment, indicating where skeletal treetops jutted above the water. "See those? They're probably eighty feet high, and until a few years ago, they were on land. The local wends have lost that land. Why else would the mantees invest so much in that dam of theirs?"

"But it's all underwater. What good is it?"

Barc snorted, exasperated by his companion's obtuseness. "Ask them! They're as much at home in the water as on land, and besides, as the pond grows, so does the length of the shoreline—and the fifty-obel-wide strip the mantees own, too."

"But why do they want to destroy Margal? There's no

shore for them. For every foot of rise, they only gain inches of new shore. And I thought there was a treaty that within the Hammad Water Gap they can only claim the water itself. The town is no mile back from the shore."

"I suspect Margal doesn't even enter into their plan. They want the wend forest lands farther south. They may not even know that they're flooding Margal out—not that they'd care, if they did."

Marboon dug in his pouch—surrendering to Barc's reasoning—and counted what creds he had. "We have enough," he announced. "Let's go look at that dam."

"See?" Barc asked, triumphantly, squinting at the far-away arc to discern details obscured by distance. "That's no fish weir. It's a stone dam—and the topmost courses, the light-colored ones, are new. They're raising it higher still. I wouldn't be surprised if all Margal Town collapses in a few years. We have to do something about it." Margal was more than just a place where his family lived. Even though he himself might not live there anymore, Margal was still—and would always be—home. The devious, un-principled mantees had to be stopped.

"Surely," Marboon agreed pensively, "but what? You can't go back to tell them. The mindskinner . . ."

"You can, though. I'll wait here, and watch to see if they follow you back out."

Arrangements were made. Barc would watch, and if Niddy was followed coming back, he would head to Karbol by a different route. If not, they would go together. If Marboon did not appear within a week, Barc should press on alone.

"Yo! Barc!" Barc, watching the shore road, did not im-mediately realize that Niddy's harsh cry came from the river. Shortly later, after stumbling down the rocky bank, he helped pull the trader's small craft ashore. "It's no use, Barc," Marboon said without preliminaries. "None of them believed a word I said. Grast thinks I made it all up, currying favor just to keep my job, while Sheb and your nasty sister can't imagine that ordinary water could harm a mountain." He spat a gobbet of half-chewed spiceroot in the river. Plunk. He shook his head. "I know. I hung on to that branch, waiting for you to show up. I saw what bites the river took from the cliff there."

"Uh-huh," Barc agreed. "How do they think those mountains formed, anyway? Water. Otherwise they'd be just big smooth bumps of high plateau. All those peaks and sharp edges were made by water."

"Frozen water," Marboon commented.

"Wet or frozen, it's powerful stuff, if you give it time. And I don't think Margal has much left."

"No?"

"Well, a few years. Maybe even ten or twenty, but once the main force of the current breaks through into the lower caves, it will tear out enough walls and columns to make the upper levels sag, even fracture. It won't be safe in there anymore. Can you imagine the devastation, the deaths, if one of the really big caves falls in?"

"Well, that's Dird's problem, I guess," Niddy said philosophically, "and Frak's, when he takes over from Grast."

Barc had considered Dird's accession to the position that should rightfully have fallen to his sister Blet—and not without vengeful satisfaction. He did not like Dird at all—she was sharp-tongued and snotty—but he disliked Blet, who had tormented him from childhood, even more. But still, Blet was family, which counted for something, and Dird was not close family at all. He supposed that the pros and cons, Dird or Blet, weighed about equally in his mind.

But Frak? That fat, roly-poly, overgrown cub? Frak the bumbler, who kept neutered, defanged mahkrats as pets, and fed them dead slithers with his bare hands? Frak, who flunked elementary geomorphology twice, and who still counted on his fingers? Frak would be responsible for saving Margal from the mantees? The idea galled Barc, who had studied hard in school, expecting that one day he would need even the oddest bits of his hard-won knowledge as the ruler of Margal Steep.

Nonetheless, he shrugged. That was over now. Instead, he would apply the same acquired lore, but as the apprentice of Marboon the trader, and someday he would take over the Karbol operation in his own right. Besides, for all their manifest faults, Frak and Dird got along with each other, which was important in a ruling pair. He and Blet would have fought constantly, and he would never have been able to get away from her. No, this was better. His thoughts remained on Karbol, home of Hotnsweet, Scents of Wonder, and all the interesting activities they, and places like them, promised. He hardly thought of Girelf at all, right then.

In the dark hours, though, Barc rolled and tossed in his bed. From his own blankets—first beneath the high-road wagon that conveyed them to Fantol, and then in the passenger cabin of a commercial barge, shared with several other travelers, Niddy Marboon heard the mumbled name "Girelf" not once but many times while Barc's sleeping mind dealt with the conflicts of hard, solid circumstance, sharp-edged desire, and the mushy obtuse reality of his untoward imprinting.

At last the glittery teeth of Karbol's towers nibbled at the flat, featureless horizon of the Lower Hammad drainage. "Ah," Barc sighed, "it will be good to get back to work. It'll take me two weeks just to catch up." Two weeks in which he would be too busy to think about lush, wet, wendish females, of hot pink cylinders of Estrokick . . .

"Ah . . . Barc?" The young bors turned, curious about the trader's cautious, hesitant tone. Marboon, he observed, still faced toward Karbol's distant shine, now topaz and garnet with sunset's rays. He did not—would not—meet Barc's eyes.

"What is it?" Barc pressed, not really anxious, but with some slight concern. "What's troubling you?"

"I didn't tell you everything," Marboon replied. "I . . . I didn't know how. I still don't. I thought when we got back to the office . . ."

"What, Niddy?" Barc was suddenly aware that Marboon's hesitancy presaged a revelation more serious than some trifling addition to his apprentice's workload.

"Ah . . . About your job. You . . . I mean, from what your mother said, you . . . don't have a job anymore."

"Did you arrange that, Dad? I mean, for Barc to lose his job?"

John Minder sighed. "I would have, had it been necessary—but no. I am only one man, after all, and I can't be everywhere. I choose people for my work, my ends, but I don't control them once they, and events, are set in motion."

"But what *did* you do? How did you get involved with Barc and Girelf in the first place? And . . . and *when*?"

Minder smiled. "Oh, I'll let you and your sisters get to the bottom of that, in time. If one of you is to be Arbiter someday, you'll have to do that sort of thing, you know."

Rob sighed. Why was it that Dad's stories always took *work* to figure out?

CHAPTER 8

Barc counted the money he had earned (and not yet spent
on females) and then counted his remaining bottles of
very expensive hormones. Twenty-five hundred creds. He
could live a month on that, the way he had been living

when he had a job, or six months if he husbanded the little vials carefully, and bought very few drinks in the bars.

Marboon had kindly allowed him to keep his bedroom in the multiplex—at least until Margal sent the trader a new apprentice, which could be months, yet. Niddy even promised to buy his lunch in return for a few hours of tedious data entry he would otherwise have to contract out. Of course Barc's terminal code was no good anymore. He could not be allowed to do any critical work.

He was grateful for the crumbs Niddy could throw his way—at some risk of Margal's eventual disfavor. Margal. No longer did he personify home as Sheb, Blet, or Grast. Just Margal. A cold, dispassionate, abstract entity endless obels up the Hammad River, linked to the multiplex terminals here by wires, microwave dishes high on distant mountaintops, and satellites maintained in orbit overhead by another dispassionate corporation in Garloom, halfway around the planet Stepwater. Margal, that in five or twenty years would crumble. What would it look like? Would the whole side of Mendeb Peak slide into the water gap, leaving exposed tunnels and tiny, distant, scurrying bors like pinchbugs in a nest torn open by the claws of hungry sucknoses? Would the apartments and corridors thus revealed look like a half-demolished building in Karbol's old spaceport district, all the walls and ceilings different colors, grimy with years of living, never before exposed to the pure, direct light of day?

Barc shrugged. That was no longer his concern. His task was to find a way to make enough creds to continue eating regularly, to pay for a place to stay, in a month or a few months, and to buy the little bottles of hormones that let him fool himself into thinking he was enjoying life, once in a while.

There were many single males in Karbol. Cities, Barc suspected, drew all the empty souls, the disenfranchised, disinherited, disowned of every race of man. There were, thus, few jobs to be had. If he planned to eat regularly, and to sleep warmly, in a bed, he would have to *make* a job for himself. But what should he do? He had already approached spaceship captains, construction bosses, the Karbol city engineering department— everywhere a well-trained, technically proficient young bors might be welcomed—but to no avail. Though bors, as a race, were fine engineers, scientists, and technicians, some were finer than others, and Barc had no special talent or training that a thousand others did not.

He needed a niche—some kind of work that no one else was doing, or that no one did well. Commerce, he thought, not labor. But whatever it might be, he had not found it yet. Ah, well, it would come to him. In the meantime, Niddy had fed him well at noon, he was restless and thirsty, and the trace of still another biologically induced urge was nibbling at the periphery of his awareness.

He had heard that there were females in some of the dives near the spaceport who only charged four creds. They could not be all that bad, could they? That way, he could stretch his money further. Barc was not ashamed of his urges or his matter-of-fact submission to them. After all, imprinting was not something he—or the M-beast— could control, was it? Ordinarily, had he imprinted properly, he would have had a proper mate, and sex whenever he wanted—or needed—it. A proper bors mate, keyed to his own emotional and physiological state, would have responded to his unique pheromones with acquiescence at worst, with eager joy at the best of times.

Since he was doomed to feel such urges intensely until he attained clesiopause at forty or so and, like Uncle Grast, had a choice in the matter, since he could not concentrate on work, finding work, or making work while his libido overrode his cerebral functions, why should he not limit the necessary expenditures as best he could? It was not as if he really enjoyed it or anything, not as if the memories it left him were sweet, like Girelf. Besides, he had not spent much time around the spaceport. Maybe

he would see something that would trigger an idea, something he could do for a living.

"Yah, I almost puked, I tell you," the fat, glossy bors
boomed, shaking his head, slamming his beer mug on the
table, waking Barc, who had been dozing in the adjacent
booth. Barc, glancing around, realized that his four-cred
wend companion had departed.

"Yah, me too," said the loud bors's companion. "Especially when the weirdo's relatives sued pee-pee and won a
hundred thousand. I thought they'd close down the whole
planet."

"We're lucky we still got jobs," the other said. "I dunno
why pee-pee signs perverts, anyway."

"How can they tell?"

"They ain't got fur."

"That's old humans," loud-voice responded, with a de-
gree of condescension. "Anyone can recognize them, but
how can they tell they're perverts?"

"Well, if they ain't, then their parents was, right?"

"I don't know. They say they aren't all half-breeds."

Pee-pee? Huh? Barc lost interest in the talk. It did not
seem to make sense. It had, however, triggered a response
in him. He had consumed three mugs of cheap house
beer with his former companion, and his subconscious
mind made its own kind of sense of the overheard conversation. He pulled the curtain aside and shambled blearily
toward the men's room. "Pee-pee?" he muttered as he relieved himself. "What kind of baby talk is that?" Maybe
it's the way offworld bors talk, he speculated. That loud
guy seemed to have some kind of accent.

He had no reason to return to his booth, and he had
paid in advance for the wend's services, but curiosity
steered him past the loud one's booth. Both patrons wore
off-purple uniform smocks with pale blue piping and
bright yellow sleeve patches that he could not read without staring intrusively. He departed.

Outside, half a block down the street, the same clashing colors caught his eye—a limousine, purple and blue, with a big chrome-yellow badge on the driver's compartment door. "Parkoon and Parkoon," he read. "Tours." Below the badge were several lines of small blue letters.

Cultural tours throughout the Xarafeille Stream
Specialty tours by arrangement
Parkoon's Gourmet Dining City Tours
Parkoon Expedition Outfitters and Safari Guides

"Aha! Pee-Pee," Barc said. "Parkoon and Parkoon." Hadn't they been in the news recently? Some old human getting killed by a prostitute in a bar? Barc shrugged. He had never seen an old human naked, but they just had to be horrible. Imagine all that skin, all wrinkly and baggy, without any fur at all. He shuddered, trying to imagine that, imagining the shock of some poor whore when the hideous thing took off its cloak. Then he shuddered again, for another reason. A stray, involuntary image had crossed his mind: a mantee, wet from the river, her short fur flat against her arms, her legs, her tiny breast-swellings . . . Girelf.

"Pervert," he muttered, disgusted with his mind's too-frequent tricks, trying to get rid of the image of Girelf without any fur, all pale, pink as her nipples all over, smiling at him. He walked faster, heading nowhere in particular. He knew he could not go immediately home and to bed as he had planned, with such thoughts bouncing around his brain. Too often, he had to tire himself out completely just to sleep, so he would not think about being unemployed and disowned—for being everything he was.

Eventually, he saw a familiar place, and realized that his hike had not been entirely aimless. He was thirsty again, and he knew that bar. He had been there a few times. "Mfapkot," he said, greeting the tarbek bartender by name. "Did you know that four of your viewscreens are burnt out?" He had noticed that as he entered. He had also noticed that several other screens were running old recordings he had seen before. He had always looked at them, because he had never trusted Mfapkot not to have made a copy, that time with Tathabel.

"You gonna complain, you buy somethin' first," the tarbek said.

Barc sat on a barstool and ordered a beer—again, the cheapest kind. "What ever happened to Tathabel?" he enquired. "I haven't bumped into her lately." He grinned at his pun, but Mfapkot did not smile.

"She run off. Some new place, only lets wends in. 'Twenny-two creds a time,' she says, an' she don't need to buy Estrokick, she's only working for other wends."

"What about the other girls?" Barc asked, glancing around, seeing that there was only one closed curtain in the place, and only two old male fard drinkers twitching their noses and quivering, talking that fast, chattery fard talk.

"They move on too, they say. New places."

"So you're just selling drinks? That's all? Can you afford to stay open?"

Mfapkot raised one shoulder—a tarbek shrug? Barc did not know enough tarbeks to tell. "Got some new ones, five-cred girls," he said. "One's in there" He gestured at the drawn curtain.

Barc finished his beer quickly, deciding to move on. This place was as depressing as he felt. He fully expected to come by another week and find it all boarded up. Five-cred girls? Poor Mfapkot. Things are tough everywhere.

Just as he swiveled his stool around, one foot on the floor, the closed curtain parted slightly and a pale shape emerged. Barc stared. White fur? An ikut, here? But so slim and small? His eyes widened further. That was not fur, it was skin. The creature had breasts like a nursing mother's.

Barc's nose twitched. Oh, no. His nose never did that, except when . . . He spun back around on the stool, and angrily confronted the bartender. "What are you doing—spraying Estrokick in the ducts? Isn't that illegal?"

"Dere's no Estrokick here," Mfapkot replied. "Jus' her." Barc's eyes turned again, but the old human—he knew that was what she was—had disappeared into the back room. Old-human, furless, and yet . . . she had smelled good. Barc's self-disgust combined with his already-shredded sense of propriety, yet he admitted to a strong, almost overwhelming curiosity. He reflected that only an hour or so past, he had been sated. He should have remained so for days. The old human had just had sex, too—out of the corner of his eye he saw a rather bedraggled male mantee shuffle from the closed booth and out the door. Prepaid, Barc thought, or Mfapkot would be chasing him. "You want another beer?" the tarbek asked him. "It kinda gets to me too, sometimes."

"Huh? Beer does?"

"Old-human musk. I bin drinkin' more, since I got them females."

Barc felt that he was not tracking quite properly. He was thinking about furless skin. Not entirely furless, he corrected himself. There had been those little patches. "Musk? You mean, like minxes?"

"Whose? Who's she? No, I mean the stuff the females put out. With them, nobody needs hormone sprays. Except us tarbeks. It only makes us thirsty. Pretty much, anyway."

The heady scent—really a scent, not an odorless pheromone—had faded, and Barc's mind felt clear again. "You mean they don't need Estrokick to do it with bors or wends or . . ." That was exactly what Mfapkot meant. No wonder he could charge less than anyone. Overhead must be minimal. "Ah . . ." Barc hesitated. "Ah . . . Do they like it too? With us, I mean?"

"Too damn much," the tarbek replied. "That's how come they're so cheap—I only pay 'em room and board. They'd be a gold mine if I could get anyone but you perverts ta come in here. I gotta play old recordings on the screens, 'cause if people saw 'em before they smelled 'em, they'd stay outside. Once they sniff 'em, though . . . An' I guess they kin be real trouble, too. One offworlder got killed las' week."

"I heard about that. How did it happen? Who killed him?"

"Him? Her, you mean. Offworld old-human tourist woman, she was. Put the urge on some guy at the port. He come to, after, an' tore her apart. 'At's why they wear all those clothes, you know—filters." He gestured at his own veil. Without it, Barc knew that he—or anyone not a tarbek—could not have remained at the bar at all.

"You mean those long robes are filters?" Mfapkot did. He explained further. Since old humans were supposed to be the ancestral human stock—Barc did not believe that, because he had been taught bors myths of their ancestral homeworld—their pheromones were generalized, and all the others reacted to them, and since wends, bors, and fards especially depended on pheromone-triggers for sex, they all reacted more strongly to old humans than old-human males did. And there was a certain quirky kind of old-human female who really got off on having men crave her. Not liking her or loving her—just *having* to have her.

"Weirdos," the tarbek growled. "Their own males aren't good enough. They gotta be in charge."

For a whoremonger, Barc thought, Mfapkot could be quite a prude. He did not say so. He paid for the second beer, which the tarbek had uncharacteristically forgotten about. "I have to go," Barc said abruptly. "I have some things to check out." And a lot to think about, too, he said to himself.

Barc found the niche he was looking for. When he reflected on his idea much later, he decided that only a pervert would have thought of it, and only a man who had already plumbed the depths of personal shame and degradation would actually have considered *doing* it—a man who could no longer be hurt by what his family or the world at large thought of him.

When he approached Niddy Marboon with his idea, Niddy also decided that only Barc could have thought of it, but for different reasons. Only someone who could think big, someone trained to consider a three-man workshop and a thousand-man factory—or even a whole principality—as different only in scale, would have done so. It took someone like Barc, trained to rule.

Barc polished his proposal with Niddy's help. It would take money up front, seed capital. "Hey!" Niddy exclaimed. "Remember that Pedimet Enterprises contract? That hundred forty-two thousand creds they owe us? They've been dragging their feet over that."

"Niddy, that's Margal's money, not ours."

"Sure it is—if Margal can ever get it out of Pedimet. Look, they're not exactly eager to drop that kind of cash, but if we sweeten the deal for them, give them a small cut of our profits—then everyone wins, right? Margal gets paid, Pedimet makes money, and *we* get the investment capital we need."

It would work! The Pedimet money was only entries in journals right now, and if they continued to stall, Niddy would have no choice but to write off the debt anyway. After all, Margal had been effectively doing so for years, and Pedimet was too good a customer to lose over freight bills—especially now, with all Margal's other problems. Even if Barc's proposed enterprise collapsed, neither Pedimet nor Margal would be any worse off than they were now.

Parkoon liked the idea, especially when Barc showed them the note from Pedimet and the lease options he had bought on a dozen scattered properties. When he unveiled architectural renderings of facades and interiors, and tables or organization for the enterprise, they contracted for the whole package.

Niddy was amazed. In a few short months since Barc

had first seen the purple and blue Parkoon limousine, his and Barc's roles had reversed. Now when someone said "I need a list of the new managers we've hired," it was Barc expressing the need, and Niddy doing the fetching. Niddy did not mind that. He often felt as if he were the young student watching the master at work. Barc, he realized, had truly come into his own now. He had found a nearly perfect niche, one that demanded much of him, but not more than he could provide.

Too bad for Margal, Niddy thought. Those fools could have had Barc running things for them instead of making a profit for himself—and for Niddy, and for Parkoon. Niddy did not doubt that Barc could even have solved the flooding problem—but they had chased him away. They couldn't accept that he, like Niddy himself, was a good man on the job, in spite of being a . . . a pervert.

He chuckled to himself. Perverts. It took a pervert to know what another pervert would want—and that was what the enterprise was all about. Barc and Niddy were building whorehouses for the offworld old-human females, and stocking them with furry men. He grimaced then. What was a pervert, anyway? Someone who didn't fit? Somebody who wanted to be different—or who couldn't help being different?

It had not been a big deal for him, Niddy Marboon. He knew the stories the Margal brats told about him, and he supposed that had hurt a little, once, but so what? He was here in Karbol, where he was important, rich, and getting richer. For Barc it was different. He was not ordinary folk. He was Sheb's son and Grast's nephew. He was *somebody*—or he would have been, if they had been smart. Bah! Barc was somebody in spite of them. And so was he, Niddy Marboon.

PART TWO

A NEW LIFE

Karbol, Margal Steep, and Garloom,
on Stepwater, and the Duchy of Erne,
on Newhome

CHAPTER 9

The wendish footman opened the rear door of a deep
forest-green limousine, and stood to attention as Barc

Doresh emerged. "Thank you, Fatharowa," Barc said, nodding slightly, obviously preoccupied. "I won't be long."

Fur Yer Pleasure was not the tawdry bar it had been only a short year before. Its pale pink door was framed in expensive azure tile, and matching rose-and-blue sidewalk pavers stretched a half block in both directions. The new entry sign, though, was small, gold, and discreetly lighted—Parkoon and Parkoon's chrome-yellow Specialty Seal of Approval below it stood out more brightly than the sign itself. Nothing but that seal hinted that there was any connection with the tawdrier, noisier Fur Traders' Lounge a few blocks nearer the port, or with the discreetly exotic FUReign Affairs Bureau on the edge of Karbol's banking district. There was no indication that all three, and many others, were all owned by the outwardly unremarkable firm of M&D, Inc., of which Barc was half owner.

"What's the trouble, Vobrot?" he asked the huge tarbek who awaited him at the door. "It's a wend, Sar Barc," he growled. "She won't leave till she sees you, she sez, an' she's scarin' the old-human babes jus' bein' here."

"Why haven't you kicked her out?"

"Long's she's buyin' drinks, law sez she can stay." Of course Barc knew that. Until now, he had depended on furred females' disinterest in places where old-human ones bought favors of young, otherwise unemployable bors, wend, and fard males. There had been no disruptions thus far, and Barc and Niddy had consistently collected as much in commissions from P&P as they made on the drinks they sold to old-human women and the booths they rented to young furred males. He did not want that to change.

"Where is she?" The tarbek indicated a booth just left of the entry. The wend Barc saw was young—and quite pretty, for one with such catholic tastes as his own. Not, of course, that he had to take whatever was available, these days. He was a rich man.

"Are you Barc Doresh?" she asked, half cringing, mak-

ing herself small. Barc was annoyed that she addressed
him by his name, not an honorific. He nodded coldly.
"Tathabel said you could help me," she murmured, not
meeting his eyes. "I lost my flute."

It was nothing Barc had expected to hear. "Are you a
musician? I'm sorry. Vobrot should have told you that all
our performers are hired through the guild."

"No! I mean, I lost my flute, and now I can't go home.
My sister—Tathabel, I mean. She used to be my sister . . ."

Barc sighed. He could tell this was going to take a
while. He slid into the booth, across from her. Even with
a table between them, she shrank back further. This one
was no brazen tart, he decided. He waved for a drink, and
did not speak until it had arrived. Then, patiently, he began to question the frightened wend.

She—Firithanet—had an interesting tale. Barc knew of
wends' musical talents, because most performers in
Karbol were wends, and he had even seen one of the odd
wood-and-electronic flutes that members of the planetary
aristocracy carried with them, but he had not known that
they were more than just musical instruments. Stepwater's
elite, the senior branches of great interstellar corporate
families, learned to play flutes in their cradles, even before they spoke. What they made was not music, even to
wendish ears, but key-tones, almost a language. By the
time young royalty—for such they were—could toddle,
they had developed unique tone-signatures, individual
combinations of sounds, harmonics, and resonances even
the most skilled others could not duplicate.

Within the palaces surrounding the Pan-Wend Archives
in Garloom, no one could pass from room to room without a flute, and the ability to play it. It was said that no
non-wend could live in the archives neighborhood without
going mad from the shrilling racket.

Firithanet had come from Garloom to find her lost sister, who had run away three years earlier, and she had
found her—but not before her pouch was stolen, with her
precious flute, near the river's wharves. She had not wor-

ried, then; she could borrow Tathabel's flute. Her sister obviously no longer had need of it. She would be able to go home.

But Tathabel had no flute, and without one, Firithanet could not access her credit account to buy passage home, to hire detectives to find her flute, or to open the grand door into her family's palace. "So, you need money to buy a flute?" Barc's conclusion was premature. How was he to know the silly complexities of the effete non-bors elite? "Oh, no," Firithanet cried, shaking her head. "One can't *buy* them." Was it special, then? Were its tones somehow distinct? No, she told him, but such flutes were not for sale. It was a matter of *sephalem,* which Barc suspected was something like "honor," watered down by silly wends.

Without her flute, Firithanet explained, she was no longer Firithanet of Arafellin Enclave, the Heir-Archivist of all the wends, but only Firithanet, unemployed orphan. She had, in the weeks without her flute, resigned herself to her sudden descent. By now the thief's trail was cold, and her flute was truly lost. "It is evolution," she told Barc. "Little ones who cannot play the kitchen door's opening tones starve; ones who go outside and cannot re-open the palace door are left for the child-stealers." That was not needless cruelty, she insisted. The small ones' flutes continued to work for a month, outside. They could keep on trying to get the tones right. But for an adult, losing one's flute was the ultimate disgrace—why, she had hardly been able to speak with Tathabel, at first, when she found out her sister too was fluteless. She would not go home to stand outside the Grand Portal and needlessly admit her shame. Let them think her dead.

"Then what in the name of the Arbiter himself," Barc swore, "do you want from *me?*"

"I just want a job," Firithanet said.

"Well, why not?" Barc asked Niddy Marboon. "Look, what we're doing for Parkoon and Parkoon is fine, and profitable, don't get me wrong, and it's easy furnishing furry men for kinky offworld skins. Maybe it's *too* easy. What we can do, someone else can too, and don't think lots of people aren't watching us. Haven't you worried about what would happen if we lost the Pee-Pee contract? If we open a few houses with *girls* in them, at least we'd have something left besides empty bars, if Parkoon finds a better deal than we can give them. Girls don't make a hundred creds, like the old-human women pay our boys, but at least we'd get a markup on the Estrokick we could sell. It's a matter of hedging our bets—and we've learned a lot about running a high-class operation. We can do the same thing with ordinary whorehouses too, can't we?"

Nidleg Marboon explained that he was not dismayed by Barc's proposed sideline venture, only by the gloomy prospect he had raised of having to work for a living again, shorn of the lucrative contract with the tour firm. His old job wasn't as much fun, and he now left most of Margal's work to his new aides, who were sharp businessmen he had hired right here in Karbol. "I suppose we could put one up behind Fur Yer Pleasure," he mused. "We own the whole building, and that bookseller, Methrap, never pays his rent on time. Maybe we'll make some money on that space, for once. And then there's that warehouse we own, over on Alabandy Street—it's right in the middle of the theater district, but there isn't a decent bar within . . ."

Barc stretched luxuriantly. He felt really good—and he smiled at Firithanet, perched anxiously on the edge of the huge round bed. "If you do that with every man," he said, "you'll be able to buy the flute factory next year."

She smiled. "I couldn't do that," she demurred. "It wouldn't be *sephalemsk*." That might have meant something like "honorable."

Tathabel shook her head. "Wait and see, Firith," she said.

* * *

Barc slid into the limousine.

"Have a good time, Sar Barc?"

"Yeah," Barc replied gruffly, slumping on the wide, soft seat. "Take me home, Fath." He had not had a "good time." It had not been Firithanet's fault, or her sister's; both had dosed themselves liberally from the hot-pink cylinders he had provided. It had not been the setting, either; the palatial bedrooms, so unlike the usual versatile booths, were a new innovation spurred by offworld old-human women's tastes. Karbol's unattached males, Barc included, considered them to be shameful imitations of the marriage beds that mated males enjoyed, and because they were shameful, they were huge erotic successes. Barc wondered quite irrelevantly if the Karbol custom of having sex in bar booths had started the same way—because it had once been an equally shameful, and thus erotic, departure from the customary beds.

His problem was not with the pharmaceuticals, either; the industrial-strength Testoslam he had sniffed could have made the Hammad River stand up on its delta end, but it could not have made the river joyful or content. No, the problem was within Barc Doresh himself. He was now twenty-one years old, a self-made bors, and could afford the best physicians—or even a private mindskinner, though as yet he had not hired one—but he could not purchase joy. Twenty-one. In nineteen or twenty more years he would be able to voluntarily turn off the urges that dominated him. In nineteen years or so, he would really begin to enjoy the fruits of his financial success, quietly celibate.

What if I'm becoming immune to Testoslam? he wondered anxiously. What will happen when the urge builds up until I can't think about anything else, but I can't do it? When an imprinted bors's mate died, he had been told, the vast genetically programmed grief he felt triggered hormonal changes even if he was not nearly forty. But he, Barc, had no mate, and he could not think of anyone whose death would cause him much more than a sniffle or two. If I become immune while I'm still commanded by my compulsions, will I twitch and thrash, or embarrass myself and have to wear a baggy workman's smock all the time? Will something inside me explode? Or will I just go mad?

CHAPTER 10

Disaster struck yesterday in the small bors principality
of Margal Steep when a thirty-ton chunk of rocky ceiling
fell, killing the ruling pair, Sheb and Grast Doresh,
the heirs apparent Dird and Frak Buckroo, and
several servants.

Several customers awaiting delivery of Margal
electronics products claim they have been unable
to get through on the net to the principality's
offices, though a recorded message claims that the tragedy
will not affect delivery dates of Margal Steep's current
production orders.

Karbol Examiner Business News
Current Outland News

Girelf had not felt a thing. She had been miles away from
Margal Steep when the roof fell in on Sheb and Grast, and
the vibration of even thirty tons of falling rocks did
not amount to much over distance. It was not until her
throngmate Simolf brought the news that she had felt the
repercussions of the rockfall.

"No!" she cried—and plunged into the dark Hammad
water, and away. Simolf, sensing her distress, unable to
fathom it, followed.

"Go away!" Girelf commanded him when he caught up
with her. "It's my fault! I did it to them!"

"No you didn't," said Simolf, altogether reasonably, as
Girelf had not been anywhere near. "And after all, they
were only bors."

"Never mind, then," she snarled, baring her teeth in threat. "Go away, and leave me alone."

Simolf did so, because he had experienced the sharpness of her teeth in play, and she looked less than playful right then. He did not tell anyone what had transpired, but he silently speculated on what could have possibly bitten Girelf herself.

Alone, Girelf dived downward into a secret cave. There were many such, and it was not the same one she and Barc had visited. There were no childhood treasures there, only darkness and quiet, only the tiny sounds of water droplets from her fur plinking into the stillness.

She imagined ripples spreading outward, and the tiny vibrations as they impacted on the walls of the cave. Could such tiny forces travel through the bedrock, the earth's bones? Could one such droplet, causing one such minuscule seismic wave, be just the one that caused a crack to form far away in another cave, and make a ceiling fall? Girelf wept alone, and quietly—for who could tell what devastation might ultimately result from the fall of a single unnoticed tear?

Barc hardly felt a thing when he got the news. Neither had Sheb or Grast, he suspected, when the palace dining room fell in. Sheb: he could not call her the M-thing, now that she was dead, but neither could he comfortably call her "Mom," nor grieve for her. Nor did Dird's demise bring hoped-for tears of grief to his eyes—and he could not imagine himself, or anyone, missing Frak at all. He wished that the incremental grief of four deaths at once had totaled up to that of one dead mate and had freed him of his male craving—but no, he could tell it was not so. He would have to visit one of his new girl-houses in a day or so.

But first, there was the annoyance of speaking with the representative of Margal Steep. Barc did not recognize his name. What did he want, anyway? No one from Margal had needed to say anything to him while his former family

had been alive, had they? So why now? Ah, well, he
thought, sighing, best to get it over with.

"Sart, I'll see Sar Bollet now," he said to the air. The office's new AI, hearing Barc's receptionist's name, automat-
ically routed his words to her. Having a human
receptionist was but one of many perquisites of financial
success. Having a big desk and sensors that silently raised
his chair so he was always just a knuckle's width above his
seated visitors was another.

Vrad Bollet tested the limit of the chair. Barc remembered him now—the big, skinny kid whom the teachers
had always made sit in the back row. "My condolences,
Sar Doresh," Bollet said. "All Margal shares your loss."

Barc mouthed an appropriate, meaningless phrase, impatient to have these formalities behind him. "Then," he
asked, "what is this visit about?"

"About? Why . . . your investiture, of course."

"Investiture?" Was the man crazy? That could only
mean one thing.

"Yes," Bollet affirmed, unsnapping the catches on the
wooden attaché case he carried. "I have here the Club of
Primacy." He slid the case toward Barc, pushing invoices,
memos, and supplier contracts aside, as if the case were
the barge of an ancient emperor and the paper obstruc-
tions no more significant than dead leaves floating on the
desk's watery shine. Barc, staring at the dark object nestled in red plush, remembered the last time he had seen
it, in Uncle Grast's hand. It was a scepter, though
Margal's unpompous bors preferred to name it for its an-
tecedent function as a club, a bludgeon. Barc could have
been no more stunned if he had been struck on the head
by it. If he picked it up, he would become, without further ceremony, the ruler of Margal Steep. He stared at the
glossy dark wooden shaft, banded with gold.

"Why?" he blurted. "Who thought of this? I can't take
that."

"You must. No man has ever refused it." Barc knew the
legends. He knew that Bollet was not telling the exact

truth: that no man had refused to take the club and lived out the month. Sometimes there had to be a way to inspire the best man to take the job.

"But I have my business. Thousands of people depend on me for their livings. and I ... I am unmated," Barc protested, unwilling to define his unnatural condition more precisely.

Bollet was less reticent. "Your quirks were of importance to Sheb and Grast," he said, "because they were most concerned with the continuance of their family line. Now few care about that, least of all the Margal councillors, who are all of an age to freely pursue their own ... odd whims. Dismiss such concerns—or flagellate yourself privately, if you will—but allow nothing to prevent your speedy return to Margal. There are worse fates than being thought a bit odd." He indicated the club. The subject was thus closed.

"As for your other 'responsibilities,'" said Bollet, "here there are a thousand whores—but in Margal are ten thousand honest laborers." He shrugged. "Nidleg Marboon can manage without you. Your function here has long since been accomplished. Now Margal needs you more at home than in Karbol."

Barc understood, and sensed the irony and implication of Bollet's precise turn of phrase. He had been too successful in Karbol. Had he contented himself to acquire only a single bar or two, disgust over his perversions and unease about his unmated state would have weighed heavily against him among the councilmen of Margal Steep. Instead he had become very successful and, because Parkoon and Parkoon had required a single firm to deal with their old-human problem, Barc had been forced to divert Margal funds to his use in the beginning. Those had long since been returned, but the fact remained that his entire enterprise had been begun with Margal money. A court might easily decide that he had been the principality's agent all along, and that the shady empire he had created actually belonged in its entirety not to him, but to Margal Steep.

For a moment, Barc considered picking up the blunt object, unsure whether to accept the honor—and thus a belated revenge against his family—or to strike Bollet with it and then flee to the spaceport. He had enough creds in his pouch for passage offworld, within Mirrim's planetary system, at least, though interstellar passage would surely beggar him.

In all his experience with Parkoon's clients, he had never encountered an interstellar tourist who was not chairperson of a major corporation, heir to immense riches, or entitled royalty who could command the resources of a country, a continent, or a whole world. That had not hurt his business, though, because there were millions of countries on thousands of worlds, millions of rich corporations, and millions of princes, too. There were tourists aplenty among the many trillions of citizens of the Xarafeille Stream.

He shrugged. Even here on Stepwater, he could probably avoid whatever goons or assassins Margal might send after him. And they might not even bother. They had other problems to worry about. Still, in spite of everything, Margal was still Margal. Deep in his blood, it was still . . . home. Yet there were other difficulties. "I have certain . . . problems," he admitted hesitantly. "Certain needs . . ."

"The council is aware of your unfortunate condition," Bollet assured him. "Your skills, in Margal's time of need, outweigh the awkwardness of supplying you with the means of your relief."

They had, it seemed, thought of everything. How it must have galled them all. Margal, he thought, was in bad shape. What had happened in the past year? When he had last checked on it, the principality's business had been prospering, but he had not followed its affairs recently. He did not think that sales had fallen off—the wharf and warehouse seemed busy whenever he passed them.

Ah, well, he thought, I'll find out soon enough, when I get there. He had, he realized, made his decision. All that was left undone was for him to reach out over his desk and pick up the symbol of his new captivity. Was he, Barc wondered, a unique kind of fool? He had left Margal Steep an embittered child, resenting his exile, yet now he was no less unhappy about returning there. But he was going to go. What impelled him? Was it simply undiscovered shreds of a conscience not utterly obliterated by his occupation and his perverse lifestyle?

Barc grasped the wooden mace and lifted it from its plush bed, thinking how much more appropriate it would have been for Vrad Bollet to have held it poised over his head instead.

The upstream journey back to Margal was long and lonely for Barc. It was always longer than downstream with the current, and now the barge had to fight the full springtime flood. Too, the Margal men accompanying him, the same ones he had once feared might hunt him down, had little to say to him. Perhaps their taciturnity stemmed from their realization of his new, high position, but, in occasional bitter, paranoid moments, he wondered if Bollet's tale was not merely a trick to entice him back peaceably. But that would have been oversubtle, he assured himself; his enemies—if indeed they were enemies—would have had to assume that he had social conscience enough to impel him to willingly return, and to have wittingly used that against him. Barc himself was not sure, knowing himself, that the assumption would have been valid, except that he was indeed on the river going "home."

When they put in at Fantol for the portage around the Great Weir, several large, comfortable motor carriages waited to take them by road to the high side of the empondment. There Barc found opportunity to test the new authority he had obtained when he had first grasped the mace, a short week earlier. "We will take the high road," he stated, and gave no explanation. Though it would add a half day to the total journey, none contested his decision. The high road it was.

At the crest of the hills, the highest elevation before the descent to the great pond, the small caravan idled on the road's shoulder while Barc climbed alone to the same rocky hilltop from which he and Marboon had viewed the stone dam. There he removed a large image-enhancing binocular scope from his shoulder pouch. He scanned the dam, noting that several courses of huge cut stones had been lifted in place atop it since his last look. Rapidly changing numbers lit in the lower right corner of his field of view, indicating the exact elevations of specific objects within the instrument's tight focus.

Barc jotted notes in a yellow plastic surveyor's field book; though the binoc was linked to five of Stepwater's GPS satellites, and though its internal memory was periodically uploaded to the navigational birds, Barc did not want to wait until he was settled at a Margal terminal to make the calculations he needed. He filled half the notebook with figures, diagrams, and sketches throughout the afternoon as he rode. By evening, when the caravan stopped at the upstream wharf, he already had a good idea of what he would find at Margal. He wondered if he would have time even to try to save the town from the rising water that had, indirectly, elevated him to single, unmated rule.

"I just don't understand why they wanted him back," Rob said. "I mean, if he was such an outcast, and all."

"Perhaps it was less important to Margal than to Barc. After all, no one really tormented him about his 'perversions,' did they? Most of his misery seemed to be in his own head . . . his self-condemnation."

"Well, I got the impression he was really afraid of what would happen if the chemicals stopped working for him."

"That may have been the origin of the taboo, among bors, to protect against such suffering," John Minder replied. "That, and the fear of misogamy leading to the reversion of their unique races to the old-human type. But I have the impression that the strength of the taboo is on the wane. Can you suggest why?"

"If there are chemical treatments for Barc's condition," Rob mused, "then the risk is lessened, and the need for such a taboo. And from what I've read, the races were once much more concerned with being genetically absorbed by the old humans than they are now. They are so widespread there seems little danger of that."

"You may be right. But Barc was not concerned with such things. Are we any closer to the root of his particular obsession?" The answer to that did not come from Rob, but from Parissa, who knew nothing much of genetics or social history of the races.

"It's because Barc's mommy was a rotten mahkrat, and his Uncle Grast was too! They should have been nice to him."

"Oh, come on, Priss. What could they have done?"

"Let's hear her out, Rob. What would have happened if Sheb and Grast had accepted Barc's condition, dear?"

"He would have married G'relf and been happy-ever-after," the youngest Minder stated confidently. "G'relf is nice, and she's a princess! She's nicer than Barc's ugly old sister and that Dird-bird!"

It might have happened that way, John Minder thought. And if it had, none of his own machinations would have succeeded. But he did not say that to Parissa, who was too young to lose her ideals.

CHAPTER 11

The gene splicers incorporated several consistent
patterns in the variant humans. It cannot be determined
if some reflected a cross-corporate agreement,
consensus among the scientists, or merely a
fortuitous accident aided by common human prejudices,
but the first consistency was basic: the variant genes
were not incorporated on any of the forty-eight old-
human chromosomes, but were consolidated on a
new forty-ninth genetic unit, the V-chromosome, named
for its shape, with the centromere near the ends of
the DNA chains. Each variant race was given the
V-chromosome, which differed from race to race
only in its detail content.

Notes to the Next Generations,
John Minder (I)

Barc arrived at the Bridge Road Gate to Margal Town literally before he knew it. Even though he had an idea of
what to expect, from his measurements at the dam and
his subsequent calculations, a half-obel rise in water level
had inundated much that was familiar to him and had
changed the perspectives from which he viewed the rest.
"Bridge Road Gate" was now a misnomer. "Wharf Gate,"
Barc mentally renamed it, because the water had inundated the bridge and much of the road, and now lapped
almost at the adit itself. Another quarter-obel rise would
bring it over the threshold and into the main levels of the
town. Barc suspected that he had not been returned to
rule over Margal Steep, but merely to preside briefly over

its demise. Without the town and its factories, the already-tiny principality would shrink below some ill-defined level of viability to become, at best, a poor enclave of bors clinging to flooded mountaintops within a territory claimed by displaced wends and rapacious mantees.

Inside the town, things looked no better. The entire palace complex had been declared unsafe, and Barc was forced to establish himself in a hotel suite high in a formerly undesirable part of town. The hotel's former patrons had been mostly wend and fard traders who would have been uncomfortable in the close, windowless confines of the lower town, so his suite had not only windows that penetrated the mountain's surface, but a windy, chilly patio cut from the living rock. He had a fine view of the water gap below, and while Barc appreciated the openness, a good part of the view was of silvery water covering land that had once been part of Margal, a discouraging sight. He would, he decided, commission a new suite with a more heartening view, if he could first save the town.

He immediately set to work, sending teams of surveyors and miners to assess the present damage to Margal, and to gauge the near-future risk. Barc was not himself a professional geologist, but he had spent much of his childhood in the deep caves, and he had a feel for rock. Too, he had been raised as a future ruler of Margal, a trogloditic community, and had thus been well exposed to geology, that most bors-like of occupations. His respect for his late uncle Grast, however, diminished as he found out just how little preservation work had been done. Grast should have known months before how unsafe the palace had become, long before it fell on him.

The palace was a mess, though work crews had carried out most of the rubble in order to reach the bodies of the casualties. Where once had been a rather pretty ceiling, carved and inlaid, was now a rough stone face. The cause of the damage was not apparent, just from looking, but when Barc examined the stratigraphic maps and sections for the area *below* the palace, he saw the problem immediately. A clearly mapped seam of ancient marl, made slippery by saturation from the rising river, ran between two porous limestone strata. The stone, itself weakened by acid-rich runoff from vast upriver swamps, had failed at the claylike stratum, and the resulting slip-strike fault had displaced the limestone columns that supported the palace ceiling. The displacement was measured in mere inches, but that had been enough. The ceiling had fallen.

Barc knew that only luck—bad luck for those who had died, but not for everyone—had caused the palace roof to be the first really big collapse. It could have happened in a crowded shopping arcade. Barc dipped into his own private wealth, which was considerable, to hire two full-time geologists from a large mining company out of Garloom.

Barc ignored anxious customers inquiring about their long-delayed orders for Margal electronics. The huge factory intake vents, low on the mountain, were mostly filled with water, and the plants were shut down. He reasoned that if there was no product, there could be no customers, and his first duty was to save the factories themselves from imminent flooding and subsequent collapse. New customers could be found later.

The arrangements the Margal councillors had made to accommodate Barc's perverse sexual needs were wholly inadequate. For the first two weeks he availed himself of the superannuated fard female they had hired for him, using massive doses of artificial hormones. By the end of his third week, a troop of young, comely wend and fard women arrived by barge, and a second barge arrived loaded with the complete furnishings for a pleasant though small bar and restaurant, complete with booths and curtains, which were considered quite exotic this far from the city.

"Mfapkot!" Barc exclaimed, greeting the gaunt, gangly tarbek. "How do you like your new place?"

Mfapkot, glancing around himself, grunted. "The bar's nice enough," he growled, "but do I only have one customer?" Barc, aware that he was the only "customer" who mattered, nonetheless assured the bartender that once word got out, he and the girls would be quite busy. Within two weeks, as Mfapkot then happily confirmed, Barc's prediction proved out. Lines of sheepish bors formed outside the Karbol Nights Bar, mostly postclesiopausal males, daring in their dotages to sample the twisted pleasures they had feared in their youths and that they had been physically incapable of during their mated maturities. The creds poured in, so Mfapkot and the girls were happy. Barc himself had a familiar, congenial atmosphere in which to ease his own internal tensions, so he was happy too—relatively speaking.

As the popularity of the Karbol Nights Bar grew—and as the rumors of Barc's own peculiar proclivities spread throughout the principality—there was much heated discussion, and the debate quickly separated Margal into two factions. The "antis" were mostly the people least affected by the ongoing physical degradation of the town—those whose investments were in outlying mines, whose residences were outside the area of flooding and geological subsidence, and those who, like Grast and Sheb, had resolutely refused to acknowledge the scope of the problem or that there was a problem at all.

The "pros" were everyone else. "So what if he's weird," they said. "He's getting things *moving,* isn't he? He's doing something, not just sitting on his fat stump of a tail." Among that majority there was an air of optimism. Among them the talk of Barc's oddness soon diminished, then faded altogether; Barc was quite happy about that.

Had Niddy Marboon been there right then, he might have observed quite correctly that someone was only a pervert when it suited someone else that he be considered so. "How ironic," he would have said. "It's all a matter of agendas, isn't it? Why, who knows, Barc? Maybe you'll start a real trend here." But Niddy was not there, and was surely quite content not to be. He was happy being who he was, and being so in Karbol, not in gloomy Margal Steep.

With the geologists' preliminary reports in hand, Barc ordered cement. Industrious—and otherwise unemployed—bors set up a plant in the dry central valley where the resources were at hand. The rocks outcropping there contained several beds of a fine oolitic limestone formed of some ancient seabed's ooze. A kiln to "burn" the limestone was easily built using machines and materials from the levels of Margal Steep that would soon be flooded anyway.

Talus slopes on the far side of the valley yielded frost-spalled granite, and a crushing mill was built on site to provide aggregate, which was then sorted into great piles of even-sized stone. Fat-tired trucks hauled cement, gravel, and sand from the Hammad River's upstream flats into Margal Town, where it was mixed in enormous drums salvaged from a defunct ore-processing operation. The resulting mix—thick enough for strength, yet wet enough to be pumped through two-foot diameter pipes—was channeled into the submerged parts of Margal, into strategic spots that the geologists had determined would block the water's flow inward. Chambers, hallways, and tunnels were filled floor to ceiling with concrete, which displaced the water in them.

"That will take care of it," said one geologist, rubbing his hands together with great enthusiasm. Barc's spirits lightened.

"Well, it *should* have done the trick!" said the indignant geologist. "There must be an unmapped seam of pervious sandstone down there somewhere. The hydrostatic head—

the weight of the water outside of Margal Steep—is pushing it up from *below* the caverns."

"What can we do?" asked a disconsolate Barc Doresh.

"I suppose we can try flooding the entire lower levels with concrete." He did not sound optimistic.

Barc made a quick calculation. "There are hundreds of miles of tunnels down there," he said, reflecting on his childhood explorations. "Even the smallest of them are ten feet wide, and as high. That's at least three yards of concrete for every foot of tunnel. One and a half million cubic yards? More like two and a half million!"

"Well, there's plenty of limestone and aggregate . . ."

"What about *time*? That's what we don't have."

"Hmm. That two-foot pipe can handle a yard of concrete a second. Let's see . . ." He made rapid mental calculations, mumbling the while. "Twenty-three days," he said, again optimistic. We can fill the entire thing in under a month."

Barc was less confident. He considered the capacity of the kiln, the crushers, the mixers, and the jury-rigged pumps designed to lift a much lighter and more liquid ore slurry from the deep mines. The pumps overheated often, or they just bogged down. They had to be repaired every few days.

"Well, even if it takes two months, or three . . ." essayed the geologist.

It did not take three months. It did not take three weeks. "It's the current!" the geologists exclaimed in chorus.

"It washes the cement out of the aggregate!" said one.

"The water just keeps flowing through the gravel left behind!" explained the other. "And even if we succeed in filling one tunnel won't it just increase the flow in others."

Actually, it would not, Barc knew.

Barc sighed. "Now what?" he asked, already knowing the answer. "What do I do now?"

"Move?" suggested the first geologist.

* * *

Other schemes were proposed. Some were tried, but most were rejected as impractical or downright impossible. Margal Town, Barc concluded reluctantly at the end of his second month in residence, was doomed. "We have no choice any longer," he told the councilmen. "If I do not have your authorization to treat with the mantees, I will invoke Executive Fiat, and do it anyway." When a Margal ruler invoked that rule—effectively declaring himself absolute dictator for one year—he thereby signed his own death warrant. A council-approved physician was required to inject him with tailored viruses that enhanced cogitation and rendered sleep unnecessary, viruses that within eighteen months contaminated his blood and consumed his vital essences so that he died of premature old age.

Rulers seldom invoked Executive Fiat. They seldom even bluffed, and Barc was sure the councillors knew he was not bluffing, either. After all, what did he have to live for? It was no secret that he himself might go mad with his internal stresses within not much longer than a year, as his immunity to artificial hormones intensified. Too, if he had been a less determined man, he would have given up on any one of several earlier occasions: when Girelf rejected him and he became unmateable, he might have committed suicide; when he found out about Sheb's mindskinner, he might have acquiesced to the treatment; unemployed and desperate in Karbol, he might have sold himself to medical experimenters in return for food and lodging; he might even have knocked Vrad Bollet on the head with that fancy bludgeon, and been later hunted down and slain.

The councillors gave him carte blanche to negotiate with the mantees, without Executive Fiat. Barc began making preparations immediately. He did not, at first, realize what was causing his steps to feel light, his head to be as airy as high altitude made it feel, and which made his sexual encounters feel less wooden and contrived than they had for a long time. When he did figure it out, he sank into a black despair. The hidden cause of lightness, dizziness, and almost-mated joy had been his unrecognized anticipation that he might once again see Girelf.

CHAPTER 12

It is ironic that the single most significant reason
the Proxima Corporation incorporated American black
bear sequences in the genomes of its slave laborers
is the least important modification, to present-day
bors. The bors were modified to exploit high-altitude,
high-latitude open-pit mines that could only be operated
during Proxima's short arctic summers, and the
decision to use bear genes was made mainly by the
corporation's cost accountants. They calculated that
it was less expensive to maintain two separate worker
populations, north and south, than to transport the
entire planetary population twice each year. Of
course it only worked because the workers could survive
the local winters largely unaided, and demanded no
fuels, food, or life support while they hibernated.

A New History of Mankind,
Rober Minder, Jr., the third Arbiter,
Unpubl. Ms., Newhome Archive

The mantee summerthrong was held in a new place, of
course. South of the water gap, where the hills sloped
ever-so-gently down to the river, a mere half-obel rise in
the empoundment had inundated vast additional acreages
of former wend forests and added many hundreds of obels
to the length of the mantees' shorelines. The new gathering place was four hundred obels "inland" from the old
one, eight fardic miles, and it was still on the shore.

One looked only subtly different from the other
through Barc's binocs, and it took him a moment to real-

ize that the difference was the dearth of typical shoreline plants where water met land. The mantees had obviously been harvesting the trees before they were submerged, and the ones left near the water's edge were not mossy, tangled riverine types that stretched almost horizontally over the water, but tall, straight upland species entirely out of place along the shore. A few clumps of speargrass and tanglefoot had been deliberately planted, and stuck up above brown, dead mats of high ground grasses whose roots had been drowned.

From Barc's vantage point on a promontory overlooking the valley he observed winding yellow threads of wagon trails that converged as new, raw roads. Those all marched south toward the Great Weir. By setting the binocs on extreme enhancement, he determined that the mantees were transporting logs and other harvestable resources south, and were bringing water-loving plant species north from below the dam. By planting them, they prepared for the day when the new shoreline had stabilized and could support the mantee ecology and economy.

Barc was both reassured and made anxious by what he saw. By gauging the distance from the present shore to the greatest concentrations of new plantings, he could see that the mantees expected to own much more territory before they were done. On the other hand, by taking elevation readings on the plantings, he determined that the newest course of stone atop the Great Weir was to be the last one the mantees planned to add. Still, by the time the waters filled the valley behind the dam, the main occupied levels of Margal Town would be fifty borrish feet beneath the water, and the Bridge Road Gate would be inaccessible to bors. What would the fifty-obel rule mean, in those circumstances? If the river ran *under* Mendeb Peak, would the mantees then own all the mountain, or would a few wet, homeless bors be allowed to cling to the upper cliffs and dig new caves there, when at last the mountain stabilized?

Sighing, Barc returned the binocs to his sack and began the long trudge downslope to the mantee encampment.

Realistically, Barc did not expect to recognize Girelf even when—or if—he saw her. The metabolic changes that a throngmother underwent would have padded her slim body with vast rolls of motherly fat. Her mobile, expressive face would be concealed within jiggling wrinkles and folds, her bright eyes reduced to tiny marbles shadowed within deep fleshy caverns. By now, he estimated, she would be mother to at least fifty young mantees, a year's contribution to the new population that would arise during her thirty-year reign. How many young males would she have been with, in two years since he had last touched her? How many fertile eggs did she now carry? As many as there were mantees in the Hammad Valley? More, to fill the new lands they had gained and would continue to accumulate? He shuddered, irrationally jealous of the males, horrified by what he knew she had become.

The young mantee males who met him at the head of the trail were expecting him. One took his shoulder sack and, after examining its contents, slung it over his own shoulder. Another patted Barc from head to foot and, finding no weapons or dangerous contraband concealed in his black fur, chattered in quick, incomprehensible Mantee to the others, who started off down the trail. Barc and his escort followed.

We aren't at war, Barc thought. Not yet, anyway. So why do I feel like a prisoner? Not yet. Not yet? Again, a subconscious thought had popped into his awareness unbidden. He had not, until that moment, really considered the possibility of outright war as a solution to Margal Steep's problems, but once the thought was freed from its subconscious hiding place, he could not avoid thinking about it.

How much explosive gel was kept in Margal's storage caves for the mining of new caverns? Was it enough to mine the Great Weir? Could Margal's bors, with no real

military training, hold the low side of the dam long
enough to bore holes in it, fill them with gel, top them
with blasting caps, then wire them together and still get
away before the rushing waters swept away every human
and human work north of Karbol itself? How many others,
forest wends and mantees alike, would die when a
hundred-foot wall of water scoured the valley? Would
Karbol itself be flooded when the empoundment's contents flowed past it into the greater river beyond, on the
long way to the sea? Barc Doresh arrived at the thronging
ground sickened and horrified.

"Girelf?" he asked, squeaking like a cub.

The throngmother jiggled obscenely and emitted a high,
tittering laugh. "Well, young bors," she said, "how do you
like me now?"

Barc's ears flattened against his head. His worst night-
mare faced him—but something was wrong. Or perhaps
everything was too right: he was not embarrassing himself
with an amorous display; indeed, he felt nothing but revulsion for the huge female. Either her terrible metamor-
phosis was so complete that Barc's body chemistry no
longer recognized hers, and his imprinting had failed,
or . . .

"You're not Girelf," he exclaimed. "You're the *old* throngmother." Where was Girelf, then?

"Of course, child," she said, no longer laughing. "Your
little lover is as miserable as you seem to be. What a
problem the two of you have caused us all!" Had they?
But how did his problems impinge on the mantees? They
did not imprint, as did bors. He asked that, politely. "She
refuses to mate! Her eggs lie dormant in her, while the
last of mine swell and ripen. For all our rich acquisitions,
we will be a poor tribe indeed, if no newlings are born to
inhabit our expanded territory."

Barc apologized softly, not sure what he begged forgive-
ness for, yet stunned by the realization that the mantees
had a problem as vast as his own. Then another part of

him brightened as he realized that where there were two problems, there was joint motivation for a solution. He asked what he could do about that. If he could motivate Girelf to accept her designated fate, could he demand that the mantees reduce the pond to its former level, and save Margal?

"You?" The throngmother laughed sharply, angrily. "Perhaps if you *die,* Girelf will forget her silly obsession, and will mate, as she must." Barc shrank back, and glanced around himself fearfully. "Don't worry," the throngmother said scornfully. "I won't have you killed, because my errant daughter threatens to kill herself if harm befalls you—and she's stubborn enough to do it. You're safe enough. But that changes nothing, does it?"

Barc agreed. He told the throngmother that he was entirely sympathetic to the mantees' plight. "But can't you designate a new heir to replace Girelf?" His unbidden thought, not quite a hope, was that if some other mantee girl became the throngmother, Girelf would be freed of her obligation, and could . . . could go with him. Of course Margal would still be doomed, but perhaps he and Girelf, alone, could find happiness in Karbol. After all, he was rich, wasn't he? He would build her a lovely grotto with a grassy waterslide even in the middle of the city, and . . . But the same shreds of conscience that had betrayed him before did so again; Margal's ten thousand had to come before his personal happiness. The only real question was: If Girelf would agree to become throngmother, could Barc require that the dam be dismantled? "What if I can change her mind?" he asked.

"As to your first question," the huge one said, "look over there." Barc looked, and saw a very small mantee sunning itself atop a large rock. "There is the new throngmother."

"But . . ." Barc wrinkled his brow. "She's only a baby."

"Exactly. In seventeen years, she will mature and mate, and will begin producing a new generation. In the meantime, my last egg will mature or will become unviable, and soon my oldest children will begin to die, without being replaced. This vast land would be almost empty, in seventeen years, but for other mantee tribes which, knowing our weakness, will not wait that long before moving into it. All our efforts will be for naught."

"And my second question?" Barc spoke quietly, knowing the fate of Margal Town might hinge on her answer.

"Then I will stop work on the last, uppermost course of the dam."

Barc sighed. It was not much. It was not nearly enough. Much of the damage already done could not be undone unless the pond was lowered so construction crews could get into the low tunnels to repair them, or even to fill them in. Still, the throngmother had made an offer. She was willing to bargain. Now, at least, the haggling could begin, and Barc, veteran of the Karbol markets, was good at that.

Barc stood, exhausted but content. The bargain was sealed. The mantees would reduce the Great Weir's height to what it had been a year before. The lowest tunnels would still be submerged—including the crystal cave and Barc's secret exit from Margal Town—but the pond would no longer encroach on the town's entrances or nibble at the cliffs of the water gap. The low tunnels could be filled with concrete, which would displace the water and provide stability to the levels above. All he had to do was convince Girelf she should do her duty to her tribe. He, Barc Doresh, had accepted his own unpleasant obligations, hadn't he? Why should she not accept hers?

"Where is she?" he asked. "I'll have to talk to her." He would have to tell her about himself. He would have to let her know that her erstwhile lover had become a pervert who consorted with whores, who used despicable drugs to further his own twisted lust, and who was a pimp for prostitutes of both sexes, who catered to the most disgusting deviates of the human races on a vast, commercial scale. She would surely forget her girlish crush when he showed her what he had become.

"Simolf will take you to her," the throngmother said. "She will not come here, or speak with any of us. I only hope she will speak with you."

Barc did not doubt it. He was a large bors, and she was a small delicate mantee—and the grotto she dwelled in, said Simolf, the male who had escorted him to the thronging place, had only one entrance. Besides, if she became angry when he barged in on her, so much the better. He would merely add rudeness and brutality to his manifest flaws.

Girelf's cave was a half hour's walk away—less, perhaps, by water, but Barc was a bors, not a mantee. He strode confidently, fantasizing that he might even return to Karbol when all this was settled, and resume his own life. The Margal council could nominate a new ruler, a properly mated one from some collateral branch of the Doresh family, when the crisis was past. His steps thus were light, and his head was filled with a certain airy delight. He felt wonderful. Surely, he could not lose. Not now.

"She doesn't make it easy, does she?" Barc said to Simolf, eyeing the dark, root-filled pool.

"You only have to swim under that big log," Simolf replied, "and then pull yourself through the root mass of the next one. I think there's a place halfway in where you can come up for air."

Air was the least of Barc's concerns. The water was cold, hopefully cold enough to slow his metabolism and reduce his need for oxygen. It was not, he hoped, so cold that he would become entirely dormant somewhere within the twisting underwater passageway and never emerge from it. Bors were not water creatures. He wondered briefly why they even had that odd ability to slow down their metabolisms. It was not good for anything, ordinarily.

The stakes were high, so Barc quelled his fears. After all, he had done this before, beneath Margal Town. He took several deep breaths, building up oxygen in his cells, and waded into the murky brown water, then lowered himself into it. He swam.

Halfway through, he emerged in a space so small he could get only his nose above the surface to draw careful breath. Even the ripples caused by the slow expansion of his chest as his lungs filled threatened to fill his nostrils with bitter swampy water. He breathed slowly, deeply, infusing himself not only with oxygen, but with fresh determination to show Girelf just what a disgusting creature he had become, to make her see that her silly infatuation with him was not only pointless, but was demeaning to her. Then, refreshed, he pushed himself beneath the surface again.

He emerged into vermilion, flame-tinted light, and his eyes took a moment or so to adapt to it. His brain took a further moment to interpret what he saw, to realize that the light was one small wick flaming in a pot of oily fat. He had not expected Girelf to have electricity in her grotto, had he? He glanced around. There was not much room. The cave was hardly large enough for him to stand up and stretch. But there! He saw a shadowy darkness, a further passageway just above the water's level. Where did it lead?

CHAPTER 13

Since few actual genes are required to dictate the
modified humans' special traits, much of the forty-ninth
or V-chromosome consists of introns, unexpressed
sequences. One area, though, holds a gene
unknown in nature; it is an entirely engineered "self-
destruct" gene, designed to return a variant engineered
population to human normalcy in the course of a
few generations.

When during the course of fertilization the self-destruct
gene cannot "find" its homozygous counterpart, it initiates
a series of actions that destroys the V-chromosome.
Thus, the old-human product of a misogamous
union is not a "hybrid" at all. It is, in every sense, a
genetically pure human of the old type.

Notes to the Next Generation,
John Minder (I)

Barc felt as if he were made of thistledown and air, as if
his considerable weight on the bed of springy, sweet-
scented moss had been reduced to nothing. He was still
wet, of course, but not at all chilly. In fact, his left side
was very warm indeed, where Girelf snuggled against it.
He glanced at her, nestled small, brown, and content in
the crook of his massive black-furred arm. Her eyes were
open. They were pale emerald green even in the orange
light of the oil-soaked wick. She was beautiful.

She was beautiful, and he felt wonderful. He felt
empty, as if his release in her had cleansed him of the vile
burden he had carried so long—as if she had absorbed

them and transmuted them into something else entirely, something that effused from her and filled the air with indefinite, undefinable, unperceived perfumes.

Barc stretched, and he became aware that he had never really relaxed . . . not entirely. All the Testoslam in the world could not have kept him like that, while he slept. He was still aroused. He caressed the smooth, flat fur of his lover's belly, and ruffled the cowlick-circles of it that surrounded her tiny pink nipples. She giggled, and rolled over on top of him. . . .

"Despicable? You? I don't think so. I think you're just fine—and I love all those wendish and fardic tricks you learned. Do you know that mantees *never* do it that way? Like we did?" She laughed smugly. "Never until now, anyway."

"But you *have* to be the new throngmother," he protested weakly. "You have to, or else . . ."

"I don't care. I don't want to stop having sex as soon as my last egg is inseminated. I don't want to be huge and fat. I don't want to do it with Simolf and fat Garunt, and old Matoof. . . . No. Absolutely not. I don't want my eggs fertilized by all those men, only by you. Ucch! Horrible. I won't do that, even for you." Secretly, Barc agreed with her. He could not imagine her doing it with anyone else. Of course, he could not imagine *his* sperm fertilizing her either, producing repulsive, hairless, hybrid infants that looked like those perverted old-human women, but . . . She had to do it, or Margal was doomed.

Still, now that he and Girelf had sealed the bond between them again and again—in every manner known to bors, mantee, wend, and fard, he suspected—he could not endure being without her ever again. Now, at last, he understood what it was like for mated males. He knew the placid contentment they felt, which allowed them to go to work day after day at dull jobs in electronics factories or dirty, grueling ones in the deep mines. Oh, yes, he understood. With Girelf at his side, he would not care if he lived at Margal Steep or Karbol, or even somewhere foreign and strange. He would be content, he knew, at least for the twenty years or so until his own desires faded entirely. "Oh, what can I do?" he moaned. "I can't let you go, but . . . I can't let Margal Town drown, either."

"You'll think of something," she murmured contentedly, not really listening, as her hands did something very strange, something that felt so very, very good.

What a difference a few hours could make. How happy the two of them had been, for a while. Of course, he had told her with a lover's confidence, her throngmother would understand when he explained it to her. Now, however, a bedraggled, soggy, exhausted, and bruised Barc Doresh humped up the trail from the summerthrong, pursued by Matoof, Simolf, Garunt, and several other irate mantee males. A fist-sized rock bounced off his muscular bors back, and he grunted in pain, too out of breath to snarl or yell. Finally, as he neared the top of the ridge obels from the pond's edge, his pursuers fell back, and he slowed his pace, catching his breath.

"I'll do it somehow!" he bellowed in the direction they had departed in. "I'll stop your fat old slug! I'll save Margal Steep, and I'll have Girelf too. You'll see!" He forced himself to be silent before, in his anger and frustration, he revealed details of the plan he had begun to formulate. "War!" he muttered as he trudged along the ridge top toward Margal. "It's going to be war."

Girelf was no less unhappy than was Barc, though she was not bruised or footsore. She, unlike him, had known what the outcome was to be—for too many separate interests were at stake; no simple, easy solutions would suffice, and none at all without a share of suffering. Only if everything worked out exactly according to plans set in motion would the various parties to the contest gain even a modicum of eventual satisfaction.

For a few sweet hours she had held her lover in her

arms, but that was not enough. She would not be satisfied with snatches of happiness in a lifetime of deprivation. She would not accept being throngmother; neither would she be only Barc's whore, or an outcast.

She dipped a hand into the water of her grotto, then swung her arm slowly over the water, watching the droplets fall, and the expanding rings of ripples intersect. If two or three tiny waves came together just so, she knew their peaks would be higher than the others. If a dozen or a hundred such waves were begun at just the proper instant, in just the right places, they might form a rogue wave all out of proportion to its origins, a wave that would slap against the shelving shore and rebound with unique results.

Had she chosen rightly? If so, she might have everything she wanted—Barc, her own honor, and the love only the throng could provide for a young female mantee. If not—nothing; not Barc, not the throng. The latter prospect brought tears to her eyes. Perhaps even a hovel in the wend forest, or a windowless room in Karbol, would be better than that.

The Margal councillors agreed to Barc's demands only because the stubborn throngmother had given them no alternative. Of course Barc had not told them *everything*. The mantees' internal problems were not entwined with their territorial aspirations, the council agreed. Whether the dam grew or fell did not affect their reproductive dilemma. For that matter, if they could not populate their new lands—or new waters—perhaps they would be wise to destroy the dam themselves, at once, thus reducing their domain to what they could successfully hold with their soon-to-diminish population.

Barc had only told them part of the story—that the throngmother refused to consider their plight. He did not explain his own part in that—that his inability to remain aloof from Girelf had lost him his one chance to convince her that her proper path was also the most desirable one. He definitely did not mention his final plea to her, after she had convinced him that she would never agree to become throngmother, whatever he did—that she flee with him to Karbol, and let the problems of Margal and the Hammad River mantees resolve themselves. What was wrong with her anyway? Was she crazy, insisting that he mate with her *officially*? With ceremony? And only if he remained ruler of Margal Steep? He imagined a troop of tiny, hairless hybrids running through the public tunnels, squalling "Daddy! Where are you, Daddy?" after him. He imagined a mantee—even a lovely mantee like Girelf—sitting placidly in a royal chamber, chatting with his sister Blet. Oh, no. It could not be.

"Very well then," he had told the council, and Blet, "you all know what we have to do. Shall we begin?" He drew a deep breath. "Margal! For Margal, forever!"

"Margal! Margal!" they responded, hooting and hurraying, then stood as one, and departed to oversee the preparations for war. There were diamond drills to be oiled and retipped, detonators to be tested, mine carts and motor carriages to be ensheathed in armor plate. Soon the damp, crumbling halls of Margal Town would echo with marching footsteps, the rattle of weaponry, and all the sounds of imminent conflict. For the bors of Margal Steep, the war began that very moment.

CHAPTER 14

Until recently, war has been unknown on the worlds
of the Xarafeille Stream, yet in the past two years over
a hundred thousand persons have died in small
"brushfire" wars. In the past, the Arbiter's forces
have arrived in a timely manner before the outbreak
of actual hostilities, but now, only pacifying words issue
from Newhome.

Where is the new Arbiter's fleet? Where are his
invincible soldiers? Must the entire Stream dissolve
in deadly war before John Minder XXIII emerges from
his grand palace in the Duchy of Erne? Have we
all, with the death of Rober VIII, lost the key to
our long and happy peace?

The Garloom Nightlight
editorial page

"Daddy, was it true? Were you really being *bad*?" Parissa
could easily imagine "bad," but she had a hard time thinking of John Minder being so.

The Arbiter chuckled. "Not bad, dear. But without all
seven of those datablocks, I was not very big, or strong.
Do you know how that feels?" Of course Parissa did, being the youngest child, and she launched into a condem-
natory exposition of that state, one that strongly
elucidated the manifold faults of her older siblings.
Minder let her diatribe run its course. "It was a difficult
time for me," he then continued. "I was quite frightened."

"What did you do?" Sarabet asked.

"I assigned a diplomat to every major town of the

Xarafeille Stream. I hoped that if people brought their conflicts to my representatives before they festered and grew into war, I could postpone the day when my help-lessness became generally known."

"Did your dippomats beat people up, Daddy?"

"Holy cubes, Priss! Diplomats only stop fights, not get in them!"

"Rober, please don't blaspheme," Minder said softly, and then explained diplomacy to his youngest child.

"That was a great risk," Rober mused when his father finished. "Your agents had to maintain a perfect record, didn't they? I mean, if a single faction defied them, and then won what they had wanted in the first place, you would have lost everything."

Minder was pleased and impressed. Rober was his most obvious heir—old enough for his adult nature to begin showing—though a female Arbiter was not an unheard-of impossibility. It was good to see that the boy was becom-ing a deep thinker. Troops, fleets, and wars were, after all, only a last resort, and were an admission of failure. "My consuls' powers were severely, publicly constrained," he explained. "They could not decree, only advise—and they could send the leaders of factions to me, here on Newhome, when an irreconcilable difference arose."

Sarabet asked, "What did you do then?" Parissa de-manded, "Did you beat them up, Daddy?" John Minder made a mental note to have Parissa's gene codes retraced. Having had only one brother himself, and no little sisters, he was not sure if her fascination with single combat was an artifact of her sex and trailing position among her sib-lings, or some unknown, aggressive trait showing up for the first time. "Sarabet will explain to you later, dear," he replied.

"Gee, thanks!" said Sarabet.

"I reserved the option of imprisoning a faction's leaders on Newhome," Minder continued, "but that was a last re-sort. I hoped that the expense and difficulty of sending their leaders here, especially when events were critical at home, would force them to exhaust all other possibilities first. And then, my consuls had certain secret orders, and funds to implement them."

"Secrets, Daddy?" Parissa frowned at Robby's pained expression. "I *like* secrets," she explained.

"Then be quiet and let him tell us," he replied. Would Parissa ever grow up? Even a little?

"The cost of a single passage to Newhome would break the budget of a small town," Minder stated. "Not the intrinsic cost, because freight and starship crews travel cheaply enough, but the imposed cost. As you once observed, Robby, there are few passenger spacecraft at all, and no dedicated passenger services, within the Stream. That is intentional. The entire Duchy of Erne, including this estate, is financed with taxes on interworld travel and tourism, but not on trade. And no ship is ever licensed that can be readily converted to a troopship or a weapons platform. When conflict occurs at all, it is kept local." So far, anyway, he thought silently, thinking of the datacrystals he had recovered—and of the ones he had not. But that was not something a child like Parissa should have to bear—not yet. Until the last one was recovered, until he had his father's power to enforce the rule of law, he could only hope no shipyards began building them. His mind shied from a future of Final War, from the terror, slaughter, and extermination that could yet be Parissa's legacy.

He shook his head. "I'm rambling. I had to insure that certain key individuals would never be denied access to me personally. My consuls knew just what kind of people I was looking for, and when they found them . . ."

"People like Barc Doresh, Daddy?" Sarabet asked. "Was he a special person?"

"An astute speculation," Minder complimented her. "Yes, Barc Doresh was one possible player in my game— not the most powerful piece on my chessboard, but not a mere pawn, either. I was thinking more of . . ."

"G'relf!" Parissa was loud enough to make all three of her family members wince. "It's G'relf, isn't it?"

"What makes you think that, dear?"

"Because she's a princess! An' cause she's going to be a queen, someday."

"A queen *ant*, maybe," Rober muttered, disgusted by mantee reproduction. He was surprised to see his father nod in agreement not with himself, but with Parissa.

"Your reasoning is a bit . . . intuitive, Pariss," he said, "but yes, in that particular game, Girelf was my queen." And Barc Doresh, he added silently, was indeed his king, a limited piece, of course, unable to leap unpredictably like a knight or to race forward and back like bishop or rook—hardly more mobile or potent, in fact, than the least of his pawns, but oh, how vital to the game. Kings, queens, and pawns, all with their own moves, according to their natures and their rules, never feeling the touch of the hand that moved them, never knowing that their fates were often decided after the very first move in the game.

Bors, Barc discovered, could not march like old humans or tarbeks did. They could stomp and they could shuffle, but not march in step with a thousand treads resounding as one. That was a minor problem; there were not enough Margal soldiers to be moved from place to place for close-order drill to be important. They could stomp, shuffle, saunter, or shamble, he decided, as long as they could fight.

Bors were good fighters, though they were not individually as deadly as gaunt tarbeks or as massively ferocious as ikuts—but there were no tarbeks to be fought, and there was not a single ikut on Stepwater. Bors were good fighters, but not good soldiers, because they were not herd creatures. Their descent, legend had it, was from solitary beasts that only acquired the rudiments of cooperative behavior late in their ascent to sapience. The prevailing theory among the human races was that of *convergence*, which lent more dignity to each than the unpalatable notion that all had descended from monkeys—or old humans. They, bors, were thus not related to old humans or descended from tree-creatures that moved in synchronized swarms, and thus they would be no match for the Arbiter's almost-mythical old-human troops. But they did not have to fight old-human soldiers, only mantees.

The problem was that each bors had to understand, individually, what tasks he was responsible for. Even "left, right, left" was taken by bors to apply only to those troops who had eye contact with the drillmaster. As he could neither directly address those farther back in the ranks nor walk backward all the time, few considered the shouted commands to apply to them. It was like that for all the tasks the bors army needed to perform. Thus Barc knew he would never march at the head of an army of bors to destroy the mantees' dam. Instead, he would watch the individual efforts of dozens of special-purpose squads, from his high-road vantage point, and hope that the efforts of sappers, transporters, electricians, and strongbacks would coincide as well as they did among the miners of Margal.

The day came sooner than Barc expected. Unfortunately, that was because he had reached the limit of what training could accomplish, not because his men were perfectly trained. Further effort would, he judged, lead only to frustration, excess anxiety, and demoralization. "Very well," he told the councillors. "Tonight we march on the Great Weir."

Barc adjusted his binocs to wide field so he could see the whole dam at once, then zoomed in on a moving speck. Yes! He could not quite make out the power cable linked to the drill, but he could see the operator and his rig. Four holes had been drilled for expansion bolts to hold the drilling rig, and the operator was tightening them with a hand wrench.

He shifted his view slightly. There! Another drill, that

one already operating; he could see the fine trail of white
dust on the dam's face. The cables snaked down the dam
and off to a generator truck hidden in tanglefoot brush a
few obels downstream. In all, he counted ten drills in
place. That was all of them. Tests on blocks of stone like
that of the dam had shown that it took a half hour to drill
to proper depth, then fifteen minutes to pack the hole
with gel, and fifteen more for the sapper to climb down
and scramble up the side of the valley to safety. Fifty minutes from now, it would all be over.

Barc continued to scan. His troops were in place, most
of them below the dam to fight off mantees attacking the
sappers, if they were discovered, and a few more holding
the approaches to the structure. It looked like the mantees planned to put a road over the top—a toll road, he
was sure. It was a quiet night. No mantees had discovered
the saboteurs yet. When they did, though, Barc's men
were ready for them; they would not escape to give alarm.
Even if they did, his troops could hold the valley floor,
protecting the detonator wires that ran up to the valley
rim. The large generator that had powered the drills was
expendable, but the detonator wires were not. Because
the mantee engineers used radios, wireless detonation was
too risky.

Still no mantees. That was strange. Nights past, observing, Barc had always seen a few of them going to and
from that little stone building at the east end of the dam.
He wondered if something was wrong—or if, for once,
things were going wonderfully, incredibly right. He
watched the last sapper descend and disappear in the
murk. Within minutes now, he would hear via his ear-
phones that they were clear. Then Prak, Barc's lieutenant,
would ignite the charges.

The soldiers who remained below to guard the wires
were all volunteers. They hoped to be able to get away after the charges blew, but there were no guarantees. The
explosives were not designed to tear great chunks of the

dam apart, to release the hundred-foot-high wall of maddened water immediately; the mining engineers assured Barc that they would only weaken the dam beyond repair, and that the people downstream would have hours, even a day, to evacuate the valley. But the dam would go. Eventually, long before the mantees could drain the pond, the dam's new flaws would grow under the monstrous pressure of the water, and the edifice would crumble. That, the engineers assured him, was inevitable.

There! Barc saw something sparkle in the moonlight. Water? Yes, there was water coming from somewhere high on the dam. But how could it be cracking already? Something was wrong! He had not heard any explosions yet. He dialed maximum enhancement on his binocs. The water—a fine sheet of it now spread over the entire surface of the dam—was coming from a tiny row of dark, symmetrical shadows less than a half obel from the dam's rim. What was happening? Moonlight silvered the dam's face; the water looked like a trickle from afar, but Barc could imagine the force of it, close up. He gnashed his teeth. The wires. Would the ever-strengthening sheet of water pull them loose? He thumbed his microphone switch. "Blow it!" he commanded. "Blow it now."

"Yes, Sar Barc," he heard. "Ten seconds."

He counted ten seconds, then ten more. "What's wrong?" he demanded to know. "I heard nothing."

"It's the wires, sar. The rushing water's pulled them all loose."

Morning. It was a gray, plain day, one that suited Barc's mood exactly. Once sure the charges were not going to go off, he had ordered his men out. Later, he watched mantees swarm over the dam, dropping by ropes from the brim. He watched them ream out the explosive gel with long poles, then pack the holes with mortar. Long before dawn, there were no signs that the construction had been tampered with. The mantees had even taken the genera-

tor truck. The war, Barc decided, was already over, though
he did not say so aloud.

The days following the fiasco at the dam were a long,
dull blur to Barc. At first the Margal council had prepared
for mantee retribution—which had lent excitement to his
depression, at least—but none had come. The mantees'
response to Barc's aggression, he realized, had been surgi-
cally precise. Now he knew what those little square
holes—really large enough for a man to stand up in—
were for. He knew also what the small building at the end
of the dam housed. The holes were small sluicegates that
could relieve the pressure behind the dam quickly. There
were hundreds of them, all over the dam's face, hitherto
unremarked by the bors. Between them and the main
sluicegates, the whole pond could be drained down
quickly, yet with minimum destruction downstream. The
little house held the water-powered machinery to operate
the gates. The mantees, economically, had only opened
the topmost row to sweep Barc's puny wires away.

In council, other propositions were put forth, discussed, and dismissed. Some were even tried.

Bors on timber rafts floated downriver and dumped
huge canisters of mining explosives by the dam's upstream
face. Mantees, underwater, cut the detonator wires. New
detonators were designed that did not need wires. Some
of those the unseen mantees disabled—or they simply
failed to go off. A few exploded, but their force was dissipated in the thick silt that built up behind the dam. A
few stunned bottom-feeding creatures floated to the surface in great clouds of turbulent sediment, but there were
no known mantee casualties; they seemed to know when
an explosion was imminent, and to get safely out of the
water.

The bors even built a steam-powered catapult that
threw great river-rounded boulders at the dam. The rocks
bounced off or shattered, seldom leaving more than shal-
low indentations in the mantee's stonework.

Someone on the Margal council proposed building self-propelled missiles. Another suggested using the catapult to throw explosive charges. Those ideas were summarily dismissed: yes, it was war indeed, but it was not, yet, *a war*. If the conflict escalated to exploding missiles, the mantees might call in the planetary guard, who would surely deal with Margal as the aggressor. Besides, the bors agreed, they were not at all sure they could make missiles that would work half as well as the simpler devices they had already tried.

"Well, that's it!" Barc said after one last council meeting had debated ever more elaborate and fruitless measures. "I am going to Garloom."

CHAPTER 15

One group of traits written on the V-chromosome
is composed of the codes that define certain unique
pheromones and a very special pheromone-recognition
capability. Intended as a safety measure to prevent
modified human populations from ever gaining permanent
genetic ascendancy over the original type, the gene-
complex codes for sexual-attractant pheromones in
the modified humans are specific to old-human
receptors, and vice versa. Thus is old-human continuity
insured, as they are universally attractive to, and attracted
to, modified humans of all variants.

Only strict cultural prohibitions among the variant
humans have prevented them from being wholly
reintegrated into the old-human stream thus far. It will
be interesting to see how long the variant beings,
already calling themselves bors, ikuts, tarbeks, and
so forth, can maintain their genetic integrity, and to
see just what extremes they go to in pursuit of that
end.

Notes to the Next Generation,
John Minder (I)

The train hardly rattled or swayed, as well it should not,
Barc thought—not considering the price he had paid for
a transcontinental ticket. From Karbol to Blednam to
Rheekwirs he had never felt more than the slightest vibration, though plains, mountains, and great canyons had
swept by outside his window. Now the journey was almost
at an end.

Who had, in those black days, first said "The Arbiter himself couldn't save Margal now?" Barc intended to find out if that was true. He peered out through the begrimed train window to see if the lights of Garloom were yet visible. He had heard that the city's glow could be seen halfway across the Belamir Desert—six hours out. If the high-speed train was indeed on time, he was only four hours from the capital city, but he could see nothing, yet.

He was both eager and reluctant. If anyone could determine the right of the matter, the Arbiter's consul could. But would Barc have to admit to the attempted sabotage, and would that be held against Margal? Who could tell?

Garloom seemed much like Karbol, a place of high glass-and-metal buildings, of busy streets and rushing pedestrians, of bright neon and laser advertisements. Barc, from the window of his cab, read those carefully. In his depression following the "war," he had given little thought to his bodily needs, but now he was damned if he would stumble into the Arbiter's representative's office with twitchy ears, red eyes, and an ache that pervaded every cell of his body. Some of those places out there had to be whorehouses or likely bars, didn't they? Garloom was an all-wendish town, but it could not be that different from Karbol. Could it?

Finally, unable to find what he sought by just looking, he sheepishly explained his desire to the cab's driver. "Wyncha say so before?" the old wend complained. "Now I gotta take you almost back to the railhead. The fardic quarter's the only place they allow that kinda stuff."

For a travel-weary, hormone-driven, and very embarrassed bors, it had been a very long night. He had not gotten more than three hours' use out of his hotel bed before it was time to leave for his appointment with the consul. It promised to be a very long day, too.

"Hey, what's that place?" he asked his driver—not the same one as the night before, he thought gratefully.

"That big thing? That's the archives. We're right on the edge of the Enclave. Actually, it's still a mile off. Pretty big, huh?"

"Yeah," Barc agreed. From here, the wendish archives, the central records storehouse for all the wendish worlds, was a great, slope-sided block, a truncated pyramid of no great distinction. It looked much like an inflated version, in stone, of a rural wendish house. "Drive by it," he ordered, thinking of Firithanet. "Aren't the high wendish officials' palaces nearby?"

"Nearby? Some of them even have bridges over the perimeter street, so the high mick-mocks can walk to work every afternoon."

"Hmm ... the Enclave. Would that be the Arafellin Enclave?"

"There isn't any other, buddy. Why? Someone invite you to dinner?" He guffawed.

Maybe, Barc decided, last night's driver was not so bad after all. Well, he could give this nose-wiggler something to think about. . . . "And the archivist's residence itself? Can you show it to me?" Barc grinned, keeping his face hidden, then said, "Dinner is at seven, and I don't want to be late. I need to know that I can find the Grand Portal when I arrive. One does not keep Firithanet's father waiting."

His jest was well rewarded. The driver first stiffened, then eyed Barc critically in his mirror. Then he chuckled. "Naw—you're joking. They don't let bors in there except to fix things. Besides, I remember, now—that Fishynet, she's the one got lost looking for her sister. Too bad. The old boy's all out of heirs, and . . ." His eyes took on a speculative gleam. "Hey? You know where she is, don't you? You do! Look, buddy, I can help you. You'll need someone like me, a wend, if you're going to try to negotiate with her old man."

"You're mistaken," Barc replied. "I only read about the family's problems, in Rheekwirs, where I'm from. I was joking, about having dinner there."

"Yeah, sure," the driver said insincerely. "Well, I don't blame you for being close. But if you just happen to feel grateful, later, I'm Bethelep, and my cab's number seven."

"I'll ask for it next time I'm in Garloom," Barc replied. "Oh! Is that the place?" He saw an elaborate entry, three sets of narrow, ornate stairs that wound and intertwined like the roots of a gnarled, ancient tree, and converged at a grand, carved wooden door, actually a pair of doors set in a single round-topped archway. Farther on, a graceful bridge arched from that building to the archive itself, across the street.

"That's it," the driver confirmed. "Now you want me to take you to the consulate?"

The Arbiter's counsul's secretary was an old-human. A male. Barc had seen old-human males, though they were not common in Karbol—but he had not seen much of them, in the sense that they usually wore long, hooded robes in deference to local prejudice. This one wore a tunic and trousers, like a bors workman's suit but cut more closely. He had no fur to rub and chafe against, Barc realized. The outfit was bright red with gold buttons and piping, and a dark stripe down the trouser seam. "Consul Marcos will be free in a few minutes," the old human said. "Please enjoy a cup of tea, meanwhile."

Barc sniffed assorted little bags of tea, but found nothing that especially appealed to his nose. There was, however, a strange burnt-and-bitter aroma hovering over the service table. He pointed at an ornate vessel, gold inlaid with black enamel, a bors product, but surely offworld. "What's in there?"

"That's coffee—an Earth beverage, originally. A stimulant. The consul enjoys it."

Barc had heard of coffee, which cost eighteen creds a cup in Karbol's fancier places. "May I try some?" He reached for the pot.

"Use one of the straight-sided mugs," the secretary said. Barc was slightly offended by that. The mugs were part of a set, matching the pot; he had not needed to be told. He had just finished pouring when he heard the swish of a door opening.

"Sar Doresh?" a different voice asked. Barc turned to see who it was—and he almost spilled his drink. The consul was an old human too, and wore a uniform identical to the secretary's. There the resemblance ended. A cascade of heavy yellow fur surrounded a face much like a young mantee's—delicate, without the great tarbek-like beak that elderly old-human women often displayed. Yes, the consul was old-human—and female.

Barc was glad he had indulged his body's demands recently—he might otherwise have hurt his petition's chances, if his sudden physical attraction had been obvious. There was, he decided, definitely something to be said for the voluminous filter garments old humans were required to wear elsewhere.

Of course, he told himself, she would be terribly ugly without her red clothes. He would have shuddered at the thought of actually touching those protuberant, furless breasts—if he had not, in spite of last night's indulgence and his inculcated sensibilities, felt quite ready to have sex with her, right then and there. He tried to supplant such feelings with anger: What's wrong with the Arbiter, anyway? Doesn't he realize what old-human women do to the rest of us? Is he stupid? Then he remembered that the Arbiter himself was an old-human.

"Sar Doresh?" the woman repeated.

"Ah . . . Consul Marcos," Barc said, trying not to stammer. "Thank you for seeing me." He hoped his discomfort did not show.

"That is my job. And your problem certainly seems like a pressing one. Please come into my office." Barc followed her. It was a nice office, carpeted in soothing gray, furnished in tan and russet, and smelling of leather. It might have felt dull or cold, but for the clear Garloom sunlight that streamed in through a broad, bowed window. Two soft-looking leather couches, curved, filled the bow's arc.

Two matching chairs faced a vast, red-toned wooden desk. "Mahogany," Consul Marcos said, seeing his admiring glance. "The local wends go mad over it. For all their forestry skills, they've never been able to get the species to grow right, under Mirrim's light."

She sat behind her desk, motioning Barc to sit, then watched him, expectantly. He felt better then. Perhaps the desk rested on a return-air grille that removed her stimulating odors. "I don't know where to begin," he said.

She smiled. "Then let me tell you what I already know. You may correct any misconceptions, and add details you feel are important." She began, and soon Barc realized that the Arbiter's intelligence service was better than he could have imagined. She knew everything. She knew the names of the men who had drilled the holes in the dam! If she knew that much, surely she could see that the mantee aggression was uncalled for. He felt reassured. Her words reassured him further. "The case seems quite clear to me. It should be no trouble at all to set the mantees straight. Being mantees, they will not defy an Arbiter's decision." Barc raised an eyebrow curiously. "If they were fards," she explained, "they would haggle over the terms. If they were wends, they would cleverly attempt to sneak around the exact wording, but mantees . . . So. All I will need from you is the deed to Margal Steep, and I can begin the process. Did you bring it with you?"

"Ah . . . the deed? To Margal?" Barc had not known there was such a thing.

"Yes, the deed. Surely you knew . . . Oh, you didn't, did you?" She shrugged. "Well, Margal will not crumble away while you return for it. I will request that the mantees not further flood it while I deliberate. They may continue to build the dam's final courses, but I hope to convince them to keep the water's level constant." She did not explain the Arbiter's firm directive, given to his agents on every world, that no ultimatums were to be given anywhere, to anyone, under any circumstances at all. "For all our experience, all the millennia of the Rule of Law," the recording of John Minder XXIII had said, "we know only how much force will suffice once an absolute command has been given. We do not know, having never experimented, how *few* such orders must truly be given in order to maintain the Rule over the Xarafeille Stream." And of course John Minder XXIII had not told his agents everything, either. He had not mentioned missing datacrystals, or war fleets, or poletzai.

The deed? But no one had ever told Barc there was a deed. Did anyone at Margal know about it? His mother might have, or Uncle Grast, but . . . He explained his dilemma to Consul Marcos.

"How strange," she mused. "Most places, such a valuable thing is kept in a dedicated place—a vault, or a museum showcase. Are you sure you haven't one?"

"I don't know," Barc replied, picturing some ancient scroll. "What would it look like?"

"Oh, just like any other large-capacity datablock." She indicated a size and shape with both hands. "I would guess, from its approximate age, that it would be green, or perhaps blue. Most blocks of that era were one or the other."

With a sick, sinking feeling in his stomach, as if he had eaten something foul, Barc realized what the deed to Margal Steep was—and worse, *where* it was. "The blue crystal," he moaned. The lovely crystal, once treasured, that now rested a full two obels beneath the water that flooded Margal's oldest levels. It might as well, Barc thought, have been on Newhome, or in the middle of the star Mirrim. Consul Marcos, seeing his dejection, questioned him. In a monotone, he responded.

"It's not *that* bad," she said then, too lightly for the circumstances. "You bors are quite clever. Surely a mere two hundred feet of water are not unconquerable. Margal's engineers will contrive a way to retrieve the deed."

"Perhaps so," Barc agreed politely, rising from his chair. He would have to go home immediately, and find out, wouldn't he? "Thank you for your time," he said, turning toward the door.

"Oh, not yet!" she said, suddenly appearing at his side. "There is another matter to be addressed before you leave." Barc could not imagine what that might be, at first. Then, when he felt her smooth, furless hands ruffling the soft blackness of his upper arm, and when he felt the rough hammering of his heart, he knew. Nobody needed Testoslam or Estrokick with old humans, he remembered, when it was already too late to matter. . . .

CHAPTER 16

Just as V-chromosome traits encourage the continuity
of the old-human phenotype both by making old humans
universally attractive to the variant types and by
guaranteeing that misogamy among variants re-
creates the old-human geno- and phenotype, those traits
also discourage misogamy between variants. There was
perhaps some concern that if slaves of different
variants were ever used together on a single planet,
they might back-breed to the old-human type at an
inconvenient time and place. As long as the nature
of the conteracting hormones* was kept secure
within corporate vaults, that risk was minimal;
considering the exclusive natures of variant cultures,
and the almost-universal antipathy toward old humans—
that I encourage on the one hand and protect
against on the other—the risk of the variants
disappearing in the foreseeable future is small.

Notes to the Next Generations,
John Minder (I)

The thudding vibration of huge pumps, for weeks felt
through the floors of all Margal Steep, finally ceased.
Grainy dust that had fallen from deteriorated walls and
ceilings at last ceased dancing on tiles and tabletops
where it had fallen faster than even the most diligent
housecleaners could remove it. "Well, so much for *that*

---

* Those hormones, now sold commercially as Estrokick and Testoslam,
were either publicly released or independently rediscovered during the
Arbitership of Rober IV. —ed.

idea," said Barc Doresh. "Now we know that the water seeps back in faster than we can pump it back out—and besides, I've been worried about the additional damage the vibration was doing."

"What do we try next, Sar Barc?" Prak was crestfallen; the pumps had been his idea.

Barc shuffled through a stack of glossy catalogues on his desk. "All these diving rigs are made offworld," he commented. "If we order one, it will be a year in transit, and by then the mantees will be raising the water again. We'll have to make our own."

Prak brightened. He was a fine engineer. The failure of his first attempt was no fault of his own. There had been no way to gauge the infiltration rate into the flooded caverns until they tried pumping them out. Now another challenge was before him. "Oh, good! I've been pondering those rebreathers, and . . ."

"Prak! Think simple. Whatever we build must be fool-proof and, above all, quick to make. We have wasted two months already."

In less than half that time, the new plan emerged— from Barc's mind, not clever Prak's. In that time Prak devised a dozen solutions, and Barc found fault with all of them. The last one, though, provided him with the nugget of his own idea, one that would not have occurred to anyone who had not actually been swimming underwater in bors caves and mantee grottoes. Prak's plan had involved portable metal walls dragged underwater and erected in flooded corridors to seal them, then pumping out the water. "Prak, Prak," Barc sighed. "It's a lovely plan, but can we build the airlock we'll need to get us to the next corridor beyond? And will we be able to move the next wall through it?"

Prak, attempting to defend his idea, unrolled a printout on the table. "Let me show you, on a chart of the caverns that . . ."

Barc, excited, interrupted him. "A map? Where did

you get a . . . No, never mind. This chart shows ceiling elevations. Are they accurate? Can we make elevations? Vertical section charts?"

Overwhelmed, Prak sputtered. Nonetheless, in short order Barc pried from him all the information he needed. "Look," he said, sketching. "The corridor ceilings are lower than the intersections. There will be air trapped in the highest places there. We need only swim from one bubble to the next, trailing a rope to guide us back."

"We?" Prak squeaked. "Us? Swim?" Barc had forgotten that his own underwater swimming skill was unknown to any but Nidleg Marboon and Girelf. He explained further, substituting "I" and "me" for the terrifying plural pronouns, and Prak became less agitated. As Barc elucidated, the truly formidable nature of the task became apparent to him. It had taken hours to walk to the crystal cavern. It would take days, swimming from one bubble of entrapped air to the next, to get there. Would he have to string ropes from cavern to cavern, retracing his way each time, dragging fresh rope over ever-increasing distances? Would he, by the time he was halfway to the crystal shrine, have to carry food with him, and some sort of inflatable raft to rest on? He shrugged. There was only one way to find out.

"Tomorrow," he said, pointing at the highest submerged caverns on the printout, "I will go through from there, to there."

He did just that. He emerged in a darkness that his portable glow lamp pushed back only a short distance. He treaded water and searched for some purchase, somewhere to brace his feet so he could pull on the tough cord in his hand, and thus bring through the heavier rope attached to it with a sheet-bend knot. He swam about, swore bors oaths and fardic curses, then, leaving his cord loose in the water, followed it back to its source.

"I need metal spikes like this," he told Prak, sketching. "I'll hammer them in, then pull the rope through and secure it. Then with the advantage of the pulley attached,

your men working from the dry end can pull through the
other things I'll need—the raft you're making, wires for
permanent waterproof lights, food in sealed packets—and
yes, an insulated bottle of that *coffee* stuff, too."

Barc, after several tries, had acquired a taste for the
beverage. Too, each sip reminded him of pleasant things,
of Consul Marcos. "Sally," he murmured to himself. Sally
Marcos, an old human, whose furless oversized breasts
did not stimulate either disgust or incestuous memory of
his lactating mother. Sally, whose office he had left feeling
only slightly less fulfilled than he had after being with
Girelf. Sally. The sense of well-being had not lasted long
afterward. Halfway across the Belamir Desert en route to
Rheekwirs he had again begun to feel the aching sickness
of bodily demand.

In Karbol, he had tarried overnight with Tathabel, but
he did not tell her he had seen the Grand Portal from
which she and Firithanet were forever barred.

Within weeks Barc advanced through six corridors to
the sixth intersection. Now, floating on his inflated raft in
the most distant one, his thoughts almost drowned by the
roar of pumped-in air, he mentally calculated the time it
had taken to get there and how far he still had to go. Each
high-ceilinged intersection conquered had taken longer
than the last. So far, each time Barc ran the rope through
the pulley, the men at the open-air end could still do the
heavy work of pulling supplies through, but Barc had to
follow each bundle, freeing it from snags, easing it around
underwater turns, all while breathing through a hose attached to a metal pot in which he placed his head.

He communicated with the base by a thin cord strung
on small pulleys, using a simple code. Each tug rang a
bell. Radios were useless in the flooded caverns, and his
engineers had not yet successfully dealt with the increas-
ing pressure as he went deeper, that forced water into the
rudely sealed cases of intercom sets that transmitted over
wires.

Pressure was a variable he had not considered until he shook the water out of a ruined intercom. Thinking on that, he began taking measurements of water levels in each cavern. As he got deeper there was less air in each succeeding bubble. At first he had attributed it wholly to exfiltration through cracks and porous strata, but later he realized that it was at least partly due to pressure alone. As he got deeper, the air in each cavern was more compressed. It did not take much calculation to determine that by the time he reached the depth of the crystal cave there would be little air indeed, even if it could be pumped in that far.

It took little more effort to calculate that he did not have time to work his way there step by step, dragging ever-larger masses of food, ropes, pulleys, and spikes, and all the sundry articles that seemed to multiply with every problem that demanded a solution. As he lay on his raft listening to the whistling roar of released compressed air, he conceded that this effort had failed. Over this distance, too many ropes broke, and larger ones would require larger pulleys and spikes, and would be even harder to pull.

It was beyond what one single bors could do alone in the dark cold, always on the brink of exhaustion, and he had not been able to train many others to swim as he did, underwater. Only half of the ones who learned could tolerate the cold water without involuntarily hibernating and having to be pulled back out. Of those who matched his own physical strength, only three proved able to tolerate the psychic pressure that bore down more heavily than the hundred-foot water column over their heads. Four bors out of Margal's ten thousand was not enough.

With a sigh, he rolled off the raft into the dark, victorious water. As it enveloped him he momentarily considered giving in, letting himself sink. It would be easy—he was so very tired. But the phosphenes that danced behind his closed eyelids that moment happened to be blue ones, an icy, familiar blue like the crystal, the deed to Margal

Steep. *There has to be a way,* he told himself, as he began the long pull back along the ropes.

"Niddy! What are you doing here?" Barc was delighted to see the trader.

"I just came by with some fresh fur," Marboon said, as coarse as ever. "And as I hear you've developed a taste for skin, I brought one of those, too—a very nice redheaded one, with little, tiny . . ."

"Niddy, shut up," Barc hissed—but too late. Several other bors had heard, and had turned their heads away in either disgust or embarrassment. Barc, after long association with the merchant, and after his own difficulties and degeneracies, had ordinarily ceased to notice Niddy's speech, but now, having labored among Margal's sheltered bors, having commanded them, he was again sensitized to their proper, wholesome attitudes.

"Sorry," Niddy replied, unchastened, but in a lower tone. "I just thought you could think better if you . . ."

"Niddy!" Barc's expression silenced the older bors. As quickly as his anger had arisen, it faded, replaced with an expression Niddy interpreted as bleak resignation. Things were obviously not going well at Margal Steep. He asked Barc to explain what was going wrong.

Barc did so. He explained the weight of spikes and pulleys, growing distances, and the failures of ropes and bors. He told how the overstressed air pumps could not keep ahead of pressure and exfiltration even in caverns three through seven, and that there were still twelve more to go, each one deeper than the last.

"Hmmph," Niddy grunted, shrugging. "So find a shorter way in."

Niddy's casual dismissal of Barc's agony angered him again. "A shorter way? There is no shorter way." Barc's ears lay flat against his skull, and his eyes narrowed to mere slits. He did not like being mocked, or having his greatest failure dismissed as trivial.

Nonetheless, Niddy shrugged again. "No? Then how

did you get *out* of Margal, that time when I fished you out of the river?"

Barc stared. As if Marboon had physically reached out and taken it from his shoulders, Barc felt the burden of failure, of dead end striving against too-great odds, lifted from him. "The tunnel," he said in a low, almost reverent whisper. "I can go in through the tunnel."

And so he did. Within three weeks Barc found himself dog-paddling within the crystal shrine itself, orienting himself, taking deep breaths of much-compressed air, the sound of his aspirations drowned by the roar from the fat air pipe at the far side of the cave.

There had been problems getting there, but they had been ones that hard work and innovation could surmount. Finding the tunnel adit itself had been the hardest of them, because the flooded riverbank was so much changed. Relocating the pumps and ganging them sequentially to step up the pressures had been next. Securing the air pipes against the current's pull was easier. Devising an open-bottomed diving canister where Barc could rest and breathe during his slow descent and his slower ascent was, by comparison, no trouble at all.

Hefting his glow lamp, Barc prepared for one more dive, his tenth. This time, he told himself, he would find it. He had found the bronze-and-glass case again, on a floor that had only a light skin of muck. *This time,* he promised himself. . . . But he did not find the crystal on that dive, or the twelfth, or the fifteenth one.

"Sixteen! Lucky sixteen!" Barc shouted. He held the heavy blue-tinged crystal in his hand. Niddy helped him climb out of the water.

"Now we'll stop them!" Barc exclaimed, performing a heavy-footed, shuffling dance. "Now we'll get their damned water out of here." Already, his mind was working out alternative scenarios. The one he liked best involved a side bargain with the mantees: he might let them keep *some* of their illegally acquired territory, if he could have . . . Girelf.

Niddy rotated the crystal in his hands, and held it up to a glow light. "Bubbles," he said. "Bubbles?"

Bark shambled over to him, dripping water. "What?"

"Bubbles, see?" Niddy pointed at several dark blemishes within the the artifact.

"So what?" said Barc.

"Crystals don't have bubbles."

"This one does," Barc countered. "I can see them."

"Well. I'll bet you never noticed them before, when you were a kid, did you?"

"No," Barc confirmed. "I never looked that closely. Again, so what?"

"Well," Niddy said hesitantly, "for one thing, datacrystals don't have bubbles, ever—but glass does."

Perhaps Barc was still fatigued from all that swimming. He did not understand what Niddy was driving at, at first. When he did, his burly shoulders sagged, and his jaw hung loose. "Glass?" he squeaked. "Glass?"

"Yup. This isn't your crystal. This is a glass casting. See? That line is a mold mark. I'll bet your crystal hasn't been in that cave for a long time."

Barc knew he was right. He also knew where his crystal was, and who had it. "That sneak! That slinking mahkrat! She took it!"

"Who?" Niddy demanded.

"Girelf! She tricked me! All this time, the mantees have had the deed to Margal Steep." Barc's fur stood on end in spiky clumps in spite of its wetness. He felt alternately hot and cold as surges of rage and waves of terrible hurt battled for dominance within him. "I'm going to get it back if I have to . . ."

To what? Wisely, Nidleg Marboon did not ask.

CHAPTER 17

DISPATCH

TO: Arbiter (eyes only, crypt. 7xc)
FROM: Samol Jebbis, Consul, Beldant (Xarafeille
         1427)
REPORT: Intervariant tensions here up from .032
         to .035. Threshold curr. est. .042. Advise.
         No resolution of ikut/bors disputes in sight.
         Ref. report last courier.
MESSAGE: John, the figures speak for themselves.
         Personally, I'm giving us six months. It would
         really help if you could arrange a high-
         profile Arbitorial resolution of a bors-
         related issue somewhere, and soon. Give
         them some hope—and me too—that a
         peaceful settlement is possible. Are
         other consuls working on anything good?

How could she have done it? Barc asked himself. They
had made love—it could not be compared with the sex he
had had with others. They had shared hopes, plans, prom-
ises ... didn't that count for anything? Were all those
things only part of some greater, more nefarious plan?
Barc hated her for tricking him, for living a lie. He hated
himself, for being a fool. His anger grew minute by minute, as he dwelled on her treachery. It was a red haze that
distorted his vision. He wanted to tear something apart.

Again, Barc was going to get wet, and to swim beneath
dark water into a place he had only been once before.
Again, the mantee Simolf stood beside him. This time,

Barc hoped, Simolf and his companions would not find it necessary to harry him from mantee territory with angry shouts and thrown rocks. He hoped, but he did not honestly think so. If Girelf would not willingly give him Margal's deed, he would beat her, if necessary. He would take the crystal and run, but he doubted that he would make it. Even a husky bors was no match for ten or a hundred angry mantees. Still, he would bash a few heads and dislocate a few mantee limbs before they overwhelmed him. Maybe he would be lucky, for once.

He waded into the pool and sank beneath the water, then he half-swam, half-pulled himself beneath the entangling roots. His anger and steadfast resolve were so great that he did not pause at the halfway-point air bubble, but continued on without waiting to suck a single slow breath. He was used to much longer passages, now; this puny burrow was nothing at all.

In the anteroom of Girelf's grotto he hardly paused to get his bearings, but plunged ahead into the dark passage to her lair, her . . . boudoir. He anticipated grabbing the treacherous mantee by her nose, and hearing her squeal. He would bare his teeth and roar, and she would give him the deed to Margal Steep. He could not stride resolutely in the low, dark way, but when he emerged, he drew himself up to his full height. His large hands stiffened, and his fingernails became like claws, to rend and tear. And there! There was Girelf, reclining on her voluptuous bed of soft mosses, her fur sleek and dry, her slim form only beginning to grow tense as she saw his rigid, angry stance. "Give it to me!" Barc bellowed, his roar flat and muffled in the close confines, but no less deadly for that. "Where is my deed?"

Girelf shrank back against the wall, terrified. This was not the Barc she had expected—not *her* Barc. This Barc did not exude the scents of arousal and love. Girelf feared for her life: she had not anticipated this; she could do nothing with this ferocious bors. "It's not here," she squealed. "I gave it to the throngmother to hide. She will never give it up."

Despite the chemicals of rage that heated his blood, Barc knew she was telling the truth. The crystal was not here, thus it could be anywhere. He envisioned the mantees' vast underwater realm, which he could not explore, the depth of the water, and its chill. Abruptly, with great finality, Barc realized that he had again failed. His heart seemed to sink low in his chest, and its martial drumbeat faded to a dull pit-pat. "I want it," he said weakly, his carefully cultivated attitude evaporating, unable to withstand this sudden reversal of his plans.

"It's not yours anymore, Barc," Girelf said quietly, but with more boldness than a moment before. "The fifty-obel rule, remember? The datablock belongs to us—as it has for years, now."

"Years?" Barc's voice broke, a cublike squeak. "How many years?" He already knew. The crystal had long since been removed when he made his escape from Margal, with Niddy clinging precariously to his root outside.

Girelf confirmed it. She had replaced the original only days after Barc had shown it to her, as soon as the mantees had gotten the duplicate made. Infatuation aside, and even love, her action had been entirely a practical matter. It had taken no great mathematical skill to count the paces from crystal to riverbank and to calculate that it was less than five obels, which was all the mantees were allowed within the water gap itself, and thus to decide that the crystal was indeed hers to take. "What will you do now?" she asked. It was not fear that prompted her question. She did not fear Barc now—indeed, seeing him wet and bedraggled, his big shoulders slumped so he looked potty and pathetic, she felt sorry for him. He was such a . . . such a poor, innocent, impractical bors.

Whether his flat, unlibidinous state resulted from his nocturnal dalliance with a redheaded "skin" the night before, from realization of his final, abject failure, or from a melange of both, Barc felt only the faint, lingering hint of his ertswhile desire for Girelf. Through the red-gray film that seemed to cover his eyes, he saw only a sharp-faced creature whose green eyes seemed to gleam with baleful light. With an inarticulate snarl he spun about and plunged back into the dark passageway.

Emerging in daylight, he strode past a surprised Simolf, who, instead of following him, plunged into the water to see if Barc had done harm to Girelf. Emerging again before Barc had gotten thirty paces on, he waved to his fellows.

No mantees harried Barc from their ill-gotten land. Weighing his ferocious expression, none dared get within a stone's throw of him, and, as he was going in the right direction, uphill and away, they wisely left him alone.

Girelf wondered if all was lost. She had never seen Barc like that. She had never been really afraid of him before. Had she lost him for good? Yet there was nothing she could do now except ride out the tempest she herself had created. The crystal had been taken long ago, and could not be returned easily. Barc's anger was established, and could no more easily be allayed. The waters behind the Great Weir rose, and would not of their own accord go down again. Alone in her grotto, Girelf wept. It was not the first time she had done so, and she did not think it would be the last.

Again Barc rode the intercontinental express past Blednam and Rheekwirs and across the Belamir Desert. This time he did not peer from his window to catch Garloom's first glow. His black mood had hardly abated since his abortive confrontation with Girelf. His fellow passengers sensed it, avoiding even eye contact with him, and kept their ordinarily noisy children quiet and out from underfoot.

Barc did not stop to dally in any fardic-quarter bars, nor did he specifically request cab number seven. He did not take a room for the night, either, but went straight to the Arbiter's consulate.

"I'm sorry, Sar Barc," said the secretary. "Consul Marcos has left for the weekend." Weekend? Barc, whose days and nights had been indistinguishable for many months, was hardly aware of such arbitrary divisions of time as weeks and weekends.

"Where is she?" he demanded.

The secretary's eye held a knowing light tempered only by his caution at Barc's forbidding demeanor. "I will contact her. Wait here." Barc did not bother checking to see if the door locked behind the retreating old human. He did not listen to verify if the secretary indeed called the consul or the Garloom police. He would see her sooner or later, and he had broken no laws—not yet.

"You're in luck, Sar Bors," the man said upon his return. "She is at her country residence, and she will meet with you there." Barc's previous visit, and his unusual lingering in the consul's office, had not gone unnoticed. The old-human male was aware of the attraction females of his race found in furred males, and a few casual sniffs of the air after Barc's last departure had intensified his suspicions. Now his superior's willingness to give out her private address to a petitioner removed his last doubts of what had transpired before, and what would again occur. "Here is her address," he said coolly, offering a paper. "Show this to your driver."

"Ummm, Sally," Barc murmured, groping in darkness for the smooth, soft, furless heat of her.

"Ummm, Barc," she said, imitating him, laughing, then reaching to guide him in newly familiar motions peculiarly satisfying to old-human women, acts he had not bothered to learn of with the paid companions Niddy had supplied.

As good as Girelf, he thought. Well, almost as good. But unlike with Girelf, his satisfaction did not last, but had to be renewed again and again, which had already exhausted both of them—and the weekend was only half gone. "We must talk," he said after their next coupling.

"I suppose so," she agreed hesitantly. "At least a little, now and then . . ."

"A lot. Now," he stated adamantly, "and maybe then . . ."

She sighed and sat up. The sight of her full, heavy breasts disconcerted him. They did not arouse him, in his presently sated state, but they had begun to represent something exquisite and erotic, something far different from carefully engendered revulsion. She pulled the sheet up to cover them. "There is only one possible solution now," she told him. "You must go to Newhome and present your grievance before the Arbiter himself."

"Newhome?" Barc was aghast. "That costs two hundred thousand creds. I can't afford that!"

"Shh! It won't cost a cred. I will authorize a travel voucher, and a thousand creds expense money. You can be there in a month, and back in another." Barc considered that. It would still give him time for his last-ditch plan, if the Arbiter could not help him. That plan was simple: a dumping of tailings rich in acids, heavy metals, and noxious by-products of Margal's refineries that would make the river below the water gap uninhabitable for decades or centuries, even far below the Great Weir itself, and then a massive frontal assault on the mantees, a slaughter of every one that came out of the water. He had told no one of that plan, and he would not threaten the Arbiter with it, either. He would take no risk that anyone could stop him before it was too late.

But Barc was not sure he could go through with that. He considered himself degenerate and a pervert, but not a monster. A trip to Newhome was far preferable. In fact, he began to look forward to it. How many provincial bors ever got to go offworld at all, let along to the capital, in a manner of speaking, of the entire Xarafeille Stream? He began to feel much better about everything else, too. "Ummm, come here," he said to Consul Sally Marcos. . . .

CHAPTER 18

The subtleties of V-chromosome design only emerge
with a lifetime to observe its effects. Perhaps the original
manipulators were not the ogres they seem. The
suppression of variant-human libidos in the
presence of immature humans of any type comes
immediately to mind. Was that intentional? Whether
the answer is yes or no, it is a virtual guarantee that
certain notorious old-human abuses would not
occur among their variant kin. Intentional or not, it
is an entirely benign modification, and it has had no
measurable impact on the overall fecundity of the
variant races.

Notes for the Next Generations,
John Minder (I)

Barc did not have time to return to Margal. He contacted
Niddy. "I'm going to tell the council, of course," Niddy responded. "They can decide whether or not to make a general announcement. You know: 'Our dedicated ruler has
gone to Newhome to plead our case with the Arbiter himself. . . .' That sort of thing. Maybe it will be enough to
stave off the war party, the ones who want to start killing
mantees, and even slow down the flow of assets out of
Margal."

"That's happening?"

"Just yesterday Benk Fedro announced he was transfer-
ring his refining operation to Morgenweep, halfway
around Stepwater, before the flooding reaches his level
and wrecks his equipment."

"Stall him! That's crazy. He can't move the blast furnaces; he'll have to build new ones. But if he guts the controls and electronics, the whole plant will take years to reopen. Stall him. I'll be back before the spring floods, and maybe we can get an injunction against the mantees. . . ."

"I'll try, Barc. You just do the best you can, and don't worry about us."

Don't worry? That, Barc thought, was easier said than done. Yet he managed. He had his own, very immediate, things to think about. The Arbiter! He, Barc Doresh, was really going to Newhome, where he would meet in person with the most powerful, most mysterious human in the known universe.

What did the Arbiter look like? In childhood, Barc had imagined him to resemble Uncle Grast, who was surely no less than the second most important human, but larger, and with red, piercing eyes. Later, he understood that the Arbiter was in fact an old human, and he then pictured him only as a pair of ice-blue eyes, large, all-knowing eyes, glowing coldly within the shadows of a hooded old-human cloak.

In recent days he had gained a new insight into the nature and appearance of old humans—of a particular old human. His innards tightened as he thought about that. Of course, the Arbiter was male, but Barc decided that just as male and female bors were more alike than bors and old humans, so an old-human male was more like Sally Marcos than like Uncle Grast. Too, just as Sally stimulated no ignorant, childish revulsion in him, neither should the Arbiter himself. At any rate, in the not-too-distant future he would know for sure.

Barc presented his travel voucher to the uniformed spaceport guide. From that moment he was neither unaccompanied nor unoccupied for two consecutive minutes. He had no idea just what was going on behind the scenes, only that he was receiving very special treatment. Did other passengers-to-be have the use of a private lounge?

Was everyone shown holographic images of suites and furnishings aboard a ship, and asked to select floor plan, materials, and colors that pleased him? Barc had no way of knowing. No wonder, he said to himself, that starship travel is so expensive. He had always imagined it to be much like barge travel on the Hammad River, but more closely confined, as in a metal bottle.

What he did not know was that a vessel now in port, whose planned destination was halfway across the Stream from Newhome, had been diverted for no other reason than to deliver him upon the Arbiter's doorstep. He did not know that the suite he requested had to be assembled in a quickly emptied part of a cargo hold, and furnished from a warehouse of beds, couches, lamps, and other articles kept for that purpose. He did not know that the "porters," the "stewardesses," and the "purser" who would see to his every need were reassigned from more ordinary duties within the port complex, or that for them his journey was the chance of a lifetime, the career break each had awaited without much hope for several years. When the voyage was over, their "traveled" status would guarantee rapid promotion and further travel, and a choice of positions and salaries. They would be quite happy to serve Barc Doresh with enthusiasm and alacrity.

Barc never saw the ship itself, to identify it among the others he had seen towering above the port like rigid, silvery soap bubbles. He saw only the inside of a luxurious cab, a tunnel, and an elevator. He saw little of the ship's insides, either—a corridor, another elevator, and then his suite, just as he had ordered it, though far larger than it had seemed in the holos. He got the impression that he would see little more of the ship in the future, so he was pleased that his quarters were roomy. His suspicion was entirely correct.

On his first day aboard, the novelty of the situation held Barc's interest. He explored his suite and experienced, with typical bors curiosity, its gadgets, conveniences, and hitherto-unknown amenities.

The second day, he discovered that his personal stewardess considered herself one of those "amenities" as well. Or perhaps, he thought (with a cynicism engendered by the profession in which he had become wealthy), she only exhibited the old-human female's attraction to fur.

The novelty of gadgets and sexual satisfaction combined did not suffice to fill the hours in shipboard days. "I am going out," he told Jane, his companion.

"Oh? Why?" asked Jane.

"I want to explore," he replied. "I am bored." She shrugged.

An hour later Barc returned to the suite. "I saw a half mile of corridors," he growled in response to Jane's inquiry, "every one the same. I saw 'off limits to passengers' signs and locked doors. That is what I saw. How do I get to see the 'real' ship—the parts behind all those locks and signs?"

Jane sighed. "You can't. It is against the rules, because you are a *passenger.*" The way she said "passenger" hinted that the word alone was explanation enough.

It was not enough for Barc. "All this luxury, this fancy suite, is very nice," he muttered, "but it is no substitute for being locked out of the rest of the ship." His bors curiosity, an innate drive, was thwarted.

"I have a theory," Jane said. "Of course it is not written in the employee manual, but everyone thinks it makes sense . . ." Barc encouraged her to go on. "Since the Arbiter controls the means of propelling starships," she said, "he must want things as they are. And if that is so, he must want starship travel to be not only expensive, but not too much fun either." She suggested that if ordinary folk could whisk about the Xarafeille Stream at will, the task of regulating the peace would become impossibly difficult. Every planet's agents and spies would be everywhere else. Even the prohibition of troopships and vessels of war would not prevent governments and princes from sending soldiers by ordinary transportation, soldiers who would gather and acquire weaponry at their destinations.

Barc agreed that it made sense. "And it is clever in other ways, too," he mused. "Since there is no overt restriction on travel, anyone who can accumulate the wealth for a ticket can go."

"But who can afford it?" Jane asked rhetorically—she had long since discovered that Barc was no arrogant rich tourist, so she spoke freely with him. "Only people who can afford to buy and sell worlds can."

"Oh, it's not *quite* that bad," Barc replied. "I am—or I was—only a proprietor of . . . of bars. Yet I could have bought my own ticket." He chuckled. "I would have had to sell everything to do it, though. Yet that is the point of the Arbiter's cleverness."

"And how is that?" Clearly, Barc's insight went much deeper than her own.

"Because it is so expensive, only the very rich can travel freely, in groups, with congenial associates to wile away the long, boring passages. Only they can *enjoy* being tourists. And there is a certain cachet to being a tourist, too. Why, when someone says 'That man is a tourist,' they could as well be saying 'He is the king of Toot.'"

"Where is Toot?" Jane asked.

"I made it up," Barc replied. "Yet the point stands. The very folk most capable of thwarting the Arbiter's desire to restrict free travel have a social stake in maintaining the status quo."

Jane agreed that it was so.

Barc did not sense when the ship landed on Newhome, though he had eagerly awaited it for two whole weeks. Two weeks, because it was a very fast ship, and it went directly from Stepwater to Newhome without stops in between. It had taken mere hours to become bored with his suite, and only days to tire of endless high-quality holoshows, no matter how perfect the equipment or how real the virtual stage. Even his acquiescent and innovative old-human "stewardess" had not held his attention for more than a few hours at a time, out of far too many hours, though in the process of becoming bored he learned new variations upon several sexual themes he believed would make Sally Marcos—or even the most widely-experienced girls in Karbol—blush hotly, yet eagerly.

When he stepped out beneath the sun of a new world, his primary emotion was relief. His second response was anger. From the moment his foot touched planetary surface, he was entirely abandoned. No one was there to meet him, and the elevator back into the ship would not reopen. There were no cabs, no throngs, only weather-beaten pavement and, at some distance, the low skyline of what he presumed was the city of Erne.

Barc walked, dragging his squeaking luggage case, cursing and swearing in several tongues. Was it a trick? Had he been lured to this place to get rid of him until the mantees finished their damn and Margal Town collapsed on itself? Was Sally Marcos really the Arbiter's consul at all, or was she perhaps some well-paid employee of the mantees themselves. For that matter, was this even Newhome or was it, as it looked, some backwater world at the edge of the Stream, where only one ship touched down in a decade? As he trudged, imagining the worst that could have befallen him, he wondered if his thousand creds were real, and if he would even be able to sleep under a roof, or eat from a table, let alone earn the money he would need to pay his passage back home.

When he reached the edge of the port pavement and entered the narrow streets beyond, no fence or sign indicated the transition. He soon found himself deep among shabby buildings, tired, hot, and footsore, angry at the squeaking wheels of his case, pained by blisters and a bare patch of gray-green skin where the case's pull-strap had worn away his fur. Then he saw the sign: ROOMS BY THE WEEK. ARBITER'S PETITIONERS WELCOME. INSPECTED MONTHLY BY THE DUCHY OF ERNE HOSTELRY COMMISSION. His fearful imaginings dissipated. He trudged up several steps and was informed by an elderly male old-human

that a room was available for three creds a week. He did
not expect to remain that long, he said, but he paid the
full amount anyway. He needed a secure place to lock up
his luggage before he attempted to discover what stupid
oversight had left him without escort or information.

An hour later, with a street map in hand, he found a
restaurant and a quarter-cred meal. Most of the patrons,
he observed, were old-humans. In fact, he realized, he
had not seen a single bors or wend, an ikut, mantee, or
tarbek, even a fard. And he abruptly noted that not one
old human wore the cumbersome filtering robes he was so
used to seeing. That, he thought, might be a problem,
unless . . .

He found a com booth and keyed up a directory for another quarter-cred. The "A" section composed almost half
its entries, and most of those were under the "Arbiter"
heading. One hour and several creds later he found an
address—halfway across the town, by his map—of a place
called "Interview Check-in and Reception." Why had he
been so well treated before his arrival, and so callously
thrust into the mires of this diffuse bureaucracy now? He
was still suspicious of everyone, and everything. He did
not know that the luxury of his voyage was usual, an artifact of an entirely different concern of the Arbiter's, and
that the clumsy diffusion of services stemmed from even
more devious concepts, but ones that only indirectly concerned him.

Erne had no public transportation system, and he could
find no listings of private cab companies. Angrily, he set
off again on foot. All of the other pedestrians he passed
were old-humans, and he realized there was no motor
traffic at all except for small freight vehicles that scurried
from one commercial doorway to another.

CLOSED, he read on a small plastic sign. PLEASE CALL
DURING BUSINESS HOURS. No business hours were listed.
Angrily, Barc marched back to his room, resisting the urge
to collar passersby and demand to know what was wrong

with this stupid place, with its people, with the mean-spirited and obviously incompetent Arbiter himself. He decided he would instead confront the concierge with his manifold complaints.

CLOSED, said the plastic tent-sign on the concierge's desk. PLEASE CALL DURING . . .

Barc awakened early. What was that terrible shrieking ruckus on the floor below and outside his window? He peered out and down. He felt momentary vertigo, thinking himself much higher than he really was, until he realized that the crowd below, funneling into a side door of his rooming house, was comprised entirely of small, short children, old-human children in white shirts or blouses and dark blue trousers. The building he was lodged in was, the concierge confirmed shortly, mostly given over to a school.

"Ah, yes. Here it is," stated the old-human clerk at Interview Check-in and Reception. "Doresh, Barc, decad seven, day five, hour five point four, a ten-minute interview."

"Ten minutes? That's all? I take months out of my life, while Margal waits, in great danger, for ten miserable minutes?"

"Sar Doresh, Sar Doresh," the clerk murmured placatingly, frightened by his vehemence, "the usual interview is *five* minutes. It is only an *initial* interview. If the Arbiter accepts your case, there may be another, at greater depth. You will be heard."

"I hope so," Barc said more quietly. "Now, what is this 'decad seven' business?"

"The date, in local months, of your interview. This is decad six, day eight, so . . ."

"A *month*? I have to wait a month?" The clerk cringed, but did not even try to speak until Barc's lengthy tirade wound itself down to mere petulance.

"Do you have enough money? I am authorized to advance up to . . ."

"I have money," Barc said, not quite shouting. "What I don't have is time!"

"A common complaint," replied the clerk, reassured that Barc's threatening noises were not about to degenerate into physical abuse. "Why, even the Arbiter himself has been heard to bemoan the shortness of days and decads. You are lucky, actually. Many wait for years. Why, I sometimes suspect that half the population of Erne consists of outworlders waiting to speak with . . ."

"Never mind that! Tell me *where* I will have my ten minutes. I would hate to get lost on the way there, and miss it entirely."

The clerk took Barc's map and marked a location on it. " 'Interview Transportation Depot One-twenty-three,' " he quoted from a list. "Be there two hours before your appointment. Transportation to the city palace will be provided."

A month was a long time for an impatient bors with a problem on his mind. Barc could only sleep so much, and the schoolchildren awakened him early. Erne provided few diversions and, as for some unexamined reason Barc felt no ferment of sexual demand and thus no need to seek satisfaction, his boredom was exacerbated even further. He spent many long mornings dozing in sunlight on a park bench, far enough from the school that he could not hear the hideous screams of old-human children at recess time. . . .

"Hi," a small voice said.

Barc lifted his eyelids. "Hello," he replied noncommittally. The wizened old-human child's eyes were on a level with Barc's waist-pouch belt buckle. "Shouldn't you be in school?"

"I am in school," the child explained. "I must meet with someone not like myself."

"That should not be difficult," Barc stated, amused by the young one's precise speech.

"But it is, really. There are presently no ikuts in Erne, and no wends in this neighborhood, and I may not walk beyond the reach of the recess whistle."

"Indeed," Barc replied, "but you have found me, and I am not like you."

"Exactly," said the child. A boy? A girl? All old-human children looked alike to Barc. For that matter, all children of all varieties did. "You," Barc heard, "are a bors."

He chuckled. "So I am. And what do you know of bors?"

"I have met only you. Your fur is black, and looks soft. May I touch it? Tactile impressions are learning, too."

Barc did not know what to say. The child, taking silence for assent, reached out and stroked his forearm, then put his cheek against it. "It is very soft," he said out of the unobstructed side of his mouth. Barc's other hand reached out as if involuntarily, and tousled the child's head fur, then jerked back suddenly. "What's wrong?" the child asked.

"Your fur feels funny," Barc answered, to cover his consternation. Truly the long, stringy stuff had felt funny, but that was not really what bothered him. Had he been introspective and a student of human behaviors, he might have understood what troubled him. Bors males ordinarily exhibit little interest in younglings, even their own. The only relationship a young bors usually experiences with an adult male is the distant mentorship of his mother's brother, yet this child's touch, and his own, had elicited odd feelings, emotions that Barc could only compare with sexual desire. Compare he could, but not equate. The rush of tenderness he felt was like being with Girelf, after sex, but he did not feel fatigue, arousal, or satiety, only a kind of one-sided affection.

"It's not fur," the child giggled. "It's *hair*."

"Fur, hair—what's the difference?"

"Fur," the small one explained, "is a complex organ

composed of hairs of different thicknesses, lengths, cross
sections, and properties that combine to provide different
levels and kinds of protection. There are guard hairs, in-
sulating underfur . . ." Barc stared. Was this really a child,
or an old, odd midget? "Hair is all of a kind," his instruc-
tor continued, "at least head hair is." He had not ceased
stroking Barc's arm or resting his cheek on it.

"Didn't I just hear a whistle?" Barc was uncomfortable.
Actually, he had heard nothing at all. "I think you have to
go."

"I did not hear it," said the gnome.

"Then that is another difference between us," Barc
stated. "Bors hearing is acute."

"It may be so," the child agreed, lifting his head from
Barc's arm. "My name is Bobby, if you want to ask for me
at the school."

"Ah . . . thank you. I am Barc Doresh." Now, why, Barc
wondered as the small one half-strolled, half-toddled
away, would I want to do that?

CHAPTER 19

DISPATCH

TO: Samol Jebbis, Consul, Beldant
           (Xarafeille 1427)
FROM: Arbiter (crypt 7xc)
ATTACHED: File, Margal Steep summary (Consul
           Marcos, Stepwater)
REPLY: Hold the tension levels below .041 by
           any means *except threat of force,* Sam.
           Successful resolution of the bors/mantee
           conflict on Stepwater (probability better
           than 50–50 in Marcos's estimate) may
           provide what you need. Repeat: avoid
           any mention at all of force, sanctions, fleet,
           or poletzai.

For several days Barc's question about the strange child
went unanswered. He explored nearby neighborhoods on
foot. The soles of his feet thickened, and at night he
awakened with cramps in his legs. In his daily wanderings
he did see a few people who were not old-humans. The
first one was another bors. Barc stayed an impulse to rush
up to him, which would have been threatening, and
merely nodded. The other, too quickly, said, "Hello."

A conversation ensued during which Barc was informed
that Ath Funderlud was from Falterrillon, Xarafeille 23, an
old world once given over to strip and open pit mines, but
now depleted. He had been on Newhome for a year, and
awaited a five-minute interview with the Arbiter, which
was now only five decads away. Suddenly, Barc's one-decad

wait did not seem so long. Perhaps, he thought, the odd prioritization stemmed from the low potential for violence of the other's situation: the mining corporations had departed, leaving barren, poisoned devastation behind, and had forfeited an inadequate performance bond rather than regrading, cleaning, and replanting an entire planet. There was complaint but no conflict, while on Stepwater genuine war loomed.

When the two bors parted, Barc thought it odd that strangers from far worlds should have talked at all, let alone like old friends, when their sole commonality was that both were bors, but another day something much the same happened when he spotted an elderly fard. That made him wonder even more. Was it merely that he in particular was accustomed to a variety of peoples, especially furred ones, or was there some undisclosed difference in the very air of this strange city full of old humans?

"I'm looking for the one named Bobby," Barc stated awkwardly, feeling odd and out of place in that office, with its row of substandard-size chairs along the wall and decorated with colorful childish scrawls on rumpled paper. He could not explain why he was there, except that he had nothing better to do—and he *wanted* to see the odd, gnomish child again, though he could not explain why.

"Of course," said the woman—the "principal," according to the sign on the door. Principal what? Barc wondered. "Sar Doresh, is it? Bobby has been waiting for you to come in. Do you have specific plans?"

"Huh? I mean . . . plans for what?"

"I take it that means 'no'? That's perfectly fine. Many of the children's companions prefer just such spontaneity." She thrust a thin packet across her desk. "That should cover Bobby's meals and incidental expenses for the next few weeks. Of course, if you need more, or if after your interview with the Arbiter you wish to stay on and continue your companionship, don't hesitate to ask for more."

"But I . . . I mean, I'm not sure . . ."

"Speak up, Sar Doresh. Is it housing that concerns you? The concierge will gladly arrange for an extra bed. Now, as Bobby has been kept waiting for days, perhaps you will step this way, and . . ."

That was how Barc became a full-time baby-sitter —a "companion" as the "principal" called it. After a while, he began to enjoy himself.

Bobby was male, he knew now. Through him, Barc met other old-human children, and before long he was surprised that he had not always been able to tell them apart. Behavioral differences between boys and girls were greater than between, say, Barc and Blet, or Barc and Dird. None of the old humans growled much, and the females hardly ever fought, even with each other, but they shrieked louder and more horribly.

Mostly, Barc and Bobby explored. Barc learned as much as Bobby did—far more than he had on his solitary jaunts. The boy's initial approach to him in the park had not, he discovered, been unusual at all. That was how young old-humans learned, in Erne. Now, with Bobby at his side, Barc had effective carte blanche to walk up to a workman in the street or a woman speaking to her computer and to ask what the other was doing—and to get not just a curt "working," but a real explanation of the task, its relationship with other tasks and projects, and sometimes even a brief history of the field or the skill itself. Even plumbers were prepared to deliver expositions on pipes and valves, and how they related to the systems that made up not only Erne, but all Newhome and, by extension, their significance to the greater policy of the Xarafeille Stream itself. And amazingly, they did not seem to worry about the time they spent at it, or what their superiors might say.

After the plumbing lesson in particular, Barc could no longer turn a faucet handle without envisioning the tenuous relationship between the water that gushed from it and the water that flowed so swiftly and silently through the water gap at Margal, and through the sluices of the Great Weir.

The Erne schools, he realized, had found a way to harness curiosity without stifling it. It was not only considered desirable for a child to demand an explanation of a stranger's activity, but once the explanation had been demanded, it would have been insulting for the child to have lost interest before the explanation was done. Children learned quickly to gauge the scope of their questions, to ask for no more than they felt they could absorb.

It was an amazing education for Barc, all compressed into weeks and days, and Bobby himself was not the least part of it. Barc learned that children were more than just small, obnoxious creatures too often underfoot. When he awakened one chill night to discover that the small furless being had abandoned his own bed and had snuggled between Barc's arm and body, he became aware of a fierce protectiveness. He realized that his emotions were not simple, and that he possessed far too few words to articulate them properly.

"Ikuts have many words for ice," Bobby told him when he attempted to explain his confusion. "*Krat* is float ice with air bubbles in it, and *frag* is brittle, crystalline ice that forms in springtime. Both are dangerous to walk on, so ikuts need such precision, but no one else cares."

"And now I need words to separate what I feel for you from what I feel for Girelf."

"For Girelf, and also for those other females, the ones you paid. Yes. One old-human language had five words, but perhaps they are not the right ones, either. *Eros* was body-love, which I do not understand, being very young. Another was *filios*, I think, for brotherly love, and *agape* seems to have been a greater love, like the Arbiter's love for all his peoples and worlds."

"Bors don't have brothers, really," Barc mused. "We have sisters—acch! I don't need a word for Blet—and we have second-sibs, from other litters, sometimes, but who cares about them? Not me."

"I suppose not. But is 'imprinting' good enough for what you feel about Girelf?"

It was not, Barc agreed. But he was not especially imaginative, and when he tried to invent words to distinguish between what he felt sharing a bed with Bobby, Girelf, Sally Marcos, and even Tathabel, he could not do so. All sounded silly and trivial.

"I will ask someone wise, and I will tell you," Bobby promised, "but today is decad seven, day five, and I don't know if I will have time before . . ."

How the time had flown! Barc experienced a pang of regret—yet another emotion with no proper word to frame it. He would return to his room over the school one more time, at least, to collect his luggage, to return the unspent balance of Bobby's expense money, and to say goodbye.

"Last call!" someone shouted. "Anyone not going to the Arbiter's palace, get off the bus."

"Good fortune," Bobby said as he climbed down from the long, open vehicle, his words almost drowned in the rising whine of multiple clutch-wheels grabbing inertia from the heavy flywheel that drove the bus, converting it into forward movement. Barc waved, but the bus turned the corner before he could see where Bobby stood.

Barc, a cosmopolitan denizen of Karbol, had not anticipated that his internal font of childlike awe had not long since evaporated. His approach to the towering arched gateway took him past black onyx colonnades inlaid with silvery metal like filigree in patterns so complex the eye only unwillingly let go of them. The gates themselves parted for his conveyance, shimmering webwork panels, electrum and bright uranium-glazed porcelain that flickered like a sun's own fires.

Amazement remained even after, for within the gates was a vast expanse: walls that diminished with distance and disappeared, a vast plain as broad as Margal's central valley, as flat as a tabletop, all carpeted in golden grass that waved, rippled, and undulated like a great sea. Far

away, small with distance, rose a fantasy structure in
white and silver, an edifice that seemed, as the bus
neared it, to be all arches, domes, spans, towers, and pin-
nacles made of water halted in motion, of silvery mist and
shadows that shifted with every revolution of the vehicle's
wheels.

When the bus stopped, Barc saw that the palace was
not moonbeams and raindrops, but white marble, glass,
and polished metal, but still, his initial impression did not
fade at all, even as he and the others were led inside. He
stood in an antechamber that seemed only less vast than
the plain outside. Again, tricks of line and light, wall, window, and subtly curved columns refused to allow his eyes
to alight in a single spot except when he peered into the
dark doorways that ringed the chamber.

As his eyes adjusted to the dimness within one of
them, he saw at some distance a high dais, and what
seemed to be a judge's bench, behind which sat a cowled
and robed figure that gestured slowly, imperatively, with
black-gloved hands. The Arbiter! Barc thought. Soon, he
would stand before that personage himself and—if he was
able to swallow his awe—he would state his, Margal's,
case.

"Fald Mettenbek," said a soft, neutral voice that seemed
to issue from the air within his ear itself. "Door twelve."
A short, rotund wend jostled forward, his head following
his eyes, back and forth, until he found the numbered
portal he sought. One by one names were called, and
numbered doors, and Barc's fellow passengers left him.
But the air remained at rest then, and there was no sound
but its passage through his nostrils. No one, no odd voice,
called his name.

When he felt a touch on his arm, he jumped. "Oh, I'm
sorry I startled you," said the person who had touched
him. Barc stared. An old-human, a male, not masked or
robed but dressed much as Sally had been, when he had
first met her. An official. Barc saw blue eyes that did not
seem cold, and a hairless face that seemed neither ugly

like a lizard's nor exotic, like Sally's. He saw hands much like his own, but adorned with only sparse, gold-colored hairs, not black fur. "Please, come with me," the old-human said. "Your story interested me so much I decided to forgo the preliminaries."

Barc, confused, wondering why he had been singled out, followed into what he was sure was a private apartment—though he could not imagine what it was doing there amid the business and busyness of the hub of the Xarafeille Stream. "What are we doing here?" he asked. "Can't I see the Arbiter?" He was suddenly afraid all his waiting had been in vain.

The old-human smiled (for such the expression was intended to be, as Sally and Bobby had taught him—though if a bors had faced him with it, he would have prepared to fight). "Of course," said his host. "You are speaking with him."

Barc stared. Impossible. This . . . this youngster? It was a trick, a cruel joke. "But out there . . . those rooms . . . the robed ones . . ."

"Those are my interviewers—and my 'public face'," said the young man. "They handle what I consider 'ordinary' cases, but as I said, with yours, I decided to participate more directly."

"I . . . ah . . . really?" stumbled Barc Doresh.

John Minder, Arbiter, seemed suddenly dubious. Was this incompetent bumbler capable of picking his nose with his finger, let alone handling the task he would be given? Minder sighed unobtrusively. Wait and see, he told himself.

The Arbiter was surely younger than Barc Doresh. A month ago Barc would have been unable to tell, or even to distinguish him from Bobby except for his greater size, but now he was able to discern subtle differences among old-humans. The Arbiter was young, but not innocent, youthful but, Barc suspected, quite wise. Barc had no inclination to condescend to him—but then, he had not condescended to Bobby, either.

The Arbiter did not sit behind a desk. He offered Barc a seat on a comfortable couch, and then sat across from him on another. Just as he sat down, from somewhere beyond the finely appointed but unpretentious room Barc heard a high, infantile wail. The Arbiter stood. "My daughter Sarabet," he explained, grinning broadly. "I am alone with her today, and I think she is announcing her dissatisfaction with the state of her diapers. Please excuse me for a few minutes."

Barc was amazed and dismayed. The Arbiter was interrupting his ten minutes just as it began! He had no idea how long it took to do whatever one did with diapers, but even his scant observation of infants and parents indicated that everything one did with them took more time than he, Barc, had. Infants shaped their parents' time, their attitudes, their perceptions of everything. Were the bowels of this one to decide the fate of Margal Steep?

"Don't worry, Sar Doresh," the young old-human said kindly. "I allow for this in my daily schedule. Your appointment will not be shortened by my child's needs. I apologize for the delay." He departed. Amazed, Barc leaned back and pondered this latest surprise. Was nothing in the universe the way his preconceptions supposed it to be? Of all the thousands of words he knew, were there so few to express his ever-changing mental states?

"Now to your business, Sar Doresh," the Arbiter said upon his return. "I have read your brief—and my own sources have elaborated on it. It is going to be difficult to resolve without the deed—and without it, there is no proof that it is yours, you see?"

Barc understood all too well. Without the deed, he could not prove that Girelf did not have the right to take it, but unless he could prove it was stolen, he could not demand its return in order to prove it was stolen!

"There is another copy of the deed, though," said the Arbiter. Barc's ears perked up. "It is in the wends' archive in Garloom." A mental picture of that forbidding truncated pyramid arose in Barc's mind. "But I cannot demand it of the wends. And there is one other datablock I need, also."

"Can they be bought, or . . . or stolen?"

"Unfortunately, planetary records are not for sale. As for stealing, I could not countenance that. But if copies were to be made . . ."

Further images arose before Barc's eyes. First was the Grand Portal of the archivist's house, followed in quick succession by faces: Firithanet's face, then that of the driver of cab number seven. "I can do that," he said impulsively.

"You can?" The arbiter's sharp, surprised expression startled Barc. For a moment he almost thought he saw an eagerness beyond his desire to help resolve the conflict between Margal Steep and the Hammad River mantees. Barc dismissed his impression as improbable.

"I think so," Barc replied, thinking quickly and deeply. "I'll have to go home, to find out." The Arbiter did not question him further. It was as if Barc's conviction alone had convinced him.

The interview was at an end. Less than an hour after he had entered the palace, Barc was again on the bus. In two hours, he was in his room, packing. Bobby was not there. "He has gone home for a week," said the principal, when Barc enquired shortly later. He was quite disappointed, but also relieved. It would have been painful to have had to say goodbye to his small friend.

In four hours Barc was once again trudging across the worn paving of the spaceport, his luggage case squeaking behind him, and in five he was back in his suite aboard ship, amazed to find everything much as he had left it. A few scratches and stains confirmed that it was the same suite, not a duplicate, but the ship's elevator had been different, as had the corridors leading to his quarters. He began to understand how that could be so later, during the voyage, when he examined the suite for the lines where it could be separated and disassembled, and then warehoused for later reinstallation in another, almost identical, ship. There was little else to do during the first days of the three-week trip, even though the holoshows in his console had been replaced with new ones, but within a week he discovered that his long-forgotten bodily drives had not dissipated forever. The old-human "stewardess" was not the same one as before, but she was just as willing. She was not as experienced as the last one either— but by the time the ship set down on Stepwater, Barc had remedied that deficiency. He had not been bored, after all.

"That was *him*? Really? How strange I had forgotten his name, even when you began telling his story."

"It's not that strange, Rob. After all, you were only five at the time, and you have had several companions since then, even another bors. And it was only for a month."

"Still, this is the first time you've told a story that I've ended up being *in*."

"I'm in it too, aren't I, Daddy?"

"You weren't even born then, Parissa," Robby growled. "Even Sarabet was still a baby in diapers. Didn't you listen at all?"

"I don't care. I want to be in a story too!"

"You can be a slither, in the beginning," her brother suggested.

"Okay. What's a slidder?"

"One of those yucky things in the cave under Margal Steep," Robby said, laughing. "You know, the slippery, slimy things mahkrats eat? Yaah! I'm a mahkrat!"

Parissa dodged behind her father. "Make him stop, Daddy!"

It had been easier, John Minder thought, when they were in diapers.

PART THREE

THE RULE OF LAW

Karbol, Garloom, and Margal Steep,
on Stepwater, Mirrim IV,
Xarafeille 578

(HAPTER 20

200	Mod 4C-2820 Datablocks, Blue, Blank	Cr 340	Cr 68,000
300	Mod 3R-2831 Datablocks, Green, Blank	Cr 420	Cr 126,000
11	Install Mod 4C-2820 w/software per quot.	Cr 10,000	Cr 110,000
3	Install Mod 3R-2831 w/software per quot.	**Cr** 10,000	Cr 30,000
	TOTAL		Cr 334000

The first thing Barc did when he stepped out of the spaceport cab was to find a phone and call Niddy Marboon, with very specific instructions. "But that's not Margal's kind of project at all, Barc," the trader protested. "And with half the factories closed . . ."

"Just get it done, Niddy. I'm meeting with a potential buyer tonight. I want to tell him it's under way."

Marboon agreed, but with ill grace. "I don't know when you started taking an interest in trade again," he grumbled. He didn't even have a chance to bring Barc up to date on Margal—not that it would have mattered: the basic problem remained, and would continue, unless Barc had found a solution. He had not said what had transpired with the Arbiter. *Ah, well,* Niddy thought, *I've be-come quite good at stalling the council.* He could surely do it one more time. The floods hadn't really gotten under way yet. Nobody had moved out in the past month. Margal still clung to the faint hope that Barc's journey would have some positive result—but he'd better come through with something, and soon.

Barc called for cab number seven, which was at the other side of town, and could not pick him up in less than an hour. "I'll wait," he told the dispatcher, who sounded like a fard. "Have him come into the restaurant."

Barc bought the driver a very expensive meal, and over equally expensive drinks they discussed what he wanted. "As you can see," Barc began, "I am prepared to be grate-ful to those who help me, and you said you could negoti-ate with the wend archivist. . . ."

Then Barc, having arranged for a room, departed, to wait.

The phone call came the next morning. "I am inter-ested in your product," said an unidentified voice. "I might be able to use five hundred of them. How soon can you deliver?"

"My managers tell me production can begin in a week," Barc told him. "Delivery of the first lot might take three weeks."

"Can I have samples, for testing?"

"I'm sorry. The prototype cannot be shipped now. It will be needed a while longer. But if you are not satisfied with the product, you need only pay for the initial run of twenty. Is that satisfactory?" The voice—which might have belonged to an elderly wend—agreed that it was. "Then if you will be so kind as to have the other instrumentation delivered here, to my hotel, I will return home at once to see to the rest of our bargain."

That afternoon a courier arrived in an unmarked limou-sine, and Barc took possession of a long, thin package wrapped in thick plastic padding. He then went immediately to the railhead, in cab number seven, and after giving the driver a tip equivalent to three days' earnings, bought a ticket for Rheekwirs. There, after ascertaining that no one had followed him, he would buy another, for Karbol. He carried the long, slim parcel with him on the train, and did not let it out of his sight.

In Rheekwirs, observing that no passengers in his car remained on the train, he stayed on board and paid the fare to Karbol directly. He made no attempt to recover the long, slim bundle of wastebin-pickings that he had mailed there. The real package was in his battered case. His concentration on "security" was probably excessive, but the stakes were high for both parties. The man who had supplied the "instrumentation" had reputation and high standing to uphold, while Barc had Margal Steep to save. At any rate, his subterfuges made him feel as if he was *doing* something.

In Firithanet's room over the bar he proffered her a long, thin, finely made wooden box with shiny inox-brass hinges and a combination-lock touchpad. "See for yourself," he told the stunned wend. She held the box with care that verged on reverence, as if its contents were more delicate than fine glass or as if the box were filled with a liquid that might spill with the slightest sloshing. She laid it on her lap, and keyed a sequence on the pad. The lid lifted with the slightest of sighs. With a sigh no louder, Firithanet fainted.

Tathabel rushed to her aid, but when she too saw what was in the box, she let her sister lie, and stared very long at its contents, without touching anything. "It looks like it's real," she said, "and only Firith knew the proper combination. But is it real, Barc Doresh?" Her eyes were wary.

"Could I have duplicated it? It is a wendish flute identical to the one she lost," Barc answered. "It is in a box identical to hers, that responds to her combination. That is her sigil on box and flute. If she plays it correctly, the Grand Portal will open for her. Does that make it 'real'?"

Tathabel stood abruptly, her sister's fainting forgotten. "I must go, or I will snatch that flute and neither you nor Firithanet will ever see me, or it, again."

Barc grabbed her hand. "Don't go far—later, I must speak with you." Tathabel shrugged. There was no likelihood that Barc had found her flute also. It had been lost years earlier. She suspected he wished to discuss who would take Firithanet's regular customers when she went home.

Home—where she, Tathabel, could never go. Her bright vision of carved corridors and echoing flute-tones were all the more cruel for the midmorning silence in that small, plain room over the tawdry bar. Emitting a pathetic squeak, she rushed away. Barc heard a door slam down the hall.

"Ah, you are recovering, I see," he said to a wide-eyed, astounded Firithanet. She did not ask if the flute was real, or hers. Perhaps the lack of scratches and wear, marks made during years of use, told her it was a duplicate. Perhaps she wished to assume that Barc, finding her flute, had taken it somewhere to be polished and restored, removing such signs of use. Perhaps a vision of the Grand Portal of her father's palace, of the broad double doors swinging wide for her, had obliterated all other concerns.

"Have you saved enough money for passage home?" he asked.

"With this," she said, picking the flute from the box, her demeanor suddenly confident, "I can get whatever I wish."

"Then shall we celebrate, one last time?" Barc edged closer to her, and held up a small pink vial.

She drew away from him. "No. Never again." She held up her flute, her expression disdainful. "I am Firithanet of Arafellin Enclave, Heir-Archivist of all Stepwater. Perhaps you mistake me for someone else—the whore Tathabel, perhaps."

Barc was hurt and amazed by the sudden change in Firithanet. Nonetheless, he concealed his feelings. He shrugged eloquently. "Not even for gratitude?"

"You will be paid, I have no doubt," she replied haughtily. "I am sure my father will give your backwater firm a contract for electronic gimmickry, at twice the usual markup."

Barc sighed. "I'm sure he will. But if you are not the whore Firithanet, whose room this is, perhaps you should leave at once. A suite at the Karbol Palatsa is reserved in the name of Firithanet, Heir-Archivist. You may wish to prepare yourself for your grand return."

The look she gave him then hinted at gratitude, but she did not step out of her role. "It will take days to rid myself of the stink of foreignness," she said, standing, clutching the now-closed wooden box very close.

When Firithanet was gone, Barc tapped on a door down the hall through which he could hear quiet weeping. "Tathabel? May I come in?"

The squeal of a wendish flute could be heard over the music in the bar below, but Barc did not care if the customers were disturbed. "Did I get it right that time?" he inquired.

"It was close," Tathabel replied, "but I don't think any doors will open to it." She sighed. "Face it, Barc. You aren't a wend. You don't have the ear for it."

"Well, play it again for me anyway."

"Okay, but it's hopeless. You'll never get into the archives." She trilled the complex sequence of tones, overtones, and undertones. "See? The K-Flat in the seventh measure must combine with the drone to produce the harmonic beat. If that is not exactly one hundred and forty-four cycles per minute—per wendish minute—it won't work."

"Yeah, well, I have to try. That was the one to open the Land Grant Hall, right? Let's try the 'files' sequence one more time."

"If you can't get in the hall, you can't open the cabinets, so why bother?"

"Look, do you want Firithanet to inherit everything? After the way she left you without even a word?"

"I don't think it matters. You can't play. If I show you everything I know, it won't change that."

"I suppose you're right," he admitted, "but if I try, you won't give me away—right?"

"I won't. And you can bet Daddy won't let Firithanet say a word." Barc had told Tathabel more of his plans than he had Firith. She knew there was a deal with Daddy. She also knew that Barc had received two flutes, not just one, in his long, thin parcel. The second one, the one Barc had just played, looked remarkably like her own. "I suppose we're both tired. We can practice later. But don't give up. I have a few clever bors tricks I haven't told you about."

Barc glanced at the strapped-down crates. "Looks like you've got it all secured, Niddy."

"As ordered. The green boxes are datacubes, and the red ones are tools and software. The blue ones are spares. I don't know why you need those. Every cube passed the tests."

"I just like to be sure," Barc replied. "We didn't have any spare wires on the mantees' dam."

"I see what you mean. Well, that's that. I'll see you to your seat."

"I can manage. Why don't you go check on our friend Tathabel, and deliver those final instructions I gave you. It's important she arrive in Garloom, at Twenty-three Perimeter Way, exactly on time."

"Sure, Barc. Have a good trip."

The railbed of the Karbol-Garloom express, and the scenery that bordered it, were all too familiar to Barc now. He was bored. At least there were no noisy children in the car, this trip. Barc's thoughts turned to a particular child, one not especially noisy, whom he would not have minded having with him right then. I wonder what Bobby's doing, right now? He missed the kid. If I mated with Girelf, our kids would be . . . But no, he did not want to think about that. Let gnawed bones have their bugs.

To get his mind off impossible hopes, he began whistling, terrible off-key notes that had no melody at all. The man in the next seat, a wend, stared curiously. "If I did not know it was impossible," he said, "I would swear that is a wendish flute theme."

"Sorry," Barc said, smiling sheepishly, stupidly. "My mother used to sing me that. Maybe she heard it somewhere, but she couldn't carry a tune in a jar." He chuckled. "Neither can I." The wend lost interest. Barc closed his eyes, and no longer whistled.

"Sar Bethelep, good morning," Barc greeted the driver of the flatbed transporter.

"And to you, Sar Barc. Everything's loaded." He gestured with his thumb at the red and green boxes, and the single blue one, behind him. "No need to call a cab. You can ride here with me."

"Like old times, huh? Sure." He climbed up next to the driver. "This is a bit bigger than number seven, isn't it?"

"Yeah, but no worry. I'm licensed for it." The transporter began to move. "We go in the back way," Bethelep informed Barc. "The Archivist's people will check everything by hand—contraband, you know—and I'm only cleared for the loading dock. You'll have to get them to move it all, from there."

"I suspect there will be enough of them with me every moment, for that."

Bethelep laughed. "You can bet on it. The only times they let foreigners in is when the equipment needs work. Just be careful, okay? I'm looking forward to spending the rest of my 'finder's fee.' "

"I'll be careful," Barc assented. But, he said silently, that may not be enough. "Wish me luck."

* * *

The wendish laborers assigned to move the crates to the archives, where Barc was to work, were ordinary enough. The supervisor, who would be with him his whole time in there, was not.

"Firith!"

She drew herself up haughtily. "*Heir* Firithanet, please," she hissed. "You could still lose this . . . this lucrative contract, if you offend."

So that's how it's going to be, Barc mused. She was still annoyed that he would make money on this deal, that he had not arranged her restoration solely from higher motives. As long as she thinks that's all there is to it . . .

"Sorry, Heir Firithanet. I meant no offense. Now, have you inspected everything? If so, show me where I am to work, and I will be out of your fur as quickly as possible." There. I suggest that I am a nit in her pelt, and will soon be gone. Surely, she wants that. She must have figured out that the flute is a fake. Does she know her father's part in everything?

She sent the laborers on with the crates. "We will take a shorter route," she informed him, "one too narrow for your clumsy boxes."

"No one told me what size to make them," he said. "Maybe if I had been talking with you . . ." He was sure she had not expected him to install the datablocks himself, and her personal attendance telegraphed her fears. She was obviously terrified of what he might accidently (or maliciously) reveal to the palace staff. Perhaps others in this warren were suspicious of her sudden return; that might take years to die down. Still, he thought, she could have been nicer about it all. After all, hadn't he done her enough favors, when she was down and out?

"This way," she said, and started off. As Barc followed, his eyes darted around at ornate wendish decor. Every column along the passageway resembled a different kind of tree. Branches arched overhead to become groins in a vaulted, sky-blue ceiling. Dark spaces between massive bark-textured trunks were doorways. Doors themselves were carved with murky forest scenes—and they had no handles or locks on them; instead, everywhere, as faint trills or echoes, wendish flutes sounded like dissonant birdsong.

Firithanet's flute whistled often, as they passed through hitherto closed portals. Sometimes she fumbled a note, and a door refused to budge until she corrected her playing. Was she merely out of practice, or did her errors stem from her fear of exposure? Barc understood why she had not wished to proceed at the head of a caravan of laborers, who would surely have noted her clumsiness.

He examined each portal and turn. A bors long used to twisting cavern passageways, it was easy for him to remember the way they went, but if he had been required to find his way with only a map, never having actually traveled the passageways, he suspected he would have become lost. At last they emerged in daylight on the bridge over the perimeter street. The slanting wall of the archival building and a dark doorway were only an obel away.

"What are you waiting for?" Firithanet snapped. "Come on."

"I was just wondering what that crowd is doing, down the street."

"Never mind that. Probably some child has gotten itself locked out of the Grand Portal. That often draws crowds—they come to laugh. It does not concern you. Come." She strode onward, and did not see Barc's carefully masked smile.

"What are those?" Firithanet demanded to know.

"Spare datablocks—in case any of the others are bad."

"Doesn't your little kingdom have any quality control? You would never get any work here, but for Father's gratitude."

"Oh really? Then *someone* here is grateful to me? I am touched. Who would have suspected?" Firithanet's ears flattened in almost bors-like manner, but she did not reply. "And now," Barc said, looking around thoughtfully, "two datablocks go in the Hall of Stepwater, and five in the Land Grant Hall, two in Census, and . . ."

"That can't be right! The Hall of Stepwater is closed. Those records are all centuries old, and older. They are never incremented, so why would Father want storage for new data there?"

"See for yourself. Here." He proffered a crumpled specification sheet. "Item seven, see?" She glanced at the paper, then shook her head.

"That is an error."

"Then go check it out. I'll finish unpacking my tools."

"I can't leave you here alone."

"Oh? Are you starting to like me again? You want me to stay longer? Good. I brought this, just in case . . ." He lifted a pink cylinder from his toolbox.

She made a guttural sound. "You're disgusting. Put that away!" She glanced around, to assure herself that no one had come in and seen Barc's gesture.

"Of course." He obeyed, then said, "What are you afraid of?" He strode toward the huge metal door to the Hall of Stepwater and began whistling, a terrible off-key imitation of a wend flute. "Do you think I can whistle these doors open all by myself? If so, perhaps I should be named Heir-Archivist. I'd be no less a fraud than you."

"I hate you! Give me that paper. Wait right here, and touch nothing." The spec sheet in her hand fluttered madly with the fast, jerky pace of her departure.

Immediately, Barc pulled a tool belt from the red case. The instruments in its pouches had been carefully selected. He opened the box of spare crystals—some green, model 3R-2831, most blue, model 4C-2820. He chose a blue one, and scurried to the Hall of Stepwater's door. Pulling a glossy black logic tester from his belt, he carefully entered a sequence on its keypad, and then glanced around himself fearfully. From the tester issued the tones, undertones, and overtones of a perfectly played wendish flute. At just the right moment, when a P-sharp emerged clear and high, interweaving with the high-register drone, Barc heard the precise 212-cycle-per-minute interference beat required to open the door. He heard also the distinctive clack of a solenoid-operated bolt. The door, all the tons of it, hardly creaked on its massive internal hinges as it swung inward.

Barc scanned the rows of closed, unlabeled cabinets and shook his head. Tathabel had not known where the block was, only the hall it should be in. He let his eyes go out of focus, and took in the whole room, lit only by daylight from a sky window high above. Special, he thought. It's a special block, and it will be in a special place. Then he saw, along one wall, a row of cabinets made of wood, not metal. It was fine, ancient wood, that to wends was like gold was to bors. He keyed the sequence "file open" as he dashed the length of the Hall of Stepwater, omitting only the final key.

"Original planetary charter," he mumbled. "The Arbiter said that the crystal he wanted for himself should be kept right by the original planetary charter. Let's try the first cabinet." He pushed the final key. Flute tones warbled. The cabinet opened. So did all the others in the row. Each shelf was labeled, and had a listed key—letters and numbers. Barc ruffled the fur on his wrist, and read the sequence written there in gray letters on his dark olive skin. Blet had showed him that trick once, in a moment of what he had mistaken for generosity. When the teacher caught him looking at it during the test, and during his subsequent punishment, he discovered her true motivation. Nonetheless, he thanked her silently now. Sisters were good for something, after all.

The crystal he wanted was in the second cabinet. He lifted it from its crumbling plush niche, and replaced it with the blank one. The doors remained open. Damn. Tathabel didn't give me a "close" code. Desperate, he punched "repeat" on the false logic tester's keypad. Again the opening tones sounded. He cringed at the noise, but the cabinet doors all swung shut as one.

He scrambled for the main doors, slipping twice on the slick, unworn marble floor, and with shaking fingers keyed the door's code. It too swung obediently shut.

Leaning on his box of tools, he panted, out of breath. He was still breathing hard when Firithanet returned. "I was right," she announced triumphantly, scornfully. "You have no business in the Hall of Stepwater. That should read 'Hall of Medical Statistics' . . . and why are you breathing so hard?"

"I had nothing to do, when you left, except to think about you," Barc said, grinning, and he reached again for the vial of Estrokick. "Are you sure you won't consider . . ."

"Filth! Pervert! Once more, and I will have you thrown off the bridge into the street, no matter what Father says."

"Ah! And just what *does* Father say?"

"Never mind. Finish your work."

"Finish? I haven't started yet," he lied. "Now where is the Land Grant Hall?"

She referred to the list still in her hand. "That's number four. Census is number one."

"Your snoopers repacked the cases after they went through them," he replied, peering into the open case. "The Census datablocks seem to be on the bottom now."

"Well then . . ." she began to say; then her face lit up with anger. "There are only two kinds of datablock, and all are blank! We will go to the Census Hall first."

"Suit yourself. If I just put the crystal in anywhere, without regard for my list of specifications—which you imply is unnecessary—I will finish in no time at all. We will have time on our hands, won't we? Is there a nice soft couch in the Census Hall?"

She repressed a reply with difficulty. Barc saw that not only were her ears laid flat, but the tips of them where the fur was thin were not pink, but white. She could not, he suspected, get any angrier without bursting. Good. He did not want her thinking clearly, not when her next unpleasant surprise arrived.

Barc reflected that he had been lucky. He had not

planned for her departure and his quick entry into the Hall of Stepwater. That had been a bonus. He had thought he would have to go through the tedious process of installing all fourteen datablocks first, before his planned diversion occurred. "Well then," he said, "why don't I put all the others—the ones that aren't getting installed—in your storage room?"

"Very well. I'll call for porters to move the crate."

"Oh, don't bother." Barc spoke quickly. "It slides well enough, and won't scratch the floor. See? This will be much faster than waiting for . . ."

"Yes. By all means, do so." She did not, in spite of her eagerness to have him finished and gone, offer to help him push the crate.

The extra datablocks were all safely ensconced in padded niches, and the storeroom door swung shut behind them. With Firithanet watching him so closely he had worked fast and nervously. "This next one is for the Land Grant Hall," Barc stated, hefting the crystal.

"They're all the same! Just blue ones and green ones! That one is blue. It can be installed in any location that calls for a Model Four-C crystal."

"Suit yourself," Barc replied with studied nonchalance. He wanted to scout out that particular hall. "But if you're wrong," he said, "and if I have to come back to reinstall it . . ."

"Install it where you will! Come! We are running behind."

How would she know? he asked wordlessly. He was not, according to his own schedule, running behind. To the contrary, he was running too much ahead. He had already stalled as much as he could, and his planned distraction had not occurred. Had something gone wrong? He could not remain in the archives forever, and he had only gotten one of the two datablocks he needed.

* * *

"There," he said, trying to keep desperation from showing in his voice. "I am finished here. Where is the Medical Statistics Hall?" Just then they both heard the patter
of padded feet on hard marble. A harried, nervous young
female—a clerk, Barc guessed—approached them timorously. She whispered something to Firithanet, whose
ears, only lately returned to relaxed state, again flattened
against her head. "It's a lie!" she spat. "That can't be true!"
She glanced at Barc. "Tathabel? Here? What have you
done?"

"Me? Tathabel?? Oh, you mean that flute I found
in . . ."

"Say nothing! I must . . . I must welcome my sister.
Girl—stay with him. Watch him carefully. I shall return
shortly." She departed. Her step, Barc thought, seemed
heavier and less lively than when she had been merely angry. Poor thing, he thought. Her whole world is about to
fall apart, she believes. Then, casting off any trace of sym-
pathy: So join the club. I know what that feels like.

"I must go to the Land Grand Hall next," Barc told the
young wend once he was sure Firithanet was too far away
to hear. "That is next on my list." The wend did not know
that he had already been there. Once inside again, Barc
pulled a crate of datablocks down an aisle between ranked
cabinets. He had spotted the proper cabinet before, but
had not dared do more with Firithanet about. "What are
you doing?" the clerk asked nervously.

"I must climb up here," he said, putting a knee on the
blue crate, "and I will then remove that dust-web. If it
were to drift into the delicate electronics . . ."

"I do not see it," she said, peering. That was when Barc
brought the datacrystal in his hand down upon her head,
hard. She collapsed to the floor. Not knowing how long he
would have, Barc worked fast. He keyed the tester, and
the cabinet opened. "M," he muttered. "These are the Ms.
Why aren't they marked?" One of the crystals was the one
he sought, the deed to Margal Steep, but which one? The
cabinets were in alphabetical order, he reasoned, so the

blocks will be also. Margal would be on the first shelf, or the second.

There were six shelves, and each one held six blue crystals. That, he thought, is not enough. There were surely more than thirty-six land grants starting with M. There should be thousands. Then he realized that just as the Margal deed Girelf had stolen probably occupied only a fraction of that crystal's memory, so these datablocks surely contained many records on each one. He did not dare take the time to be sure. He wished there were labels.

For the first time since he planned this, he remembered the Arbiter's requirement that he copy the deed and the other crystal, not steal them. "Bah!" he muttered. "Does he want them or not?" Barc wanted them. Oh, he felt a guilty pang or two; he was more the criminal than was Girelf, who at least had the dubious fifty-obel rule to justify her theft. Too, her act only affected Margal's ten thousand. His, if the Margal deed shared a crystal with even a hundred others, might impact a hundred thousand, a million people.

The repercussions of his theft, he realized as he pondered the unlabeled crystals, would go even further: of the thirty-six crystals, all letter M, where would he find "Margal"? Near the beginning, of course. A was a common vowel, as was E, and the others were less so, Y least of all. How many "Ma" entries were there? How many before "Mar"? He could not be sure. He needed to take more than one crystal—but how many?

The clerk was waking up! He didn't dare hit her again. Wends looked fragile to him, a big bors. How could he know whether another blow would kill her? *Hurry!* Which crystal is it? Which one should I take? If only there were more time!

"Ach!" he growled. "I have ten spare crystals—no, nine now—and four of them are blue. If I replace the first four with blank ones . ... No, not the *first* four. 'Mar' will not be on the first one. Mab, Mac, Mad ... Mah, Mai ...

The second through the fifth. 'Margal, will be on one of those." Four crystals. How many thousands of deeds? How many lives might be impacted for want of some ancient proof? He would, he decided, have to find a way to return them—all of them; the Arbiter was right—but that would be later. Now, he had to take them.

He rapidly replaced the deed crystals with blanks, and settled the stolen ones in the blue crate. There! It was done, and just in time—the clerk moaned and stirred, and lifted her hand to her head. Quickly he dragged the crate back a few paces toward the door, then picked up the slight wend, and placed her beside it. He slapped her cheeks and pleaded with her to wake up. Finally, she opened her eyes. "Oh, I'm so sorry," he bleated. "Are you hurt?" He felt her skull. "Oh, what a terrible bump. Is there a medic nearby? What shall I do? I feel so stupid, dropping that crystal . . ."

"Never mind," said the wend, wincing as she touched her head. "How long was I . . ."

"Only a moment. It's not serious?"

"I . . . ouch! I don't think so. But hurry, will you? I want to go home and put ice on it."

"Of course," Barc agreed, and he did hurry. By the time Firithanet returned, he was packing his tools.

"How is Tathabel?" he asked her.

"She is . . . the Heir-Archivist is resting from her journey." Firithanet no longer looked angry, only hurt and beaten. Neither Tathabel nor Barc had known what reception the elder sister would receive. Now, considering the situation, he realized that their father had to reinstall her in her position of first heir—to do otherwise would have raised more questions than it might have deflected. And Firithanet had no choice but to support her sister's claim; if doubts cast on one sister caused their fraud to be revealed, both would fall together, and both knew just how unkind the world beyond the archive and palace walls could be. "She explained briefly why you are here,"

Firithanet added. "I was a fool to be so angry. I was so afraid. . . ."

"I understand . . . I think. You won't betray me?"

"How could I? For my own selfish reasons, your secret must remain safe."

"Those are the best reasons—the most honest, anyway." Enlightened self-interest, every trader knew, was the firmest basis for a good contract. In mating, commerce, or politics, security lay in understanding the needs of one's opposite, and in knowing that those needs, and one's own, were met. Such contracts were seldom broken.

Firithanet leaned over Barc's toolbox, and palmed something within it. "I may one day decide to travel again," she said, holding the pink Estrokick cylinder up between two fingers. "I may need this, then."

"Really? I mean, it wasn't . . ."

"It was not all that bad. Really. Sometimes I . . . I even enjoyed it." She would say no more. Barc did not wish her to say anything else.

"If I return the crystals after I have copied them, then can you . . . or Tathabel . . . see that they get back in their proper places?"

"Of course. Again, we have to, don't we?"

"I suppose so." Barc shut his toolbox, and Firithanet pushed the pink vial into her waist pouch.

"Push the crates aside. There," Firithanet commanded, recovering some of her diminished aplomb. "Sithamet, see that the porters remove them. Sar Barc—can you carry the blue case, the unused spares, yourself?"

"Easily," Barc assured her. "It weighs very little." Indeed, as he carried it through the maze of halls and passages, the stone and wooden forest that was 23 Perimeter Way, his burdens—all of them—seemed light indeed.

"Tonight," Barc announced as he laid a fat envelope on the transporter's seat, where Bethelep could see it, "you are going to buy *me* a very, very expensive dinner."

"Tonight, I suspect that I will be well able to afford that," said Bethelep, chuckling as he hefted the white parcel.

"Maldepan, Malefash, Malebendelink, Maloon . . . Oh, good there are no 'Mali' entries," said Barc as he raised his head from the screen.

"Why is that good?" Nidleg Marboon inquired.

"Because I'm already on block number four, and I am nowhere near the 'Mar' entries."

"So?"

"Well, I'm getting scared. How many 'Mam', 'Map,' and 'Maq' entries can there be? Niddy, maybe I *missed* it! Maybe 'Margal' is on block *six*."

Niddy reached into the cobbled-together datacube reader and removed block four, and replaced it with the unread crystal five. "Move over," he said, and pulled up another chair. Images, text, and survey maps flashed across the screen.

"What are you doing?" Barc asked.

"What you should have done," Niddy responded. "I'm going to start at the *end* of block five."

"I didn't think of that," Barc admitted.

"I know. Have you paid any attention to the girls since you got back? I think you're a bit fuzzy-headed."

"Uh . . . I haven't had time. I had to build this crystal-reader from scratch, you know, and then . . ."

"It never pays to ignore the needs of your littlest brains," Niddy said with great solemnity. "Everything the big one does has to be routed through them first. Ah, here we are! Marfat, Marfallon, Mareeb, Mareck, Marabat, Maquelind, Maprak . . ."

"I thought you were going to start at the *back* end of the list."

"I did," Niddy said, pushing his chair away from the terminal.

"But you didn't say 'Margal'!"

"You're right. I didn't." He shook his head slowly. "Do you think Tathabel will trade crystal number six for these?" He indicated the four useless datablocks, which ended with "Marfeth."

Barc sat down at his console. "Barc the bumbler," he muttered to himself. "Barc the clever fool." Everything he did worked, up to a point, and then he did something stupid and ruined it all! Every plan he made was a good one, and every one fell apart because of an oversight, or an unwarranted assumption, or . . .

He began to type. "Dear Tathabel and Firithanet," Barc wrote. "I have a very big favor to ask you both. . . ."

"Dear Barc," he read. "I'm so sorry. Because of all the questions surrounding our return to Arafellin Enclave, Father decided to send both of us on an extended 'vacation,' for a year or two, until things quiet down.

"I am writing from Sithalemin, on the Frastack Coast. It is a lovely resort island right on the equator, so it is warm all year. In fact, Tathabel is on the shore, sunning herself, right now.

"I'm sorry neither of us can help you right now, but when we get back . . ."

A year? For Barc—and for Margal—a quarter of that time would be too long to wait.

Barc Doresh had been unhappy before, and if his life followed its usual course, he would be so again. Still, somehow he doubted that any single episode of his now-customary unhappiness would ever surpass in depth, breadth, scope, or intensity what he felt right then. He had not been able to say anything positive to the council, to the people of Margal Steep. "I'm working on it" just didn't suffice anymore. Half a dozen big power-loaders had arrived that very morning to start moving another manufacturer's equipment—and, incidentally, to remove one full seventeenth of Margal's gross revenue. And he, Barc Doresh, supposedly in charge of things, wouldn't even be there to wave goodbye.

He marched up the steps to the Arbiter's consulate. At least he would see Sally again. He had put off a very necessary visit with one of the girls in anticipation of this reunion. Then, afterward, he promised himself, they could discuss his next trip to Newhome, to deliver the Arbiter's datablock copy, which even then rested safely in the consulate safe.

"Ah, Sar Barc," the secretary said. "You did not call for an appointment."

"I need to see the consul right away," Barc informed him.

"Well . . . Oh, well, I'll see what I can arrange. One moment." He departed. Barc waited. It was a very long moment, and Barc's thoughts did not range far from that quietly decorated office with its comfortable couches. It would not be as nice as it had been at Sally's residence, but then . . .

"The consul will see you now, Sar Barc. I believe you know the way. . . ."

"Yes! I mean, yes, I do, thank you." He kept his steps slow and resolute. The secretary, watching him race out of the room and down the passageway, merely smiled, and shrugged.

"Who are *you?*" Barc blurted. He was disoriented. The office was not there! This room was decorated in harsh umber and violet, raw reds and a particularly horrible vermilion. Heavy drapes concealed the wide windows, and where the cushiony couches of his memory had been were metal benches. Even the desk was different, of harsh painted metal. A uniformed old-human male faced him across it, with one eyebrow raised at Barc's dismay.

"I am Consul Rand," he said dryly, "and as this is my office, and you are my visitor, isn't it only polite for *you* to identify yourself to *me?*"

"But . . . Where is Consul Marcos?"

"She is on her way to Medlor, I suspect. At least, that is where she was posted."

Barc, his blood surging with hormones produced by abstinence and anticipation, was not, at that moment, brilliant. "But," he said, and then, "but . . ."

Even in Barc's shocked and befuddled state it did not take long for the new consul to clarify the devastating state of the changes that had occurred. Sally had been transferred, but not before she had forwarded to the Arbiter the datablock that Barc had left with her. "But without the deed to Margal Steep, he is as helpless as you are," said the consul. He shook his head apologetically. "There is one thing, though . . ."

"What?" Barc grasped at the proffered straw.

"Before she left, she received several letters from the Arbiter. One was left behind." He shuffled papers on his desk. "Ah, here. Perhaps you will understand what it means. This one arrived after she left, though she took the others with her. Perhaps she meant to write, to explain them to you."

Barc snatched the sheet. He skimmed past salutation and introductory sentences. ". . . And Barc Doresh may yet prevail even without the deed, if he can reconcile the contrasting elements that bind Margal Steep, the Hammad River, and the desert of Musal Bhjak, across the mountains that mediate between them."

"What is he talking about? Reconcile what? And to what?"

"I'm sorry. As I said, this is not the first letter. The others . . ."

"I know. The others are halfway across the Stream with Sally." Barc slumped. It was not enough. Contrasting elements? Mountains mediating? What sense did that make? Without the deed, he could do nothing.

Without further words or courtesies, he shuffled from the office. At the reception desk he asked for Sally's new

address, even though a letter would take months to get
there and a reply, even by the Arbiter's special couriers,
would take at least weeks to return, and any understanding she could contribute would arrive too late.

CHAPTER 21

The desert-dwelling fards of Stepwater are typical
of their race, though their culture is more primitive—or
more pristine—than elsewhere. Stepwater's fards
are colorful, in their bloodred desert robes, but their
mineral-dyed fabrics are not displayed in boutiques
or shops, because they only make strips of their special
weaves to order, and those who wish them must
dicker with the fards themselves.

Should a tourist wish to view these unique fards in
their purest state, the deserts north of Karbol provide
the perfect opportunity. Barge transportation is not
luxurious, but staterooms are available, and even
deck passengers will find the inconvenience worthwhile
for the magnificent scenery. The great mantee dam
on the Hammad River provides impressive holocam
shots, and the quaint principality of Margal Steep
offers clean, comfortable accommodations on the very
verge of the fards' desert habitat. In Margal, the traveler
can contract with guides and outfitters, who
guarantee a safe and rewarding introduction to the
tribe of Musal Bhjak.

Parkoon's Guide to the Worlds of the Xarafeille Stream,
Volume 177, Parkoon and Parkoon,
Newhome, 12125 R.L.

"Quaint? Comfortable accommodations? Guides and outfitters?" Barc snorted. "Whose idea was this, Niddy?" He
waved the facsimile page of the *Parkoon's Guide.* "And
how much will that thirty-seven-word plug cost us?"

"It was Parkoon's idea, Barc," Nidleg Marboon answered calmly, "and as we are their prime supplier of 'hospitality' on Stepwater, it won't cost us a cred. In fact, they're offering to help pay to set us up."

"Tourists? Here? Niddy, this place is falling apart. Look at that ceiling. The liability insurance alone . . ."

"Not *here,* Barc. Notice that the guidebook doesn't even mention Margal *Town.* All we'll need is a new wharf for the barges, just downstream of the water gap, a hotel somewhere, and an overland road. . . ."

"The only place flat enough for a road is out on the salt pans, and that's right across fard land."

"I'm dealing with them, Barc. I can handle old Wridth Hasselteek."

"Yeah? What's he going to want from us?"

Niddy hesitated. "Well, he wants water, mostly."

"Water? Water? And are you going to pay the mantees for a pipeline easement to the river?" When pressed, Niddy admitted that he was indeed "dealing" with the mantees.

Barc exploded. "Haven't you learned *anything,* Niddy? We depended on them to maintain the river level, and what did they do? Now you want to convert Margal to a tourist trap that depends on mantee barge pilots for access, on a pipeline across mantee land, and on mantee water? Why don't we make it easy on ourselves, and just *give* Margal to the mantees? No! Absolutely not. Tell Parkoon thanks—but no thanks."

"I really think you should look at these plans, Barc. I've spent a lot of time on them." Barc shook his head. Niddy waved his roll of printouts. He continued to press Barc, who finally, with ill grace, gave in.

"Oh, all right," he sighed. "Let's see what you've got."

Hours later, Barc pushed the prints aside. "The barges I can put up with," he said. "If the mantee bitch raises pilotage fees, we can use the land route. We own the right of way, so we could even lay rails all the way from Karbol—or threaten to. But that pipeline . . . That's our jugular vein. We can't afford to be *that* dependent on mantees, but . . ." His eyes took on a calculating gleam. "Are those printouts of the caves still handy? You know— the ones we used when we were trying to get to the crystal room? And how about that topographic map of the whole principality? And isn't there a copy of *The Geomorphology of Northern Stepwater* around here somewhere?"

Marboon found them. "Here, Barc. What are you thinking?"

"Look. We need to get water from here"—his finger stabbed the river, on the map—"to here, right?" He indicated the salt flats just northwest of Margal Steep, out on the fard-owned plain. "Why can't we just leak a bit of the water that's flooding our 'basement'? We can run a pipeline along the railroad tunnel's roof, then out across the valley, and . . ."

Wridth Hasselteek, the fard headman, was not impressed with Barc's bargaining. "If they are our own wells already, why should we pay you for the water in them?" he asked—or rather, he asked something like that, but in the spitting, chattering variant of fardish homespeech that his primitive people spoke.

"There is no water in the wells now, is there?" Barc was becoming exasperated. "You can't even *use* the northwest desert, because it's too far to carry water, right?"

"*Flak whirith spat. Blettik frewel nish?* So what? If the water comes back, it's *our* water."

"What if it comes back—and then I turn it off again?"

The chief drew breath angrily. *"You?* Turn off our water? We will kill you. Only a bors would talk of stealing water."

Barc sighed. "Okay, what if I just never turn it on in the first place?"

It was a long day. It had started early, and the morning was spent educating Wridth Hasselteek in the elementals of hydraulics. If Barc could pump water from Margal's caves instead of the river, and then build a pipeline across the central valley, he could fill the old, dry reservoirs of Musal Bhjak. Finally, the headman accepted that though the water inside the wells would belong to him, the pipeline, the means of delivering the water, was Margal's. For one day, that was enough.

By sunset, Barc was only halfway home across the central valley, which was enclosed on all sides by Margal's mountains. His rough-country groundcar trailed a long plume of alkaline dust, even though he was, of necessity, going slowly. The "road" was no more than the tracks his car had left that morning. Though the ancient glacial lake bed was flat, there were sinkholes, and in some places the surface was only a thin crust over hidden solution caverns in the weak limestone below.

Such caverns had been formed by water, he reflected. Water had once percolated between strata and through cracks, and had made caves. Mineral-laden water dripping from cave roofs formed stalactites. Water. Always water— and none had flowed beneath the valley in thousands of years, not since glaciers had crept down from Margal's mountainous heights. Wet caverns were "alive" in a sense, growing new stalactites and other formations, constantly changing. Dry ones, on the other hand, were static, and only crumbled slowly. Thus the sinkholes under the central valley were dangerously unstable, and had to be avoided by surface travelers, lest they fall through. Barc did not dare travel in a straight line.

Barc pulled a map from the back of his car. By waning light he traced the mountains on it, and compared them with the horizon. There under Mendeb Peak's shadow lay Margal Town. Even its deepest caves were hundreds of feet higher than the valley floor. Once water was pumped up over the threshold, and down through a pipe to the valley, the siphon effect would keep it flowing—he thought.

Looking out the opposite window of the car, he glimpsed the toothy arête that was the valley's western wall, and the low pass where the two-track road wound among the rocks and out into the fards' desert. Would he need another pipeline over the pass? More pumps? He would have to check out all the possibilities.

At least he had gotten his terms across to the old headman: he not only wanted a right of way for his road across the salt pans, but he needed the fards' agreement that they would trade with the tourists, not kill them—as Wridth Hasselteek's folk were too often inclined to do. In turn, the fards would have water.

Now, though, there was much work to be done. Barc rolled up the chart and started the engine again. He was too eager to get started to camp out for the night. He was pretty sure he could keep on his track with only the headlights.

CHAPTER 22

The early geological history of the northwest plateau province is dominated by two processes: the formation of limestone by oceanic deposition, and the overrunning of those deposits by vast lava flows, resulting in interlayering of soluble and insoluble rock.

Later epochs saw steady uplift and stream erosion that continued for almost fifty million years, without a great deal of crustal fracturing or faulting. The border between the plateau ranges and the salt pans and deserts is a series of low-energy drop faults.

The rough mountains of today result from glacial erosion mostly channeled by preexisting streambeds in the lavas and solution features in the limestones.

At the periphery of long-lived mountain glaciers, meltwater created different topographies as it flowed over exposed volcanic strata or limy deposits. Where limestones outcrop and surface water is plentiful, karst terrain is typical; the land is potted with sinkholes, which are the collapsed remains of solution caverns in the underlying rock. Vast systems of caverns below determine the terrain above; there are no surface streams, no valleys or gorges, only sinkholes that make the topography resemble that of an airless moon.

The caverns underlying the principality of Margal Steep are part of the same complex as those of that outcrop in the Margal central valley and at

several places in the fardish deserts to the north
and west, but the strata are often isolated by
discontinuities at the fault faces.
> *Geomorphology of Northern Stepwater,*
> Flad Bustep, University of Garloom,
> 12025 R.L.

Again, Margal Town echoed with the sounds of machinery, though its flooded factories were silent beneath many
feet of water. The year was up, and the mantees had
closed their new, high sluice gates. Day by day the water
level inside the caves rose inches or so at a time. Had it
been springtime, the Hammad River would have been fat
with meltwater from the still-glaciated mountains hundreds of miles north, but, happily, it was only midwinter,
and there was still time. . . .

Time? Time before the town's highest caverns began to
crumble, to slump into the watery ones below? "No, don't
stop," Barc commanded. "Put on another shift." The engineer nodded. Privately, he thought Margal's ruler had
gone mad. Probably all that perverted sex, he thought privately. Why, Blet Doresh—who was supposed to rule with
her brother—had locked herself in those crumbling rooms
of hers and would not come out at all. Shame. The engineer, in her circumstances, would not have come out either, though he doubted he would have slept under his
bed, for fear of falling rock, as Blet was rumored to do.

He thought Barc's plan mad: with Margal falling apart,
shouldn't all their effort be directed toward shoring and
reinforcing? If the town was going to collapse, what was
the madman's point in building a huge new cavern? And
for what? A railway tunnel! But they were building *another* railway across the fard's desert too. What use was
there for *two* railroads? What use for even one? Ah, well,
he consoled himself, at least I'm working. A job is a job.

Barc, of course, was quite content. He had not spoken
with his teat-stealing sister since he had returned from
Garloom, and little else would have pleased him more

than to have that continue—except, of course, for the progress on the work at hand.

The thoughts of Margal's factory workers, designers, and engineers generally reflected the supervising engineer's. They had work, Margal had work, and how long could either have lasted without it? No one was unemployed now, though Barc knew that the present situation could not last; most of the money came from the shrinking Margal treasury, and when that was gone only the funds that trickled in from Parkoon and Parkoon, and from the profitable Karbol enterprises, would be left. If the new excavations could be finished before Mirrim's springtime light lingered overlong on the snow-covered mountains to the north, then everyone would remain employed—the factories would be rebuilt, and the toolmakers and precision workers would no longer have to haul rocks and worry about crushed fingers.

The new tunnel began a mile north of the farthest extent of Margal's caves at the edge of the central valley, and it drove through the base of Mendeb Peak toward the town. It was a huge hole three-quarters of an obel in diameter, large enough for five railway trains to travel side by side. The rail-laying equipment, mostly adapted from machinery on hand in the town, was presently occupied southwest of Margal where the Hammad River, the mountains, and the fard's salt pans abutted each other. Already, crushed rock ballast had been laid running several miles north, and ties and welded rails followed the roadbed a dozen obels behind.

"Two routes? Two? And the one wider than the entire railhead at Karbol?" Blet, for all her isolation, was no less confrontational or irascible than before, and she unfortunately had the ear of several Margal councillors. Barc had to conciliate her.

"Look, sis—Parkoon is paying half the bills, and I'm paying the rest. Margal needs the work."

"*You're* paying? With Margal money!"

Barc sighed. Dealing with Blet was never easy. She had a lawyer's mind for details and a mahkrat's conscience.

"Margal's investment was paid back," Barc insisted. "You signed off on Niddy's and my Karbol enterprises."

Blet grudgingly acknowledged that. "Still, it's too big a tunnel, and it doesn't go anywhere."

"I explained it. The rail tunnel will lead to the tourist hotels, which will all be in the central valley. Visitors can experience the desert there in perfect safety because it's Margal territory, not fard desert, and the fards who come there to trade must remain polite at all times, and kill no one. The travelers, who after their introduction to the fards wish to visit them in their camps and buy their goods, will need rail tickets. We can charge them for the trip back through town and north by rail to the fard encampment. Just wait! We'll make good money. The tourists will have to stop in Margal, and they'll buy things. . . ."

"If there is any Margal left!" Blet snarled. "This morning my bedclothes were covered with crumbled rock."

"We'll stabilize the lower caves. I've sent for offworld engineers, experts . . ."

"If they get here in time! If I'm not crushed and buried beneath my own ceiling."

"Aw, sis!" Barc replied noncommittally, savoring the very thought of it.

The desert railroad was complete. Only the old-fashioned fuel-burning steam locomotive was yet unfinished. Ten passenger cars waited at the Hammad terminus, complete with window grilles to protect against fardish projectiles. These were unnecessary, but they would give the impression of risk and adventure, and Barc had not revealed the extent of his deal with the fard headman to anyone—others would merely have protested that there was no way he could keep his end of it, because the fard wells had been dry almost forever, and he had not even started construction of a pipeline.

The rail tunnel was ninety-five-percent complete. It ran from the central valley almost to Margal Town. Already, the rail-laying equipment had been moved into the town in anticipation of the last half-obel of rock being removed. That was to be done this morning. Most of the tunnel had been cut with huge mining moles, but Barc insisted that the last fifty feet would be better removed with explosives placed on the tunnel side, away from the town. To that effect, Barc held in his hand a small black box with three controls: a white rocker switch labeled OFF and ON, a red crystal button whose internal glow indicated it was active, and a blue one that did not shine. One push would arm the blue button, and a second would fire an array of buried charges. The red button only needed a single push to initiate the first series of blasts.

Pleas that the blast's vibration would surely damage Margal Town fell on deaf ears. Barc was adamant. "Are we ready?" he asked over his hand phone. Confirming messages came in from the tunnel workers who had evacuated the entire passage and had returned to town. "Then on five, I will . . ."

A disheveled, hard-breathing Prak ran up, waving a roll of construction prints. "Wait! Wait! We've made a terrible mistake. Don't push those buttons!"

Barc, holding the detonator, shook his head. "Everyone's out. There's no reason not to. . . ."

"But there is! Look!" Prak unrolled the sheet. "Here," he said, pointing, "and here." He was not speaking loudly now, and Barc's frown kept other curious bors away. "This figure is wrong, and that one. The slope of the tunnel is all wrong. The head of the bore is not just beyond that rock face there"—he pointed—"but down there, almost two obels *under* Margal Town. It will come out level with the lowest of the old tunnels, and will fill with water, and . . ."

"Nonsense!" Barc shook his head. "I checked every calculation myself. They are all correct. Now watch, and ob-

serve the first day in Margal Steep's new life." He pushed
the red button. Prak moaned, and slumped.

Deep within the rock, explosions shook Margal's walls.
Fine dust sifted down. In moments, the initial rumbles
ceased, but there was no return to silence. A muted roar
continued, like the sound of distant locomotives. The rock
face did not crack and collapse, but remained solid. The
continuous vibration caused fine dust to work loose and
fall everywhere. It could be felt underfoot. Somewhere far
below, water roiled and surged through the now-useless
new tunnel, where no rails would ever be laid.

Prak looked ill. His ears and whiskers drooped. "I was
right," he groaned. "It's just like the dam—we failed."

Barc wrapped an arm around his assistant's shoulders.
"Ah, well," he said softly. "I guess I've grown so used to
failures, this doesn't bother me much. Come, let's go see
what damage was done." The blue button, as before, remained dull and unlit.

CHAPTER 23

FROM: Barc Doresh, Margal Steep
TO: Fenethfeth and Tansal, Architects
          1318 Waterside Way, Garloom
MESSAGE: Gentleman, I am contemplating
construction of an extensive summer palace to
augment the existing official residence here at
Margal Steep. Attached is a bank draft which I trust
is sufficient retainer, and my rough conceptual sketches
for the buildings and grounds. Please be so
kind . . .

   Scrawled note: Feneth, this looks like a live one!
A million Newhome creds—and that's just the retainer?
Let's jump on this before the crazy bors changes
his mind! Tansy

"Poor Barc," Sarabet murmured. "Everything he does goes
wrong. Couldn't you have helped him, Daddy?"

John Minder sighed. "He did not have the deed. What
could I do?"

"Make him a new one!" Parissa suggested—or demanded; Rob could not tell the difference. "Just tell that
awful G'relf to go away."

"It was not that easy, dear," said the Arbiter. "Besides,
remember that all these things happened years before you
were born."

"Besides," Rob said in the scorn-dripping tones he
saved for his youngest sibling, "law is law. It must be the
same for everyone, or it won't work. Dad is *Arbiter* of
the law, he isn't a dictator."

"I don't care! I want Barc to be happy. Besides, you got the datablock you wanted, Daddy."

"Then perhaps I should continue Barc's story—and then you can decide whether I made the right decision. . . ."

Barc visited the mantee summerthrong once again. He had no great aspirations, but he felt obligated to try to resolve things amicably, one more time. Rumor and hearsay said that Girelf had not given in to her throngmother's importunements, and that the young Elleth sat at the old one's side, the recognized heir. What, Barc wondered, did that make of Girelf? What position did a rebellious ex-heir have in the mantee throng?

Perhaps, Barc hoped, if she was ostracized and unhappy, she would consider . . . But no, he chided himself, it was silly to think she might abandon her throng, her own kind, for someone like him. Girelf was no Karbol prostitute. Besides, how quickly had Tathabel and Firithanet abandoned him for the chance to return to their own kind?

The spring melt was well under way, and even now, to the north, icy water was trickling and rushing down from high slopes into the Hammad tributaries, and the smooth river would soon rise, and would carry roots, branches, and streamside debris with it. Were the mantees celebrating the territory they would gain when those springtime melts began to pile up against their enormous dam?

The summerthrong gathering was held far inland from the last site, of course; last year's gathering place was now underwater, and the mantees anticipated that their new location would soon be at the water's edge, so carefully had they calculated the volume of meltwater and the height of their dam. Their arrogance annoyed Barc. He did not tarry with the throngmother and her elfin heir, once he was told that Girelf's grotto was not yet flooded, and that she still resided there.

Entering the hole, Barc had to hold his breath longer

and swim underwater farther before he emerged inside. The shelving area where he had rested before, breathing entrapped air, had shrunk. Keeping his head above water, he could not reach the submerged floor anymore. His nose almost scraped the rough ceiling when he stuck it up to breathe.

Had Girelf known of his arriving? She met him, hand outstretched, as he surfaced, and even wet and chilled as he was, her touch had a tingling, electric quality that incited him to pull her close to him. Her dry fur and his dripping pelt slid against each other as if they were one, and no conceivable dose of artificial pheromones could have stimulated the pulsing ache in his groin, the constriction of his throat, the hot, red blurring of his vision, or the mewling tone of his growls as together they tumbled backward onto Girelf's mossy bed.

What happened next was, Barc decided later, the best ever. Afterward, deliciously sated, not just relieved, as they lay entwined in a way that made her slender limbs seem to defy the rigid nature of bones, joints, and tendons, Barc's self-conscious warmth defined the limits of his universe. Girelf. Momentary remembrances of others littered his consciousness, but those hardly distracted him. Those other liaisons now seemed like terrible, struggling dreams—even his memory of Sally Marcos's big, milkless breasts seemed to belong to someone else entirely. Even though he could not see Girelf's nipples, he was sure he could feel just where their tiny twin pressures indented the fur over his ribs.

Girelf made tiny cooing noises in her sleep, long after their second coupling had exhausted both of them. "Perfection," Barc decided, was an imperfect noise. "Close" described the relationship between the sun Mirrim and its planet Stepwater, an astronomical distance that bore no relationship to what he felt when he had merged with Girelf—or to what he felt still.

He could not sleep. He instead reflected on his strivings and his obsession, his bors rigidity of behavior that seemed modifiable only when he went to ridiculous, chemical extremes. He had bitterly resented both the need for chemical stimulation and the underlying craving that turned his brain into wet mush. He had hated knowing that purely through an accident, his natural bors compulsion had been directed not toward a bors female, but instead toward a mantee, a specific mantee—Girelf. Now at this moment, warm and contented, driven by no force but an admittedly irrational affection for that sometimes disagreeable, often contrary female, he was pleased to be allowed the latitude to admit that there was more than just sex between them. Strangely, inexplicably, in spite of all that had gone between them . . . he *liked* Girelf.

Her noises intensified, then stopped as she became awake. He liked her. He felt warm and protective of her— and thus, he had already decided, he had to warn her of the nastiness he planned for her people, the disaster that would befall them if they did not reach an accommodation with him, and with Margal.

"Stop that!" he murmured, feigning annoyance, removing her tiny hand from his fur and enclosing it in his own large one. "I must tell you some things."

"Later?" she asked with a patently false whimper, knowing already that he would not be swayed.

"We must discuss our choices, our future," he insisted— and he explained to her what he planned, and what she could do about it. Boiled down to essentials, it was this: if she agreed to go back to the throng and to take her rightful place as throngmother, the mantees would, as promised, lower the water somewhat, and Margal would survive. He did not mention that his own misery would from then on be complete, or that he would be doomed to an endless succession of ever-less-satisfactory liaisons with furred females and little pink cylinders, of skinned females with swollen, unnatural breasts—liaisons punctuated with days or weeks of ever-diminishing mental capacity as his demanding glands overrode the rational impulses of his brain.

Did she even know about that? he wondered. Did she
care?

If Girelf refused to be throngmother, to mate with all
the males until her last egg was quickened, then to become huge and horrible, a gestating machine for a seemingly endless new generation of mantee pups . . . then he,
Barc Doresh, would be forced to do something incredibly
cruel, that would result in the displacement of all her
people from the entire Hammad River drainage. Terrible
suffering would ensue.

"How?" Her voice had a skeptical edge. "You had big
plans to destroy the dam, and you failed."

"If I have to, I'll show you how—you, and your fat
mother. I can do what I promise, and I will, if I must.
Take my word for it, for now. It would be best for
everyone"—Everyone except me and you, he added
silently—"if you go back to the throng, and . . ."

"And let myself become ugly, and so huge I can't even
swim without help? Ha! Would *you* do that?"

I'm doing something just that repugnant to me, Barc
thought. If you do what's right for your people, and I do
what's right for mine, we'll both be miserable the rest of
our lives. He did not say that aloud, either. He had to give
her one last chance, but deep inside he hoped she would
not take it. Of course, when he revealed the exact nature
of his threat to her, she would hate him for it—but would
she recover from that? Even exiled from her own folk,
with nowhere to go, would she choose to stay with *him*?
Still, there was a chance of it, and otherwise no chance at
all. "I don't know what I would do," he admitted. "We're
talking about *you*."

"No!" she said.

"No?"

"Didn't you hear me? No. No."

"No what? We're not talking about you?"

"No, I won't do it. I won't be the new throngmother.
Not now, not ever."

Barc sighed. "Then . . . will you mate with me?"

She looked at him as if he were indeed a strange creature, and not too smart. "Already? Didn't we just finish . . ."

"Not like that. I mean forever. What do the old humans call it? Mating for life?"

"Marriage? Is that what you mean? Are you crazy? Then I really would be exiled. I would really be a traitor, then. Refusing to be throngmother is bad enough, but someday, after Elleth takes over, maybe I can return. But not if I'm a traitor." She purposefully avoided mention that she herself had proposed just that, before she had thought out all the consequences.

"But you don't have anything else, no place to go . . ."

"I don't have anything better than to be your permanent whore?" Her eyes sparkled with anger. "I would sooner work in one of your disgusting Karbol bars and . . ." She turned away, and he could barely hear her next murmured words. "If you could find a way for me to keep my honor among my own folks, and for yours to respect me, too, maybe I might . . . think about it. It's not that I don't want to be with you, Barc Doresh." She sighed. "Now you must go. It's all in your hands, now."

Barc heard the firm decision in her voice. He did not even try to caress her as he stood up and walked the short distance to the water's edge. "I will be back. I *will* find a way."

What a terrible creature I am, thought Girelf. Poor Barc is such an innocent, and I am pitiless toward him. Yet when she thought of his best solution to the problems that beset both of them, she knew that he had not stretched his imagination far enough. She did not want a partial solution to her own dilemma. She wanted everything—and for that slim possibility, she would risk everything, too. The solution had to come from Barc, not from her. And it would, she assured herself, though not without doubts, if he would only consider things from her point of view, not just his own.

* * *

The steam barge's huge cylinders chuffed great watery gouts of exhausted steam, and the steel-webbed timber walking beam rocked regularly, ponderously, causing the vessel's three-story-high paddle wheels to thrash and churn the Hammad empondment's serene waters. Those waters, except where the barge disturbed them, were unusually placid for the time of year.

The mantee Simolf, who had come to investigate why the water gap upstream was not yet roiling with the seasonal meltwaters that should already have been gnawing at the foundations of Margal Town, was distracted from his mission by curiosity. What were the bors up to now?

The barge, he observed, was oddly configured—really two barges side by side, with some kind of oversized ballast box between them, filled with rough, broken rock, bors mine tailings. Spanning the ballast, which threatened to sink the low-freeboard hulls if the water roughened, was an engine, a great tangle of tubes, pipes, valves, and cylindrical boiler whose unidentifiable parts clattered shrilly and moved in ways mysterious to Simolf, even had he not been all but submerged in the water. The monstrous toothed scoop that had loaded the barges stood aloft, immobilized by cables. He swam closer.

With a great rumble, the ballast level in the house-sized box dropped. Within a moment, Simolf could see no rocks at all, and the hulls rode high in the water with suddenly increased buoyancy. Then, beneath the surface, which was yet hardly disturbed, a hard mass of moving water yanked his floating body first this way and then that. Simolf tried to see what had caused it, but when he dipped his head under, he saw only a thick cloud of mud mushrooming from the pond's bottom, directly under the barge. It swelled toward him like an immense fungus growing at incredible speed.

He fled. Even as he thrashed ashore, the water around him became extraordinarily muddy. What had the bors done? He reviewed what he had seen: the barge had held rocks, and then had none. The water had roiled as if a great mass had been dropped in it, and muddy bottom soil had spread first as a cloud and then, as with a cluster of pebbles dropped in, had spread in an expanding ring, clear in the middle, murky everywhere else. The barge, he concluded, had dumped a load of rocks. It should not have been so, he reflected. The bors did not have mantee permission. What if a seaweed farmer had been tending his crop directly underneath? What if a troop of immature mantees had been playing in the water-killed forest there? As yet, that seemed the worst possible speculation.

The barge was now steaming rapidly—as great puffs of smoke and sparks from its funnel indicated—toward the Margal shore. That shore was, after a winter landslide, a cliff perforated by openings, the entrails of Margal Town revealed to view. Since Simolf could not catch up with the barge to ask what they were doing, and why, he went instead in search of his throngmates.

When the newly laden barge returned to the open water, seven mantees observed it. Simolf, rested now and again ready for a strong swim, dove deep just ahead of the vessel, and observed it from below as it thrashed by overhead. As he had suspected, the bottom of the ballast box looked like two huge doors. He was no mechanic, but it took no expertise to speculate that the four enormous, shiny cylinders mounted to the doors were filled with high-pressure steam that held them shut and the ballast in place. The immediate purpose of the barge was thus to be filled with rocks, and then to dump them elsewhere. Was there more to it?

Simolf followed the vessel, which seemed to be following the reverse of its heading ashore. That made him suspicious. Was it going to the same place as before? That would imply purpose beyond the mere disposal of unwanted rocks. The barge halted, and Simolf saw a bors with a glittering hand transit climb up the ladder to the rudimentary pilothouse roof, from which he took bearings this way and that, and then called commands through a speaking tube. He remained atop the pilothouse while the vessel's wheels again pushed against the water first one way then the other, obviously adjusting the barge's position according to a previous sighting. The barge again stopped.

With great trepidation, Simolf ducked underwater. He could not see far because the last dumping's sediments made everything murky, but he soon enough found the huge flattened pile of rocks that had been dumped. It was confirmed—the bors not only wished to dump rocks, they wanted them to fall atop the previous load. But what use were rock piles under the pond? The bors could not fill it, not in a thousand years, a million. The barge was a black patch in the brown water overhead. As he studied it, the blackness seemed to expand.

Simolf swam faster than ever before! A great mass of rocks was coming down, right at him! He swam like a fish, expending all his store of energy in desperate flight, and felt turbulence as the sinking rocks passed mere inches behind his flailing feet. He was tossed upside down in the backwash. He heard the sharp clatter of new rocks striking others already there. The air was driven from his lungs, and he could not tell up from down. He swam, not knowing if he traveled toward the rocks or to safety, but at last, when he was afraid it was too late, he emerged in air and precious daylight.

Exhausted, bedraggled, filled with a weight of gulped water and with a foreboding he could not explain, Simolf pulled himself ashore where his companions awaited him. They huddled close to him until he recovered enough to speak; then Simolf recounted what he had seen, and what he inferred. The bors were not just dumping unwanted rocks. They were . . . building something. But what? And why? With the depth of water, it would take a thousand bargeloads to build the rock pile to the surface, and a thousand barges that many trips to build an island more than one hundred obels in extent, on which a solitary bors might stand on new land beyond the fifty-obel border

claimed by mantees. What insanity was that crazy Barc
Doresh performing now?

There was only one way to find out. Weary Simolf
sighed, and lurched to his feet. "If I survive this," he
vowed insincerely, "I will join a tribe of fards, and will
never again look at more water than can be held in the
palm of my desiccated hand." Nevertheless, he waded
back into the empondment. "I will *ask* the crazy bors what
he intends." The other mantees, less tired, followed to
support him if he collapsed and was unable to swim. The
barge, he saw, had already taken on another load of rock,
and was steaming out, on the same course as before.

"I am going to build a summerhouse here," boomed
crazy Barc Doresh. "I have hired the finest architectural
firm. I will have a delightful wooden fane with lattice and
corbels and a colonnade of paired cedar trees, all around
a fountained courtyard, with captive fish in a pond and
lamed corkers lounging about and singing for me." Simolf
shook his head. Crazy indeed. Had his dilemma driven
him so? "I will sit on my fine porch and observe songbirds
flitting in the smoke trees and zebelisks darting across my
greensward," continued the bors. "Perhaps I will ask your
lovely Girelf to join me there, from time to time."

At the mention of Girelf, Simolf frowned angrily. He
had looked forward to mating with her, to the pleasure of
it and the satisfaction of having his seed, which he was
sure were strong, coopt a fair share of her eggs, thus war-
ranting the continuation of his line. The thought of Girelf
remaining unquickened—and the thought of having to
wait until tiny Elleth matured before experiencing the joys
of sexual congress—turned frown to ferocious scowl.

"This is mantee water," he growled. "You have no right
to dump rocks here. And besides, it is far too deep to be
of use to you."

"I don't need a mountain," Barc replied. "I want only a
gentle rise to my retreat." Again, he rhapsodized about
greenery, gentle swales, lawns, and wildlife scampering

across a valley that currently rested everywhere at least a quarter-obel under the mantees' water. Surely the bors had snapped, and was delusional. Simolf verbally implied as much.

"Examine your great dam," Barc commanded him gleefully. "There you will find a clue to my motivations."

Simolf felt sudden fear gripping at his middle. Thinking of the explosives they had defused at the Great Weir, he said no more. The throngmother had to be warned. As he swam away in haste, Barc's voice followed him. "Too late! Tell your fat old mother to come to me in Margal Town, to discuss the terms of your survival."

Soon mantees swarmed over the Great Weir, but they found no new boreholes, no explosives, fuses, or wires. The vast structure stood firm, as before, proudly walling off the waters from the wendish forest in the valley below it. Simolf did not understand. A clue? What had the unbalanced bors meant?

It was the throngmother herself who first noticed it. "The moss!" she cried out. "Look at the moss on the dam face!" Simolf did so, but saw only seaweed turning dry and gray in the afternoon sunlight. "That is water-moss," his mother exclaimed, "and it is now dry."

Dry! Now Simolf knew. The moss should have been wet. It should have been below ever-deepening water, but it was not. The pond's level had not risen; worse, it was lower than it had been in the fall. He knew that if he were to examine the gentle, sloping shores upstream, he would find them brown with silt, where mantee water had once again become mantee land—and beyond the shore, that fifty obels of mantee land had once again become bors and wendish land.

Within a day the pond's recession was thoroughly documented. The water level was falling. Where was the spring melt? What had the bors done with their water? Quickly made calculations indicated several things. First, they indicated that at the rate the pond was dropping, an entire year's gain would be lost before the Pointing Hand, the summer constellation that showed where south lay, was entirely overhead at midnight. Second, they promised that even if the water stabilized, by fall the mantees would own scarcely more land or water than they had when their dam had been indeed only a pervious fish trap made of sticks and withes.

Third, the Hammad River downstream of the Great Weir would cease to exist. By the time that the trickle still flowing in its bed reached Karbol, even augmented by the few tepid tributaries that flowed in south of the weir, there might be enough water to wade in, but no more. Visions of disaster filled Simolf's head. The wends downstream would blame the mantees when their forests dried and died. The fine folk of Karbol would curse them when their shiny faucets belched air and muddy brown slime instead of clear, cool water.

Fourth—and not last, but in Simolf's jaundiced view, worst of all—the demented bors would be proven right! The rock pile his bargemen were building would not be a hump beneath the waves, nor a reef, nor even an island, but a low hill in a lower valley many obels from the shrunken remains of the Hammad River. Mantee spies had gone north as far as the Margal Bridge, and had verified that the flow through the water gap was no greater than in midsummer. The bridge was again high over the white rapids there. The mantees were barred from explorations farther north by the broad jumble of new rapids and cascades that formed where the river's reduced flow tumbled over the wreckage from the landslide, rocks and rubble intermixed with occasional pathetic reminders that those rocks had once been part of the bors' dwelling places: here, a broken doll sunning itself atop a boulder; there, a rock face with paint and stencils clinging to it, the remains of some family's dining-room wall; and elsewhere, a rectangular gout of water forced through some still-unbroken slab pierced by an erstwhile window or doorway.

It was as if the spring melt had never occurred. It was worse than that—as if some great hole had opened up in Stepwater's face, a gaping mouth that gulped the mantees' precious sustenance before it reached them. The throng-mother had sent to Karbol for a photoreconnaissance plane to overfly the river north of Margal, at great expense, but Simolf suspected that would only pinpoint the location of the disaster, and not its cause or reason. For that, they must go to Barc Doresh.

Simolf moaned. His enormous mother—to give her credit for her levelheaded acceptance of what was and what would be—had commanded him to prepare her litter for the long journey to the water gap and Margal Town. "And remember to bring the wheels," she reminded him. "I will enter the bors warren in style, not flopping up their ramps and streets on my poor belly." Simolf barked orders at his half-brothers. Soon, very soon, the sad, fearful, humiliated procession was under way.

The throngmother rested in a soft net of woven sea-weed. Even with half her bulk underwater, slung between poles buoyed by hundreds of inflated fish bladders, her weight pressed her ample flesh through the net, where it erupted as hexagon-shaped protuberances. Simolf, befitting his position as an older son, swam beside her head. Others pushed and pulled her floating conveyance. Still others, behind, towed the wood-wheeled cart that would support her hammock poles when they dragged her ashore. Only when she approached Barc Doresh in his own chamber would she allow her pride to force her to stand on her own inadequate feet and to approach him, to beg for her people's lives.

Though it really made no difference to the mantees' survival, two questions remained uppermost in her mind: How did he do it? Where did the water *go*?

CHAPTER 24

DISPATCH

TO: Arbiter (crypt. 7xc)

FROM: Samol Jebbis, Consul, Beldant (Xarafeille 1427)

MESSAGE: Things are hotting up! Latest rating is .040. John, you promised me some good propaganda, and I can't wait much longer for it. They aren't killing each other yet, but once that starts . . . Are your you-know-whats on full alert?

REPLY: Hold them! Help is on the way. Sam, you won't be disappointed. I'll send the footage as soon as it's available. And no poletzai. This *has* to be done without them.

Many months went by in the lands bordering the Hammad River. Those months brought slow, creeping changes, but no great or shaking events met the eye. The mantee pilgrimage had been turned back at the rapids when they emerged from the water. "All is not ready yet," they were told. "When all the principals have been contacted, you will be summoned to talk. For now, go back and enjoy your brief remaining tenancy of Margal land."

The bors continued to dump bargeloads of rubble in the same spot. As the level of the empoundment dropped and the pile of tailings grew, first a shoal appeared, then a small island. Bors workmen arrived with wagons and wheelbarrows and off-loaded cartloads of soft, dark soil, which they spread about.

Other bors hewed fractable rubble with edged steel hammers and expandable wedges, and began laying the rustic foundations of an extensive structure. Gardeners planted trees in pockets of deep soil and flowering shrubs and vines where the new soil was thinnest. Rafts of fine, smooth-grained deodar were floated across the lowering water, and blocks of dark, contrasting wood were hewn and carved into pedestals and column capitals by hired wends, whose eye for artistic detail was unsurpassed.

Even when construction of the new palace was well under way, the barges did not stop delivering new stone. It seemed the bors never stopped digging, somewhere inside Margal's mountains. If the sheer volume of detritus were considered, the mantee watchers might suspect that enough had been removed from the mountain to hollow out a whole new Margal Town.

Finally, in the fall, an imperative message arrived from Margal at the mantees' gathering place. It was just in time, for the summerthrong was about to dissolve and the mantees to scatter to their winter lairs. It was a sad ending for a dismal summer. The waters that had previously risen had killed all but the hardiest waterside willows they inundated, and when they receded they left vast acreages buried in fine silt. That silt created thick, greasy muck along the shores, and it dried into an obnoxious, irritating dust elsewhere. The mantees spent much of the summer in the water, and were otherwise muddy and dusty at once.

When they received Barc Doresh's summons, they gathered poles and mesh hammock, and the throngmother's floatable cart, and set off for the second time on their unwelcome journey.

The Margal police showed little respect for the mantee delegation, holding them back from the bridge while a caravan of laden carts rolled by. Each cart was like a min-

iature forest, filled with young trees whose roots were
balled and wrapped in hempen cloth. Bors youngsters ran
from river to caravan with buckets of water, which they
poured on the roots of particularly fragile species, keeping
them cool and moist.

Trees? Inside a mountain? It must, Simolf thought, be
Barc's idea, because it was so patently insane. Yet his
mother did not treat it so. "Find out where they take the
trees," she commanded him.

"Excuse me, Sar smoke-bush," Simolf imagined himself
saying. "Please tell me . . . where are you bound? May I
see your writ of passage?" He steeled himself to speak
with a fat bors pulling a cart, and asked much the same
question.

"We are planting them in the desert," the bors said.
"They will, I am told, shade the soil and provide shelter
for violets, begonias, and seek-the-darks."

"That is a crazy idea," Simolf blurted. "If trees and begonias wished to grow in dry sand and gypsum flats, they
would already be doing so."

"I am inclined to agree," said the bors, whose fur Simolf
noticed was dull, tatty, and dry, as if he did not eat
enough fat, "but I am employed now, hauling trees there,
and I will eat a meat sandwich with real butter on this
very night, and tomorrow I will break my fast on a heap
of rootmeal standing like an island in a sea of sweet
cream, so who cares? When these trees die in the heat of
the desert, I will fetch more, and will continue to buy myself princely meals."

Other caravaners said much the same things, with variations that depended upon their particular cargoes and the
nature of the dietary insufficiencies that had recently
plagued them. They brought trees, bushes, roots, corms,
rizomes, bulbs, seed heads, and even cages full of birds,
spilts, natterlies, and other small woodland creatures. Margal
trucks took their cargoes inside through the mountain or
along the river road, no longer submerged, to the new
railhead—which was yet another of Barc Doresh's insanities.

Simolf relayed what he had learned to the throng-mother, who was unsatisfied. "He is not *that* crazy," she stated. "I really want to know what he is doing." She would get her wish—but not as soon as she would have preferred, and she would not be happy with her knowledge.

"Where is the mantee Girelf?" demanded a portal guard when the mantees arrived at the town entrance in the wake of a train of wagons. "If she is not with you, then step aside—over there will do. You may wait in the shade of those rocks until she arrives."

"Girelf!" spat Simolf. "She is not here. She is not coming."

"Then perhaps you wish to send one member of your gang or herd ahead, to buy a tarpaulin from one of the suppliers on Outwater Way," the policeman suggested. "The rocks will shade you this evening, and the sun heat in them will warm you through part of the night—but you will need shade from dawn to midday tomorrow, and the day after, and . . ."

"Enough!" said Simolf. "Throngmother, I will fetch your wretched daughter. I will pull her by her stubby ears, if she resists."

The old fat one agreed that he should go after Girelf, but cautioned him against mistreating her. "I have a most uncomfortable suspicion that we may need her goodwill, no long time hence."

Barc Doresh savored his moment. All was arrayed before him just as he had imagined—and planned—it. The last of the plaster was dry now, and painted. His eyes caressed the suite's glossy malachite columns, the pink granite arches, and the subtle black-and-white flecked biotite floor tiles. He sat alone at a waxed gallwood table imported from the Bidbhek forest, in the tallest of eighteen similar chairs. Nidleg Marboon, his scruffy fur now curried and trimmed, stood behind Barc's chair. He wore a tan leather sambrowne belt with a leather loop, from which hung the Margal club, and he stood stiffly, as if he were a military guard—which, in fact, he considered himself to be. This was Barc's great moment. He, Niddy Marboon, would use the silly club if he had to, if things got out of hand.

Beyond was a loggia curtained with embroidered, translucent Musal Bhjak muslin that allowed enough cool, northern light through to flood the room with a soft glow. The conference table, and Barc, faced the opening, and stood to the left of the portal where the mantees gathered. Yes, all was perfectly arranged. There was the fat throngmother. There was Girelf, looking disheveled and angry. And there . . . Simolf, and two of the other mantee males who had tormented him. All looked tired. Had they slept poorly, huddled against the rocks outside Margal? Had the long, upward hike to this high chamber fatigued them? The steep, winding passages had not permitted them to use the throngmother's cart, so they had been forced to shoulder the poles of her hammock. He shrugged. If all went well and this conference ended amicably—or at least to his personal satisfaction—he would show them the elevator.

He gestured offhandedly at the chairs. The throngmother, true to her promise, was now standing. She waddled laboriously to the chair opposite Barc—a chair identical to the others, but wider, just as Barc's own was taller. Simolf and the others seated themselves, which still left the two end chairs and four others empty. Stiffly, hesitantly, Girelf seated herself at one of the latter.

Barc nodded to his left. A bors at the portal called to another in the hallway beyond, and shortly, three persons entered. The first was Barc's sister Blet, who blinked in the bright, diffuse light as if in unfamiliar surroundings—which she was. The last time she had emerged from her safe haven, there had been no malachite-columned chamber, only solid rock—rock that now rested in Hammad Pond and formed the foundation of Barc's other foible, his summerhouse island. She took the near end seat. Her fur was as dusty and dull as the mantees', as if fine dust clung to her also. Several patches of fur were missing, exposing pale olive-gray skin—some of which sported white medicated plasters—and others revealing lines of small, black stitches. Next came a foul and pungent odor, and swishing, rattling sounds, followed by three desert fards whose beads and bone pendants clattered, and whose scent of never-washed flesh and fur had preceded them. They eyed the unfamiliar furniture askance, never having seen either table or chairs. Realizing that if they pushed the chairs away and squatted as was their habit, their chins would rest on the table edge, they chose to imitate the others present—though not without lengthy and unseemly rustlings, wigglings, and discontented, uncomfortable grunts.

Following the fards came two bors: Sard, the Margal council head, and Prak, whose station in the community had risen in Barc's service. They seated themselves, nodding politely to the others present—except the fards, to whom a nod meant something other than greeting, and who would have departed with many insults had they thought a nod had been intended for one of them. As it was, they wondered why the bumbling bors and the sneaky mantees tolerated it.

Last came three wends, followed after a tolerable distance by two tarbeks. "Mfapkot," Barc said to one of the tarbeks. As Barc alone knew who the wends were, their entrance caused no more stir than had that of those now seated. Only the tarbeks caused unease, a fear that some trace of their fierce exhalations might escape their filter veils. Barc inclined his head ever so slightly to the old male wend, who was highly placed in Garloom. He did not acknowledge the two females with him—his daughters Tathabel and Firithanet.

When all were settled, one end chair remained unoccupied, but Barc ignored it as if its presence were an oversight, or as if its claimant was to arrive at a later time. Niddy clicked his heels—or he would have, if his feet had

been shod—and ceremoniously lifted the mace from its
loop. He handed it to Barc. Barc, in turn, hammered it on
the table—though there was no need to get anyone's attention. He set it conspicuously in front of himself, and then
spoke. "We have much to resolve," he said, "now that all
the principals are gathered . . ."

"Let us start with our water," interrupted the throngmother. "What have you done with it? We want it back."

Barc pointedly referred to a paper before him, peering
as if nearsighted. "Hmm. That is item four on the agenda," he murmured. "We must deal with each item in order, as all are intimately connected, and the resolution of
one stems from the resolution of the one before. You have
copies. Take a moment to familiarize yourselves with
them."

A rattling of papers ensued. The throngmother's eyes
widened perceptibly as they traveled down the page.

Item One: Modification of the rules of succession and inheritance of Margal Steep, with particular reference to
the governorship of the principality.

Item Two: The marriage of Governor Barc Doresh, according to the Newhome Convention of year 12099 of the
Rule of Law.

Item Three: Revision of the fifty-obel rule as applied
within the traditional and historic boundaries of Margal
Steep.

Item Four: Finalization of water rights and right of way
agreement between the fardish tribe of Musal Bhjak, the
bors of Margal Steep, and the mantees who inhabit por-
tions of the valley once occupied by the erstwhile
Hammad River.

The throngmother was flabbergasted, astounded, and at
sea. What did one thing have to do with another? What
did she, for instance, have to do with Margal succession
or the crazy bors's mating? What had she to do with fards
whose land was nowhere contiguous with mantee territory? Water rights? She considered the Great Weir, half

out of water now. What water would be left to bargain with, at year's end? The bors's arrogance ... "erstwhile Hammad River" ... was too obviously well founded. Equivalent confusion was evident on the other faces around the table, except among the fards, who could not read, and who did not seem to understand why they should be there at all. One, a small fellow whose spicy odor was larger than he himself was, licked his lips continually, as if he expected platters of whatever noxious stuff fards customarily relished to arrive momentarily.

"Item One," said Barc, capturing everyone's attention. "My sister Blet will address it."

Blet rose. She eyed Barc dully, blinking often as if plagued with dust. "I no longer wish to share rule in Margal with my brother," she muttered, hardly audible at the far end of the table. "I do not wish to live beneath hanging rocks that fall on me, or over the encroaching waters that cause them to fall." She sat down.

"Please forgive Blet's terseness," Barc said. "Last night, for the third time—and hopefully the last one—part of my sister's ceiling fell on her. You may all know that our beloved mother and uncle died under just such a rockfall." He sighed. "Blet is not herself, so, for the purposes of this meeting, we may take her silence for assent. She will remain awhile, and will speak up if she wishes to contradict what is said in her name." His eyes fixed on Blet, and did not leave her until she nodded weakly.

"Blet," Barc continued, "has accepted from Margal the grant of a nitweiler farm on the edge of Margal, on wendish land purchased from the wends there. She deems it a sufficient asset and settlement of her inheritance claims, and dowry enough for her to acquire a husband and a sire for her younglings yet to come." The smallest fard, who alone of the desert men understood Barc's words, translated for his companions in a quiet, chattering tone. The fards shrugged. What did that matter to them? "As you may also know," Barc said, "residency would be required for those younglings to inherit status in Margal Town, and

Blet's new residence is outside Margal territory. To insure a smooth succession, I propose—as I have little fear of falling rocks and intend to risk remaining here—that my children by the wife I will take be irrevocably declared heirs to the governorship of Margal, and their children, male or female, after them, by a method of choosing yet to be determined by their mother and myself."

Those gathered listened silently, all likely hoping to be able to link the disparate threads of Barc's puzzling revelation by some word or inference to the other equally mysterious points of the agenda yet undiscussed.

"I refer you to the relevant Article of Margal's Charter," Barc said then. "It is printed on the third page of your copies." Paper rustled, and muttered comments followed, as all but the fards examined their sheafs of documents. "As you can see," said Barc, "a quorum is required—two of whom must be recognized leaders of human subgroups neither bors, who might be biased, or wends, whose general claim to the planet Stepwater might be construed as creating a prejudice against subowners and charter owners under their race's sway. Here we have Shillemeh, throngmother of the Great Wall mantees, formerly the Hammad River mantees or the Great Weir mantees, and there is Wridth Hasselteek, headman of the Musal Bhjak. Here also"—Barc nodded in the direction of the wends—"is Ethelemin, the Chief Archivist of all Stepwater, from Arafellin Enclave in Garloom and the Pan-Wend Archives, who will record all these proceedings.

"The third document you have before you is an affidavit which I hope all of you will sign, witnessing Blet's concurrence with what has been agreed thus far. Please examine it. When all have signed, we can proceed to Item Two." Few missed the threat and the promise in Barc's last sentence. Whether from curiosity or from high stakes in the outcome of the subsequent items, all intended to get Item One over with quickly.

What do I care? thought the throngmother, Blet, Barc,

or someone else? She signed her witness to Blet's agreement, and her acquiescence to the open-ended nature of future Margal successions. The other mantees, seeing their mother's act, followed suit. The fards did not. A bors aide brought them a black stamp pad and each fard pressed his nose against it, and then against his affidavit. The smallest fard thereafter licked his nose incessantly, and his tongue turned purplish black. Both other fards maintained their dignity, such as it was, though they continued to twitch, tap their feet, and play games with their busy fingers beneath the table. They were fards, after all. The others present each signed their copies, and laid them before themselves on the table.

A rumble was heard and felt underfoot—another cave-in somewhere in Margal Town below—and Blet stood up, her ears flat and her nose an odd, pale gray. She was not required to sign. "Am I done now?" she bleated. "Can I go?"

Barc felt almost sad. Had the feisty Blet he knew been driven entirely away by her multiple traumas and her fear? That, he reflected, would be a great pity. He would be sad if it were so. He then imagined his sister living contentedly in a hut made of roots and logs, thatched with reekvine, warmed by a fire of dried nitweiler dung. He imagined her oblivious to the stinks. He imagined her with two noisy cubs clawing greedily at her breasts, unbothered by their fighting and her own scratches, and equally unannoyed by her smelly husband, whose feet tracked blood from the slaughterhouse or nitweiler-skinning shed on her trampled dirt floor—and Barc was sadder still.

Then he imagined Blet recovering her wit and spirit—and finding herself irrevocably locked out of Margal and committed forever to the nitweiler farm. He imagined her rage. He imagined the sufferings of her husband and her brats that would ensue when her devious mind and nasty disposition again returned true to form. Suddenly, Barc Doresh was a happy bors again. "Of course you may go, sister," he said in a kind, quiet tone. "Your carriage is ready at the north gate. And may I wish you a very speedy recovery?" Blet did not respond. A bors led her away.

"Quick!" Barc hissed to another aide as he gathered up the affidavits. "Take these to the vault below. Record them and have the crystal delivered here, to the Archivist, who will escort it to Garloom. And has the vault's code been changed? Is Blet's password revoked?" The aide assured him it was so. "Good," he sighed. "Then have the miners shore up the tunnel they dug over Blet's chamber. We do not want any *accidental* rockfalls."

"And now," he said, addressing all present, "to Item Two." He grinned. "I wish to marry. That is, I wish to mate for life, with the female of my choosing as do the old humans—as does the Arbiter himself. I wish my union to be recognized not only by those who may approve of it, but by all, as an irrevocable contract with the force of law. I will read the relevant passages of the Stepwater Code and the precedents set by the Arbiter and his predecessors in that office." Barc read. Most of it went over the heads of his listeners, especially the fards, who had no comparable institution to marriage at all.

Barc's revelation elicited a few comments, but several shrugs—after all, it was important to no one but Barc Doresh and whoever he "married." An odd custom, thought Simolf. Will he get to futter anytime he wants, not just one intense week of his life? Never having so indulged, Simolf had no basis to determine what was preferable. The fards did not shrug, because a shrug might have been interpreted as a gesture of *thewk,* a mortal insult, but their raised eyebrows were a universal expression. The tarbeks, who ordinarily deposited semen in acid-rich hot springs where females of their kind were known to bathe, and thus propagated their kind in a quiet and respectable manner, and who considered such remote intercourse the acceptable limit of congress between the sexes, did not care what perversions bors practiced among themselves.

The three wends listened with mixed feelings—mixed

between them, if not within themselves. Tathabel, who had actually enjoyed her unions with Barc and considered him a superior lover to the singularly meagerly endowed wends she had encountered on her extended vacation in the tropics, was slightly sad that a door left slightly ajar was now firmly closing.

Firithanet, who had in spite of herself believed that Barc was hopelessly enamored of her, was offended that he had so easily turned from her to another—even though she knew all about his problem. Only she, and the mantee throngmother, had the slightest inkling of what was coming next, and did not gasp aloud when Barc stated his next proposal: "I wish," Barc said next, "to marry the mantee Girelf."

A hubbub ensued. "No!" spat Girelf, embarrassed and humiliated. Shillemeh, throngmother, knew immediately that she would have no choice but to acquiesce—no, to support Barc's demand enthusiastically—because the marriage was Item Two, and until it was settled, there would be no resolution of Item Three (which she suspected would not favor the mantees) and Item Four (from which she might, just might, be able to wring concessions that would allow her throng to survive).

The fards, once the implications were made clear to them, would also acquiesce. The matter was internal to Margal Steep, and they were only concerned with Item Four, and water rights.

Mfapkot saw nothing wrong with mating outside one's own kind—for others. He would agree to whatever his friend Barc wanted, as would his companion, his chief.

If the wendish archivist thought the union perverse, he would nonetheless go along with it—his daughters, who had themselves experienced similar liaisons, and did not wish to have it acknowledged or bandied about, would make sure of that.

The listeners who were most appalled by Barc's proposal were the bors. Superficially simple, the implications and repercussions were terrifying. First, Barc's children—in the male line of descent—would inherit rule over all the bors in Margal. That was untraditional, uncomfortable, but could be tolerated. Second, they would be Girelf's children as well. They would not be bors. They would not even be mantees, who were at least furred, and smelled decent, and whose sexual practices were strange, but not disgusting. But the children of Barc's and Girelf's mating would be . . . old humans. Furless, stinking old humans who would, upon maturing, wish to mate with their mates, with their children . . . with anyone, with everyone. No! That could never be. Sard, the Margal councillor, marshaled his arguments. Even with so strong a case as he believed he had, he was deeply afraid—Barc Doresh had saved Margal. What was gratitude worth? Sard was also acutely aware that he alone would not decide the issue and that, if it went against him, he would have to deal with the repercussions of his resistance to it.

Prak—who had seen the old-human women, the "skins," who occupied his boss's nights and who had, uncomfortably, shamefully, been close enough for him to react libidinously to them—stood up suddenly, knocking over his chair. "No!" he shouted. "This cannot be allowed!"

Sard welcomed the distraction, which gave him time to marshal his thoughts and his attack. When Prak subdued himself and sat down again, the old bors spoke softly, but in a trained voice all could hear. "Whatever my personal feelings, Sar Barc," he said in even tones belied by his fur, which was standing stiffly upright along his spine and on his neck, "this cannot be. You have assembled a quorum sufficient for lesser decisions—Blet is gone, and cannot legally return to rule—but this matter is of a higher nature, and the law is quite specific. Old humans—or halfbreeds of old-human semblance—cannot inherit except among themselves. There is a case for your children's children, but none at all for your offspring of the first generation. That is not Stepwater law, but interstellar precedent established in the beginning by the first Arbiter of all. It

is a cornerstone of our very civilization, made necessary by
the nature of our genes. If hybrids, who nullify our very
forms when we mate across proper lines, could inherit our
assets as well . . . all would be chaos. They would usurp
all, and soon the Xarafeille Stream would have no inhab-
itants but the hairless ones.

"For that reason such an inheritance is perforce limited," Sard continued with hardly a breath. "It can only
apply to the governance of the principality of Margal
Steep and the personal property of the parents. If there is
no direct heir, the heritage reverts to the line of second
resort *at the time of the decision*—to the successors of
Frak and Dird Buckroo, because no collateral relation-
ships are recognized under the law, which is specifically
designed to forever limit the effects of just such usurpa-
tion, by hybrids of the old-human type, as is contemplated
here.

"But that is not all. The requirements for a decision of
such moment are clear. A quorum must consist of one
ranking member of each race but one. I see mantees, with
throngmother Shillemeh among them. I see tarbeks—one
Mfapkot, and Duke Thastokpot of the Lead Valley
tarbeks. That is two of suitable rank. I see the Archivist
of all Stepwater, and that makes three. Then there is
Chief Wridth Hasselteek, a fard, and you, Barc Doresh,
who are governor of Margal Steep." Sard took a rhetorical
pause for a breath that was as good as words. "But," he
went on, "that is only five. There are *seven* races of Man!
Where is the ikut who will vote, or the old human? I see
neither, and *one*, at least, you must have. I therefore move
that Item Two be struck from the agenda, and that this
conclave go on to Item Three."

"Indeed you are right, Councillor—as you are always
right," Barc conceded, "but you lack a vital fact I have up
to now withheld."

Sard said nothing, so Barc continued. "One chair here
is empty, unneeded before. I now ask that its proper oc-
cupant attend us here." All eyes turned to the vacant seat,

and then to the entry portal, which was in shadow, as the sun Mirrim had moved several degrees across the sky while the meeting had progressed. The shadow in the entry moved, and emerged into the room, a black-robed figure taller than a wend but less so than a tarbek, whose face was entirely covered by a thin, opaque veil.

Barc stood. "All rise for the Arbiter John Minder . . ." he said in sonorous, stentorian tones. A hush like night at the bottom of a bors mine shaft obtained, but was followed almost immediately by the scrape and rattle of chairs, the rustle of accoutrements, and by amazed, indrawn breaths. ". . . in the person of his council, the Respectable Sally Marie Marcos," Barc finished his sentence.

He stood behind his own chair and offered it to the Arbiter's representative, who doffed robe and veil, and sat. Barc then picked up his club and conspicuously handed it to Niddy, who again hung it from his sambrowne and then stepped back twice, and again stood at attention. Only the bors present and peeking in the door knew that the seeming ritual was not ancient and solemn; Barc and Niddy had invented it only hours earlier.

All eyes turned toward Consul Marcos. "You may be seated," she said briskly. "We have much to accomplish in the short time I have allowed for it." All the wide eyes focused on her, and the teeth of those kinds of people who expressed amazement with gaping jaws, reflected red shards from her crimson tunic. "Sar Sard," she said, addressing the elderly bors, "Barc spoke correctly. The fact withheld is that I am here, an old human, and that I hold a position of sufficient responsibility to qualify this meeting as a proper quorum. Thus we are enabled to continue deliberations on Item Two. State your case."

Sard rose, bowed to the consul and then to the others present. "Consul, I no longer have a case." He sat.

"Are there others, then?" Marcos asked. "No? Then I will . . ."

"Wait!" It was Girelf. "I object to this! It is a charade,

a perversion of law. I am the subject of this travesty—am I to have no say?" She stood stiffly, defiantly, and darted loathing glances first at Barc, then at Shillemeh, and then at Sally Marcos.

"You are Girelf?" Marcos said, rhetorically. "You are a mantee, and thus mantee law and precedent pertain. Is there a precedent?"

Girelf, revealing no knowledge of law or precedent, remained silent. Shillemeh rose to her inadequate feet with the aid of Simolf and another mantee. "There is, Respectability." The throngmother grinned widely. "It is called the Rule of Secondary Obligation, and it requires that a mantee female who refuses appointment as throngmother with her birth-throng cannot refuse the lawful order of her own throngmother to mate 'with those individuals the throngmother may designate outside the throng.'"

"No!" Girelf hissed. "That old rule refers only to the budding off of new throngs! There is no new throng intended now. There is only the misogamous intention of a randy bors with a sex-addled head. The rule was not meant to extend so far."

"Ah," said Shillemeh, "but does the rule specifically state it? It does not. Can anyone here confirm or deny my assertion?"

"I can confirm it," said the wend archivist. "It is common to all mantees. Though the intent of the rule was surely to provide throngmothers for new mantee settlements on underpopulated planets, it is nowhere so stated. By the letter of the rule, Girelf must mate as directed by Shillemeh."

"I will not!" Girelf shouted. "I will die first! I will . . . I will . . ." She eyed Shillemeh malevolently. "I will," she said then, "assume *your* position as throngmother, instead."

"You cannot. You have turned it down," said Shillemeh. "Elleth is to replace me. It is decided."

"No. You cannot refuse me." From her waist pouch Girelf lifted a small object, which she palmed in such a way that only Shillemeh could see it. "Shall we withdraw for a moment to discuss it?"

"You may," said Consul Marcos. "But be quick. My ship awaits me."

"You cannot humiliate me so," said the throngmother, when both were hidden from the room by the loggia's curtain. She recognized the tiny medical vial—the vial that held an egg that she had ejected unfertilized. "I have other eggs, and some are still . . ."

"You do not know that—and Elleth is far too young. The mantees will accept me over you, if I . . ."

"No! I beg you. You are my daughter. Can you be so cruel?" But Shillemeh saw that Girelf was adamant. She also saw something else, that a daughter could not hide from the one who had given her life—a faint trace of an expression she could not interpret, but which she somehow knew did not bode ill for her.

"It is all a charade, Mother—as I said before. The game must be played. Surrender this point to me, and you will gain everything else you want. I promise that." Now Girelf's eyes brimmed not with harsh, angry light but with barely suppressed tears. They spoke together in quiet tones, and then Shillemeh nodded, pulled the curtain aside, and hobbled back to her wide chair—but even Barc noticed that her slow footfalls seemed less heavy than they had on her way out of the chamber.

"Respectability," the throngmother said once she and Girelf were again seated, "may I speak once more with my daughter before we proceed?"

Consul Marcos nodded, and for once did not mention haste, or her pressing schedule.

"Girelf, my daughter, I find I cannot *command* you to accept this burden. I could not bring myself to mate for a day with a creature so foul as a bors, so repugnant as that particular bors, that Barc Doresh." She sighed, and kept her eyes on her daughter, avoiding Barc's glare. "But," she said, "for the sake of our people—for the sake of the

repulsive and perverted Barc Doresh's Item Three and
Item Four, yet to be negotiated, I will allow myself to *beg,*
not command. Daughter, will you marry the bors and bear
his hairless, ugly . . ." She suddenly glanced at Consul
Marcos, and reconsidered her words. ". . . and bear his
children?"

Girelf sighed also. She blinked—or at least it looked
like a blink, as her head was turned away from Barc. From
another perspective, could it have been . . . a wink? "On
one condition only will I do so, Mother," she said in the
same solemn tones Shillemeh had employed, yet with a
trace of an odd, quirky expression that Barc failed to notice, as if she were secretly amused. She looked at Simolf,
then at each other mantee in turn. "For the sake of my
people, for their survival, I will mate with . . . with that
hideous, debased, and wholly inadequate creature. But
there is a condition that must be met." Her gaze fixed on
Barc, who looked much like a small cub who had been
doused with a bucket of cold water. If she was secretly
amused by her own theatrics, there was no trace of it in
her gaze now. "I will do so if and when you, Mother, declare yourself satisfied with the resolution of the last two
points of the agenda yet to come." She addressed the Arbiter's representative next: "Is that fair? Sacrifice for sacrifice? Will you ratify these proceedings if my condition is
met?"

Sally Marcos kept from laughing, but she had to cover
her mouth with her hand and pretend to cough, wishing
she had been able to keep her veil on. "I will," Sally Marcos said solemnly. "Girelf, of the Great Wall mantees, I
honor you. Your sacrifice will be recorded in the annals on
Newhome. Seldom has a female promised to endure such
a fate—surely worse by far than death—for the sake of
her folk." Surely, she thought, no one here *believes* this
nonsense, do they? She looked about her. The wends always looked like they were laughing at everyone; their ex-
pressions could have indicated great solemnity, for all she
could tell. The mantees, far down the table, seemed to

find no humor in what she said—except, perhaps, for Girelf, of course . . . and Shillemeh? The tarbeks? Who could tell? And the fards wriggled and jittered as fards do. It could have been laughter, but they seemed to be ignoring the proceedings. Then she looked at Barc—and had to look away quickly before she lost her composure entirely. She drew a long, deep breath, and continued her "solemn" speech.

"When the remaining points are resolved—*and I am sure they will be,*" Sally stated emphatically, staring at Barc, who had shrunk still further and could surely shrink no more, having now heard not one but two lovers' abysmal opinions of him, "your people will revere you, locked forever in misery in this stone heap, mated to . . . him, so that they may splash freely in the waters of the restored Hammad River." She nodded to Girelf, and sat down.

As the consul had stated, so it went. The last two points were dealt with swiftly and—as all present agreed—fairly. "In sum," said Sally Marcos, referring to her notes, "point three: where water flows *under* land or through a gorge, a water gap, or along a precipice, the land adjoining it will not be subject to the fifty-obel rule. Where it is artificially empounded, it can only be with the consent of the owners of backwater land, who shall retain their claim to the acreage submerged, and who will gain certain rights to the water over it. Margal Steep agrees to grant certain uses of the land abutting a much-reduced Hammad Pond to the mantees of the Great Wall.

"Point four: Margal Steep is granted permanent right of way for its railroad across the fardish desert. The Hammad River will be restored to its level of two winters back, and the modified fifty-obel rule will apply. Wridth Hasselteek's wells, now full, will continue to produce water of reasonable quality, judged by traditional fardish standards, and all parties to this agreement will so warrant it.

"Further and finally, all lands fed by the Hammad but

not part of its original watercourse will remain in the hands of their traditional owners. Mantees of the again Hammad River throng will be permitted access to open water in such places, and gathering and basking rights on the shores, but shall have no claim upon it."

Consul Marcos took a deep breath. "My attorneys will draw up the documents in the spirit of what we have agreed upon. Is that satisfactory to all?" There were no demurrals. "Then I declare this meeting closed." She stood. Barc rushed to help with her robe and veil.

"Wait!" the throngmother protested suddenly. "What does the last thing you mentioned mean? What land is fed by the river, but not part of it? Do you refer to where our water has gone?"

Consul Marcos glanced meaningfully at Barc, her veil not yet in place. Barc in turn raised one eyebrow and smiled, recovering slightly from his earlier humiliation. "Come," he said, "I will show you. Perhaps when you conferred with your daughter on the loggia, you were too occupied to notice." He pulled the curtains aside and gestured for the others to step onto the porch.

There before them, spread out as a great bowl of tan, ocher, and many shades of gray and dun, was Margal's central valley, a vast arid depression cupped in the jutting fingers of mountains. Girelf gasped. She had not realized, in spite of the climb within the mountain, just how high Barc's meeting chamber was. It was surely less than a quarter-obel from the top of Mendeb Park. "There," said Barc proudly. "There is your water—Margal's water." He pointed, and then the mantees saw what they had ignored before: a glitter, a flash, and a metallic shine. The valley's sinkholes were no longer empty or filled only with dust. Each round, rocky vessel sparkled with sunlight reflected from water.

They saw too that the desert floor in places was not dun and dark, but a fine, hazy green. And there at the base of Mendeb Peak was a puff of white and a thread of silver, almost at their feet, where the waters beneath

Margal Town belched and rushed from a great, unseen hole in the mountain's base. It was Barc's "railroad" tunnel, now half-filled with water that gouted and splashed upon the rocks below. Already the force of the waterfall had cut a pool in the soft, chalky limestone before running downward to the desert and disappearing in the honeycombed ground.

"Where is the rest of our water?" demanded Shillemeh, not understanding how much of it the riddled limestone had taken up, much as a sponge absorbs washwater from a basin.

"It is there, filling the caves under the valley," Barc explained. "Each pool you can see is like the narrow mouth of a jug, and most of the water is unseen below. The valley is filling from one range of peaks to the others, and the excess percolates outward beyond that low pass to the west, to fill Wridth Hasselteek's wells. Of course, the water that migrates that far is salty or alkaline, depending on what strata it passes through, but the fards relish it, and they will sell its crystalline precipitates to my coming tourists, and will grow wealthy."

"The trees!" exclaimed Simolf. He pointed. There on the valley floor were small spots of greenery, their shadows long in the afternoon light.

"They will shade the karst pools and the moistened soil," said Barc, "and though the land itself is of use to us bors, the pools and sinkholes and the vast flooded caverns are not. Perhaps your mantees will find some use for them. It is your right."

"But will the river still return to the Hammad Valley, with so much of its water trapped here?" asked Shillemeh.

Barc explained. The riverbed had been drained by the initial rush of water to fill the empty valley, but beneath the soluble limestone lay the granitic roots of Margal's mountains, an impervious barrier. The valley was already mostly filled, and the water's flow was limited by a wall of rock left standing in the "railroad" tunnel—the still-solid rock that the blue button of his igniter would have caused to shatter. With the flow into the valley limited so, the following spring's floods would restore the flow almost to normal except for ordinary losses to evaporation and the seepage that filled the fards' wells. Even some of that water would eventually, through slow percolation, rejoin the river farther down, as bankside springs. With careful conservation by the mantees and proper management of their great dam, even the flow south to Karbol would not be greatly diminished.

"You can see the layer of mist that forms late in the day," Barc said, pointing to the waterfall. "It will fall as dew on the slopes, and great redwoods, now seedlings, will tower there." He glanced at Girelf, then turned away, a troubled expression on his mobile face—one he did not want the others to see. Sally Marcos, though, noticed, and followed him inside. The mantees remained, gazing on the desolate valley that had absorbed their dream of a vast mantee realm just across its enclosing mountains.

"Give it time, Barc," she said softly, placing her hand on his rigid forearm. "There is less distance between you and Girelf than it seems, right now. She has an image to create and maintain with the mantees, but soon . . ." She paused, having noticed the object Barc had removed from a niche along the wall. "May I have that?" It was a request and a command; there was steel in her voice. Reluctantly, Barc handed her the black device, its red and blue crystals both uniformly dull. "You feel insecure, I know," Sally said, taking it from his hand, "but there will never be a need to push that blue button."

The blue button: the switch that could activate the second series of charges planted not only under Margal Town but beneath the low wall of the western pass, charges that would shatter the remaining rock holding the Hammad River pent in the central valley. Had Barc pushed that button twice, the lip over which the waters now flowed would have been lowered, and the entire river would have been diverted to the central valley, to rush then out into the fards' desert and there to be forever dissipated in a

great alluvial fan, dooming the mantees to migrate elsewhere or live entirely upon bors sufferance.

"Even the threat is unneeded, Barc," she assured him.
"There is no need for the mantees even to know of it."
She snapped the case open and removed the power
source, then reached deeper within and pulled out a
handful of chips, tiny wires, and electronic parts. She
dropped them and crushed them beneath her foot. Barc
shrank further. His last resort was now gone. In days or
weeks the remaining charges would deteriorate. Yes, the
choice was now gone—but he knew that in handing the
box to Sally, he had already decided.

The fards were content with their wells. The mantees
would again have their river and their pond, though a
lesser one than they had once envisioned. Tathabel and
Firithanet had their archives and their respectability. Sally
would return to her new posting and her promotion. For
Mfapkot and the others, all was much as it had been before. Their lives would progress. They would eat and
drink, mate, sell, trade, and eventually die. What else was
there?

But what lay before Barc Doresh between this moment
and his eventual grave? He did not know. Blet would no
longer torment him, of course. He was really free of her.
But he had seen the steel in Girelf. He had heard her bit-
ing denunciation of him. Of course, he had heard her
contented murmurs as well, her affectionate giggles there
in her damp grotto. Which Girelf had he committed himself to? Even now, he heard her voice raised in laughter,
there on his loggia, overlooking the evidence of his tri-
umph, which now seemed hollow and sour. What did she
and her fat mother find so funny?

Would he and Girelf mate again, or did her sharp words
signify the end of that? If they did, and there were children
. . . they would be strange creatures, old humans, neither
bors nor mantee. Then he thought of a small face, light-
years away. Bobby. He felt a rush of warmth. Yes, they

would be old humans, but that was not all bad. No, it was
not bad at all.

Again he heard laughter. Were they laughing at him?
Had he again, as so many times before, made some terrible mistake? He did not know. Only time would tell him
if he was indeed the fool he suspected he might be. Only
time, and the flowing Hammad River, and the slow percolation of its waters beneath the small realm called Margal
Steep.

EPILOGUE

DISPATCH

TO: Samol Jebbis, Consul, Beldant (Xarafeille
         1427)(crypt. 7xc)

FROM: Arbiter

MESSAGE: I understand you've defused the situation
on Beldant and tensions are at a low of .029 and
holding. Two for one, Sam! We did it—this time.

   I know you have all the footage of the decision at
Margal Steep—you used it well enough—but I thought
you might like to see the "behind the scenes" stuff
too, so I'm sending the whole file.

   You handled Beldant well, and I particularly liked
your "people solving their problems themselves, without
need for intervention" slant. If only they knew. Of
course you made Sally Marcos look like she was
just rubber-stamping things, but I'm sure she doesn't
mind. You and I—and Sally—know how hard we worked
for it. John.

"What happened next, Daddy?" demanded Parissa. "Did
they live happily ever after? Did they?"

"Only *they* can say, dear," John Minder replied. "They
are both human, and human lives are long. No one is
happy all the time. But when I last saw them . . ."

"Yes!" interjected Rob. "You said you'd been to
Stepwater. What did you see? Did you meet them?"

"I did, after a fashion, though they did not know it because I was in the guise of an itinerant potter, yet I managed to take a holo or two. Would you like to see?" All

three children did—even Rob abandoned his studied equanimity to plead as enthusiastically as Parissa. Their father reached for a datacrystal high on a cluttered shelf, and inserted it into the reader. All the shelves were cluttered except one, which held a simple wooden rack containing blue, green, and vermilion datacubes. There were seven spaces on the rack, but not all the spaces were filled. John Minder sighed as his eyes passed over them. Seven datacubes, seven planets, and—he fervently hoped—seven stories to tell his children or his grandchildren. He hoped there was time to complete the task. So far, he had been wise enough or lucky enough not to need a fleet, troops, or more than the visible trappings of his office's power. Oh, Shems, he said, but only inside his head, would you have taken those datablocks if you had known what a burden you placed on me? If you had known the risks? He was sure he knew the answer to that. He willed himself not to think about it, not right then.

The data module contained a simple holo taken from a distance and later enhanced; thus the four faces were not quite distinct. Rob was first to recognize the scene: a stone pier jutting into a placid lake. The gray-green of distant foliage lined a far shore, and beyond that rose mountains, pink-tipped with faraway sunset. "Mendeb Peak," Rob said, indicating the tallest mountain. "And that is the island Barc built. See? There is his summerhouse, behind him."

"Is that Barc?" Parissa demanded. "Let me *see*!"

"Don't push," snapped Sarabet. "That is Barc Doresh, and there is Girelf."

"Are they happily-ever-after? I can't see."

"You can't *see* that," Rob commented.

"Perhaps not," his father commented, "but much can be determined from indirect evidence. Parissa? Look closely, and tell me what you see there."

"I see Barc, and his arm is around Girelf, and there are two . . . They *are*, Daddy! They *are* happily-ever-after! They have two children. See?"

"That's happiness?" Rob scoffed. "Children?" He nudged Sarabet and rolled his eyes toward Parissa.

"It may be so," John Minder said to his youngest daughter, ignoring Rob's adolescent cynicism. "Surely it indicates that their reconciliation progressed to a certain point . . . and at least twice."

"What are their names, Dad?" asked Sarabet.

"The boy . . . Why, that's Bobby. Couldn't you have guessed? And the girl is Sally, after my consul, who had a great impact on their relationship."

Parissa arose, sniffling. She kicked her brother's ankle, hard, and ran from the room. "Ow!" Rob protested. "What's wrong with her?"

"Why don't you find out?" his father suggested. His expression made it clear that it was *that* kind of suggestion. Rob obeyed.

"Why did you kick me?" he asked when he found her, in her room.

"I hate you!"

"That's fine with me—but why?"

"They named *him* 'Bobby' after *you*, didn't they?" she sobbed. "How come they didn't name *her* 'Parissa'?"

"You weren't born yet, that's why. Someday you'll understand."

Someday, John Minder repeated to himself. And someday he would tell Parissa of his *first* voyage to Stepwater, to the city where he had met with a sad and angry young mantee named Girelf. "It's not *fair*," she had wept. "You are an old human and can mate as you please—and with someone you love. I am forced to choose between my mother and my people, whom I love, and Barc Doresh, whom I also love. Is there no other alternative?"

John Minder's eyes had taken on an unreadable, faraway look. He gazed out through a broad, uncurtained window and down the length of Perimeter Way, to the bridge that spanned from the Archivist's palace to the Pan-Wend Archives itself. He knew only that within those archives was a certain datacrystal, one of seven, that could decide the fate of more people than he could ever know, than even he, the Arbiter, who purportedly knew all, could imagine. He could see the archival building as well, and busy wends in the street before it, and traffic speeding past it.

As yet, at that time, he had not known that the archivist had two daughters, Firithanet and Tathabel, who by fate and chance would become lowly whores in Karbol for a while. He had not known of the cabdriver Bethelep or of Nidleg Marboon. He had not even known that Consul S. Marcos was called Sally, and was a very pretty girl. There was much that he was destined to learn about those and other seemingly insignificant people. With his next words, he began that long lesson.

"There may be a way," he told Girelf. "Much depends on this young bors you love. Answer me honestly, now. Is he clever and resourceful? Has he flaws?"

Girelf answered positively to both questions, but did not embellish. She did not glaze over Barc's flaws, which were many and quite obvious. She was very much in love, yet she was no fool, nor blind. She wanted Barc, and she had no desire at all to mate with any others, or to be throngmother—but neither did she wish to be an outcast among her own kind, or a despised alien in exile within a bors principality. She wanted it all—Barc, the love and respect of her own people, and acceptance by the bors folk of Margal Steep. She wanted children—Barc's children— but only one or two, not hundreds. That those infants would be as hairless as the Arbiter himself did not bother her—the small boy-child, Bobby, who even now toyed with her short, brown fur was strange, indeed, and quite unlike a mantee pup, but he was not at all repulsive to her.

Because she was basically honest, and because she wanted so much, she told the Arbiter everything he wanted to know.

* * *

Later, when Girelf had gone, when all the months and years had elapsed, and when all the events that would unfold from that meeting had transpired and been recorded on datacrystals only future Arbiters would see, John Minder watched his last child, Parissa, toy with elaborately carved chessmen scattered across the thickly carpeted floor. The queen was indeed shaped as a graceful mantee, and the king a large, broad-shouldered bors. When Parissa grew tired of her unorthodox game, he would pick up the chessmen and arrange them carefully in proper rank and order upon their white marble and rich, green malachite squares, preparing them, and himself, for one more game in a long contest that was not yet nearing an end.

Special Sneak Previews
for the
Next Two Novels
in the
Arbiter Series

FELLENBRATH

An Arbiter Tale
on sale early 1996

Fellenbrath was a harsh and lonely planet circling a star of the same name in the 271st inhabited solar system of the Xarafeille Stream, where the seven races of Man commingled in an uneasy peace, and where the mysterious Arbiter with his great fleet and poletzai legions watched over it all.

On Fellenbrath were a few tarbek tribes, but mostly fards—desert-wise, hard, enduring fards who wrestled livelihoods from the driest deserts. Every seep, every spring, every damp spot on Fellenbrath's habitable zones had a name, and was owned. The fards who owned them were harsh men, and they bred sons as hardy and as unrelenting as were they themselves.

To every rule, there is an exception, of course. Among the sons of Fladth Wrasselty, lord of the spring named Valbissag and the stone town that surrounded it, the exception was the child of Fladth's old age, called Slith. Slith Wrasselty was tan-pelted like most fards, with soft white belly down and short, creamy fur from digits to knees and elbows. His whiskers were long, black, and fardlike, projecting from the corners of his mouth and from his brows. He was quick of movement, and his pink, mobile nose was never still. His long-tufted ears, like hyperactive radar antennae, never ceased their scanning. Fards did not seem quick to other fards, of course. Among them, Slith seemed ordinary, or perhaps even a bit sluggish at times, but members of the other races of

man would have deemed him jittery and abrupt—like all
fards.

Mentally, Slith Wrasselty was quite un-fardlike, mainly
because, unlike his brothers, he actually *liked* his aging father Fladth (which was quite strange) and he had no desire whatsoever to slay him (which was unnatural and
almost unheard of, if not quite perverted).

Slith's strange, un-fardlike attitudes had shaped his behavior in other ways, too. Because he had no wish to be
a patricide—and because he made no secret of it—his
two older brothers and two younger ones had no use for
him at all. They did not even bother to plot his death,
though all of them nursed glorious schemes by which they
hoped to slay or emasculate their other siblings as soon as
one of them succeeded in assassinating old Fladth.
Though men of other races deemed such fardish preoccu-
pations cruel and inhuman, the contest over succession
and inheritance unquestionably bred quicker, smarter, and
more ruthless fards, and the Wrasselty clan, longtime
owners of Valbissag, stood high among those. Slith, should
his brothers not change their minds and slay him as a
matter of principle, a mere trimming of a loose end,
would be an unusual Wrasselty indeed—a living brother
of Valbissag's owner.

Of course it might not be much of a life. If he pledged
fealty to whoever won the struggle, he might be so lucky
as to be granted a seat by the spring, where he could
breathe its life-giving vapors and ladle its flavorful water
to his lips. He might even be allowed a patch of sand to
sleep on in an outer courtyard within the palace walls. If
his elder brother Gleph inherited, he would surely make
Slith work all day, likely at some noisome task, for every
privilege. If Thradz, the next oldest, won, Slith would be
lucky to catch a single breath of Valbissag's steam, let
alone a sip, unless he paid for it in solid coin. If either
Thplet or Splath, his younger siblings, took claim of
Valbissag, palace, and town, he might have an easier life
of it, because both seemed to look on him with distant af-

fection, but there was no guarantee of it. People changed when they became successful, and the nature and direction of such change were always unpredictable. It was not wise to count on anyone whose self-interest was unclear.

GLAICE

An Arbiter Tale
on sale Fall 1996

Tep Inutkak of the *ikut* race of man on Glaice, stood over two meters tall and was covered with white fur. His fellow students at the Metok University, most of whom sprang from other kinds of parents, considered him a man mostly because he was half again the height of a lissome *mantee* male, weighed three times as much as a jittery *fard,* and was not afraid of a good rough-and-tumble with the *bors* males in his dormitory.

But tonight, he was working on his paper which was a week late. He had filed his long, yellow claws to blunt nubs that did not slip off his terminal's keys or obliterate the letters on them. He had adjusted his chair just so, to accommodate his stub of a tail. Those things helped, but they didn't aid the flow of words and ideas from his brain to fingers to keys, from the keys to the multi-terabyte data-storage crystals somewhere deep within the clammy basements of the university.

It wouldn't be the end of the world if Tep didn't get the paper in by the end of the week, but he was afraid it might be the end of his academic career. He envisioned his ignomious return to the Inutkak ikut band, and his future thereafter. There was nothing wrong with the Inutkak life, Tep assured himself. Someday when he was much older, he'd be ready to challenge the old *shahm,* to take his place as chief. But now he was too young, and enjoyed city life far too much.

Tep struggled with the paper for another hour before he pushed his keyboard aside and waited for a printout.

"Maybe somebody down at the bar can help me with the last part," he muttered. Maybe a beer or two would loosen his head just enough so he could finish it himself. In all likelihood someone at the bar *would* be able to help, because the Last Atopak Tavern was a hangout for Metok U. grad students.

As luck would have it, Tep recognized a group of potentially useful fellow students the minute he entered the bar. Also as luck would have it, they were wholly engrossed in a discussion, and did not welcome his persistent efforts to change the subject to his paper's topic. "Tep Inutkak," said Velanda, a bors archaeology student, "don't you even care if the mantees kick you off your own planet?"

"Huh? Kick me off Glaice? I was born here."

"Don't you watch the news?" Velanda and the others seemed surprised, but not excessively so. Most of them were old enough to know what it was like to be a second-year grad student. There was seldom time for anything but study. Velanda took pity on Tep, and brought him up to date.

It seemed that an ikut band somewhere on the other side of the planet had purposefully disrupted their usual migration pattern so they could mate with another band that occupied the same territories, but in other seasons. Everyone knew how finely choreographed ikut migration cycles were, and how disastrous it was if a band got off schedule. If a band missed its regular voyage through the equatorial waters, they would also miss out on certain kinds of fish they needed to stay healthy.

The Ketonak band missed the southern half of their migration and ended up back in their northern camp at just the time the local mantee throng arrived to mate on the offshore rocks. Happily for the Ketonak, the mantees contained many of the trace nutrients they had missed by not completing their voyage south. Unhappily for them, the mantees did not willingly submit to being eaten.

"Cannibals?" exclaimed Tep. "They killed and ate other people? Are they still living in the stone age?" he asked shaking his head. They were, his fellow students agreed.

"But that's only part of the story!" insisted Blent Dagro, another bors, a chemistry postdoc. "The Warm Stream mantee throngmother is taking them into Metok High Court. She's brought murder charges against their *shahm.*"

Tep had just drained his second mug of beer and, realizing that he would get no help with his paper from anyone present, decided to go back to his room and try again. "Well, it *is* murder, isn't it? Mantees are people, too." He stood, and set down his empty mug.

"It's killing—but *murder*? The Ketonak only did it to live. In the old days before there was a High Court, all ikuts ate mantee, didn't they? You tell us, Tep. You're the expert on food chains."

"I wish I was," Tep said, sighing. "I never will be, unless I get this paper done, though, since all you guys want to talk about is mantee stew . . ." He turned to leave.

"Wait, Tep!" said Velanda. "I'll go with you. Maybe I can help with your paper, and then I'll tell you the rest of the story about the Ketonak and the mantees."

"Sure," he said. "You can tell me some on the way. Especially about how what the Ketonak did affects *me*. I didn't eat any mantees."

Velanda told him. "It would have stopped right there. The court would have awarded the Warm Stream throng damages, and probably would have ordered the Ketonaks disbanded and scattered among the other bands, which is traditional, isn't it?"

"That's what people did centuries ago," Tep agreed. "But I don't think there's been a similar case in generations. I suppose now that there's a formal court and all, things are different. But you still haven't said how—"

"As I said, it would've stopped right there except that Professor Rakulit, who's been putting together a book on radiocarbon dating of prehistoric sites on Glaice, and—"

"Rakulit? Isn't he a seel, too?"

"Tep! Don't call them that. Prof. Rakulit is a *mantee*. Calling him a 'seel' even makes him *sound* like he's something to eat."

"It's the ikut word for 'mantee,'" Tep protested. "It doesn't mean anything bad."

"Hah! If there was an ikut encyclopedia, I wonder if 'seel' would be cross-referenced along with *bors* and *tarbeks* as 'other human subspecies' or with *ritvak* and *etolat* under 'traditional ikut meals'?"

"So did they eat your committee chairman, or what?" Tep asked facetiously.

"Tep! Professor Rakulit has proven that the mantees have been on Glaice longer than anyone else." She rushed to finish the tale. In short, Rakulit proved that the mantees inhabited Glaice in 650 R.L. and that the ikuts didn't arrive until around 800, and the bors a century and a half after that. That meant that the mantees were the original charterholding colonists of the planet, and the others were there only on their sufferance. The Warm Stream throngmother heard about Rakulit's work, and before long she had gotten all the mantee throngs on Glaice to join a class-action suit against all the ikut bands, to have them declared displaced persons who had to apply to the mantees for licenses just to remain on the planet where they were born.

"They can't do that!" Tep exclaimed. Suddenly his own problem didn't loom so large. "I belong on Glaice just as much as they do! I was born here, too!"

"So was I," Velanda replied. "So far, the mantees haven't included us bors in the suit, but it's still scary. Where could we go? We'd have to appeal to the Arbiter himself, to find us a new homeworld."

"The Arbiter! Hah! I sometimes think the Arbiter is a myth, like the bogeyman who lives in holes in the ice, and—"

"Just for your information, Tep-with-your-head-in-the-snow, the Arbiter has opened a consulate right here in Metok. It's right down the street from the Last Atopak, as a matter of fact."